SOUL CONFESSIONS

SOUL CONFESSIONS

MONIQUE MILLER

www.urbanchristianonline.net

Urban Books, LLC
78 East Industry Court
Deer Park, NY 11729

ISBN 13: 978-1-60162-873-2
ISBN 10: 1-60162-873-0

First Trade Printing April 2008
First Mass Market Printing December 2010
Printed in the United States of America

10 9 8 7 6 5 4 3 2 1

This is a work of fiction. Any references or similarities to actual events, real people, living, or dead, or to real locales are intended to give the novel a sense of reality. Any similarity in other names, characters, places, and incidents is entirely coincidental.

Distributed by Kensington Publishing Corp.
Submit Wholesale Orders to:
Kensington Publishing Corp.
C/O Penguin Group (USA) Inc.
Attention: Order Processing
405 Murray Hill Parkway
East Rutherford, NJ 07073-2316
Phone: 1-800-526-0275
Fax: 1-800-227-9604

Dedication

This book is dedicated to the loving memory of my grandmother

Caroline Hodges Miller

Acknowledgments

There are some people I'd like to acknowledge for their support and encouragement during the writing of this novel. I'd first like to thank God for giving me this gift and opportunity to touch the lives of so many.

To my Mom, Gwendolyn F. Miller and my Dad, William H. Miller, your continued support of me has been priceless, as the commercial says. I could never thank you both enough. Mom thanks for again spending quality time with "Cricket" while I worked on the completion of this novel.

Meliah, thank you for being my publicist in training. You are truly destined for greatness. God has a wonderful plan for your life and I am glad He included me as a part of it. I love you, sweetheart!

From the oldest to the youngest of my siblings—Denita, Penny, B.J. aka Will, Christopher and Christina. Thanks for being the best sisters and brothers a sister could ever want. I love you all for your support and words of encouragement over the years. Penny thank you for your assistance with my photo shoots!

Family: Erma, Valeria, Sheila, Giovanni, Lauren, Tonya, Jonica, Sherika, LaQuita, LaTricia, Tiffany, Lizzie, Wanda Gail, Alonda.

Author friends—Jacquelin Thomas thanks for seeing something in my writing starting with the Blue Sky days. Toschia thanks for believing in me and my being able to call you friend and Soror. To my other author friends thanks for the networking and support: Suzetta Perkins, Sherri Lewis, Kendra Norman-Bellamy, Annette Dammer, Stacey Hawkins Adams, Dorothy Pettis, Vanessa Davis Griggs, Tia McCollors.

Friends: Thanks to so many of my friends—Clitondra, Darlene, Elizabeth, Halona, Lori, Diedre, Lorrie, Kenydra, Nancy, Paula, Crysta, LeKaja, Alicia . . .

Sorors—Thank you to all my Sorors of Alpha Kappa Alpha Sorority Inc.—Especially Tau Omega Omega, Alpha Zeta Omega and Chi Iota Omega.

Writer friends: Special thanks to the members of New Vision Writer's Group—Durham, NC—Jacquie, Angela, Suzetta, Sandy, Cassandra, Titus, Lesley, Karen, Pansy, Tonya, Pamela and Shatoya.

My agent—Again thank you to my agent Sha Shana Crichton for seeing something special in my writing so many years ago.

My editor—Thank you to my editor Joylynn Jossel for your sharp eye through so many words and pages. Keep on, keeping on!

Readers—Thank you to you, the reader, for your e-mails with support and encouragement. I really appreciate it!

Urban Books and the Urban Christian Family—Thank you Carl Weber, Kendra Norman-Bellamy and Joylynn Jossel for working so diligently with me and other authors to share our gift of writing with the world. Thank you also to the fellow authors in the Urban Christian Family.

There are so many people, and if I've left your name off please know it was not intentional. Thank you so very much,

_______________________________________!

Your Name Here

☺

Thank you all so much for your support!
E-mail me at: *authormoniquemiller@yahoo.com*
Visit my website at: *www.authormoniquemiller.com*

SOUL CONFESSIONS

Prologue

Phillip Tomlinson

Phillip's body tensed as he stared at the name, Jeana Sands, printed on the manila folder he had just retrieved from the back of his bottom file drawer. He had forgotten it was there. It had been years since he'd stuffed it in there in the first place. Years since he thought about Jeana Sands and the child he fathered so many years ago.

He flipped through the pages. The folder held a certified letter he'd received informing him that Jeana, an ex-girlfriend from college, wanted child support for her son. It also held a copy of the DNA test, which proved Jeana's son was biologically his and documentation of a bank account not connected with any of his other accounts.

Phillip remembered the day he had gotten the certified letter asking for child support for a child he hadn't known existed. The boy was nine-years-old when he received the letter. After going to court and having a DNA test performed, he found out the test proved he was the father to a 99.97% chance.

It was, at that point, a secret account to pay automatic monthly child support payments, was created. Soon after the account was set up, Phillip placed all documentation connecting him to Jeana in a manila folder. He scrawled her name on the tab and hid it in the very back of the bottom file drawer.

There was no way his wife would find out about the child. It wasn't *his* fault that he told Jeana she needed to terminate the pregnancy, and she had gone ahead and had the child anyway without telling him. And, it wasn't his fault she waited til the boy was nine years old before she contacted him. He had no emotional ties to the boy, and didn't even know what the boy looked like.

Legally, he would provide the child support payments, but that is where the ties ended. His life was progressing just fine. Soon after setting up the account for the boy, Phillip found out his wife, Shelby, was pregnant. He and his wife had been trying for over two years to conceive, and now he had the family he always envisioned and wanted.

Jeana and her son did not fit into his plans. Phillip made it very clear to his lawyer that he didn't want anything whatsoever to do with the boy and did not want any contact from Jeana. Jeana had complied with his wishes and never bothered him again.

There was a knock at his office door. "Hello, anybody in?"

Phillip shoved the file back into the drawer and looked up to see one of his best friends and fraternity brother, Will. "Of course I'm here. I just got promoted. I can't start disappearing now."

Will placed his hand on one of the moving boxes, which sat on Phillip's desk. "You need any help packing up your things?"

"Naw, thanks, man. I won't officially move to my new office for a few more weeks. I've got more than enough time to pack." Phillip closed the drawer he had been looking in.

"Congratulations again. You deserved this promotion," Will said.

"You're dog on straight I deserved it. I should have gotten it a couple of years ago." He shrugged his shoulders. "But hey, I ain't complaining."

"Everything happens in its own season. This is your time. God had his reasons for you getting the promotion now instead of then."

Phillip pulled one of the filled file boxes off his desk, placing it next to the office door, "Well, it is about time, is all I can say."

Will looked at his watch. "Hey, I just wanted to step in for a second and see if you needed any help. I've got to check my emails before my meeting in an hour."

"Naw, I'm just packing a little at a time until the carpet is replaced in my new office." Phillip's office phone rang. "Hold on a second." He picked up the receiver. "Hello, Phillip Tomlinson speaking." He waited for a response from the other end of the line, but none came. "Hello, hello," he said again. There was no verbal response but he did hear a distinctive click.

Will looked at him questioningly. "Same crank caller?"

Phillip placed the receiver down harder than he intended. "I guess. It's kind of hard to know when they don't identify themselves."

Will shook his head. "It's crazy. Why would someone waste their time calling all day long and not say anything?"

"They must not have anything better to do. I wonder how many other people are having the same problem as me with these crank callers," Phillip said. "Shelby has even been receiving calls at home."

"I don't know, but I'm glad they're not calling me."

Phillip shrugged it off. "I'll just be glad when they finish replacing that carpet. Hopefully, when I move, the calls will stop."

"Or, maybe the person will get a new hobby." Will looked at his watch again. "Gotta go man. See you later. Maybe we can do lunch or something."

"Sounds good. Give me a call later."

Once Will left the office, Phillip closed and locked his office door. He returned to the file cabinet and pulled the manila folder back out. Looking around his office, he spotted the paper shredder sitting in the corner of the office next to his fake ficus tree.

He retrieved the shredder and placed it on his desk. After plugging it in, he pulled the contents of the folder back out. One by one he took each sheet and shredded it. Phillip shook his head wondering why he had kept all the information in the first place. His lawyer had copies of everything safely tucked away in his own office. He should have destroyed it all years ago.

Once everything in the folder was destroyed, Phillip then shredded the manila folder also. Wiping his hands as if he were removing imaginary dust, he said to himself, "Let the past stay in the past."

Chapter 1

Shelby Tomlinson

Trust

Shelby heard a growl just before the phone was slammed down in her ear. She looked at the caller ID; it displayed 'unknown'. She breathed a sigh of frustration, tired of being hung up on. It was the second time that day. And she had lost count of the number of times they had called in the past month or so.

She wished who ever it was would stop calling her house. It was really getting annoying. Shelby figured it was probably some kids playing on the phone and hoped they would get tired of calling.

She wobbled over to the bottom of the staircase. "Nyah, darling," Shelby called to her daughter.

"Yes, Mommy?" Nyah replied.

"Do you have your shoes on?"

"Yes, Mommy."

"Come here so I can see if they're on the right feet."

"Okay, Mommy."

The phone started ringing again. Without looking at the caller ID, Shelby snatched it up and said, "Hello," loudly.

"Hey, baby. What's up? You sound a little upset."

"Oh, Phillip. I thought you were that person calling to hang up on me again," Shelby said, relieved it was her husband.

"Nah, it's just me. We're going to need to have the calls traced somehow. It seems to be getting worse."

"It has," Shelby confirmed.

"I'm coming through the front gate now. I'll be there in a minute. Are you and Nyah ready?"

"Yeah, we're ready."

"Good. I'm ready for Dr. Silva to confirm the fact that we are having a boy," Phillip said excitedly.

"You really do want a boy don't you?"

Shelby rubbed her stomach. "Yeah. I do."

"What if it's a girl? Will you be disappointed?"

"No. I'll love her just the same. But I am hoping we're having a boy. I can tell Nyah isn't going to be the type of girl who will shoot hoops or play football. She's so prissy."

"She is not," Shelby said defensively.

"I love my little angel. But whether you want to admit it or not, she's prissy just like you."

"Phillip!" Shelby said, chastising him.

"That's what I love about you two," Phillip tried

to say quickly before Shelby could say anything else.

"I don't know what your definition of prissy is, but Nyah and I are not prissy. We're just ladies. We don't accept just any old thing that comes our way. We know what we want when we want it."

"Like I said, that's why I love you two so much."

"I can't believe you . . ." Shelby started to say.

"Hate to cut you off but I'm pulling into the garage now. See you two beautiful ladies in a few seconds."

"Hello again, Dr. Silva," Phillip stated.

"Hello, Mr. Tomlinson. It's good to see you," Dr. Silva said in his thick Spanish accent.

"It's good to see you again, Doc," Phillip said.

"Hi, Miss Nyah. How are you doing?" Dr. Silva smiled.

"Fine," Nyah said shyly, attempting to hide behind her father's leg.

"Shelby, how are you feeling?" Dr. Silva asked.

"I'm feeling a little better. This pregnancy is nothing like my pregnancy with Nyah. It seems like I'm sick all the time," Shelby complained.

"The sickness usually subsides by the second trimester," Dr. Silva said.

"I wish it *would* go away. I'm almost in my third trimester. I'd like to enjoy this pregnancy a little bit," Shelby said.

"How's the nausea medication I prescribed for you?"

"I only take try to take it when I feel I really need it," Shelby answered.

Dr. Silva nodded his head. "Try not to let your stomach get completely empty and continue to keep your fluid intake up. I don't want you to get dehydrated."

"I definitely don't want that to happen again. I hated having the IV in my arm. This baby is really giving us a run for our money."

"He sure is," Phillip interjected.

"You think it's a boy, huh?" Doctor Silva asked.

Shelby rolled her eyes playfully at Phillip, "My husband has it in his mind that it's the baby boy he's been waiting for," Shelby said chuckling.

"I know my little man is in there. He's already starting to give us problems and he isn't even here yet." Phillip patted his wife's belly.

"My mommy's gonna have a baby," Nyah told the doctor.

"Yes I know, Nyah," the doctor replied. "Do you know if Mommy's going to have a boy or girl?"

"Daddy said Mommy's gonna have a boy."

"Mommy's *going* to have a boy," Shelby corrected her daughter.

"Yeah, that's what I said, Mommy," Nyah said and smiled.

"Well, that's what you're here to find out. Let's try to do this ultra sound again. He *or* she is stubborn, that's for sure." Dr. Silva said.

"I'm praying this third try will be a charm," Shelby said.

"I hope so too," Doctor Silva agreed.

Phillip moved closer to Shelby's stomach and rubbed. "Son, I need you to position yourself so that we can show everyone that you're a boy."

Shelby smiled. "He's moving."

"You said *he*. So you must agree," Phillip said.

"No, I was just talking. It could still be a girl," Shelby said.

"Let's see if we can put everyone's minds at ease."

As Dr. Silva performed the ultra sound, Shelby thought about the first time she came to Dr. Silva's office a little over four years ago. She and Phillip had been trying to conceive for two years. Shelby had been concerned that she was the reason why they couldn't get pregnant.

Shelby tried to bring up the subject of their childlessness with Phillip on numerous occasions, but for some reason, Phillip continued to avoid the subject.

One night, Shelby got the house ready for a night of romance in hopes to get her husband to relax and discuss the problems she was having. He became so good at avoiding her, that she set everything up so he wouldn't be able to escape. That night, she tried to talk to him after giving him a bath with a massage. She made sure he was full of his favorite foods from his favorite soul food restaurant.

Once his stomach was full of food and he was in bed that night, she voiced her concerns. To her disappointment, he had again come up with some excuse to get out of the bed and flee. At her wits end, she prayed God would help her by giving her some kind of answers. She was frustrated and wanted to give up on the whole thing.

When he finally came back upstairs, Phillip had found her crying in the bed and much to her surprise, asked her what was wrong. They started to talk about her concerns. She told him she thought something was wrong with her. She felt that was why they had not conceived. She wanted to talk to a doctor, and find out what the problem might be. She revealed to him she was frustrated that she couldn't talk to him because he would always run and hide.

After they finished talking, he apologized for avoiding her. Philip told her he'd be there to discuss any concerns she had in the future. He agreed that it would be a good idea to seek professional help.

She was happy and relieved after their conversation. She spoke with her boss, an infertility specialist at the OB/GYN she worked at, the following week. The doctor referred them to her colleague, Dr. Jose Silva, for infertility counseling.

She felt comfortable with Dr. Silva from the first moment she met him. Shelby liked his bedside manner. He was warm and friendly. He answered all of her questions and seemed to be very caring. He didn't play around. He ran tests for blood work during her first appointment. He did an ultra sound to make sure her ovaries didn't show any abnormalities.

Her first ultra sound had left her with an empty feeling. Working at an OB/GYN office, she was accustomed to seeing the prenatal patient's monitors with the figures of babies soon to come. Her heart sank when she saw hers, which didn't have anything that resembled any of her patients.

She commented to the doctor that the ultra sound looked empty. He assured her he would do everything in his power to achieve the goal of one day doing an ultra sound that would show a baby.

After a couple of months of basal temperature charts and more tests, Dr. Silva determined there weren't any problems for her. The doctor wanted to perform tests on Phillip to see if there was a problem with him.

At first she was hesitant, fearing he would revert back to his evasive behavior. She felt he had a phobia of needles. When she told him he would need to undergo some tests, Phillip quickly agreed to have them done, and she was surprised.

After having a semen analysis performed, it was determined that Phillip had the infertility problem. He had a low sperm count. Phillip took the news from the doctor personally at first. He was offended by the doctor telling him there was an abnormality in his test. Phillip told her the doctor was calling him a freak.

Shelby reassured him that wasn't the case. She was happy the doctor found a reason for their infertility issues, so they could move on and do some In-vitro fertilization and try to conceive.

That's when Shelby learned about a secret Phillip had been keeping from her their entire marriage. Phillip's ego wouldn't allow him to let Shelby think he wasn't man enough to get her pregnant. He felt that God was punishing him for a mistake he had made years earlier. Confused, she asked him what he was talking about.

He revealed to her that in his sophomore year of college, he had gotten his girlfriend pregnant. He told Shelby when he found out about the pregnancy he told his girlfriend she needed to terminate the pregnancy, because neither one of them was ready to become a parent.

Shelby was bewildered when he told her about the ex-girlfriend and the pregnancy. She couldn't believe her husband kept such a big secret from her. She was even more astonished to hear that he was so callous in telling the girl to get an abortion.

When Shelby started asking him questions, getting louder and louder with each one, he quickly explained that he'd changed his mind and told his girlfriend not to get the abortion. He then said that the girl had a miscarriage a couple of weeks later.

She was livid, because he kept the secret for so long. It hurt her. She was more upset when she realized the only reason he even told her about the secret was because he didn't want his male ego to be bruised.

Shelby let him know he was selfish for not telling her earlier. She told him that God was good and would not punish him like that, but it was wrong of him to hold something back as important as his secret, especially since he really believed that he was being punished. Because that would mean she was being punished also.

Phillip apologized and agreed to do any of the procedures necessary by the doctor. He did everything in his power to get back into Shelby's good graces. Shelby forgave him for his deceit.

Dr. Silva started In-vitro fertilization procedures, and Phillip bent over backwards for anything requested of him.

In their first round of IVF procedures, there was a successful harvesting of twelve eggs. After the fertilization process, they had seven embryos. Dr. Silva placed three of the embryos into Shelby's uterus in hopes that one live pregnancy would occur. The other two embryos had been frozen for a later attempt for another IVF round.

After ten days of waiting and a negative home pregnancy test, they were told by Dr. Silva that the test he performed was positive. They were pregnant. Two weeks after that an ultra sound confirmed, there was one fetus starting to grow.

Shelby was on cloud nine. Even though she had a couple of other ultra sounds and felt the baby's movements, it still hadn't seemed real until the contractions started.

When the doctor handed her the baby for the first time, she knew her daughter was the most beautiful baby she had ever seen in the world. She couldn't believe after all the waiting that she was finally holding her baby girl.

They were back in Dr. Silva's office with her second pregnancy. The doctor transferred the other two embryos and they were blessed to have had one of them grow. The pregnancy so far had been an ordeal for her. She was sick the entire time and hoped the sickness would subside quickly.

"Ahh, let's see. There's the head and one leg. There's the other leg. Wow he's spread wide open. There's no doubt," Doctor Silva said.

"Yep, there's no doubt," Shelby said. "It's definitely a boy."

"Even I can see that," Phillip said. "I told you all it was a boy."

"Boy, boy, boy," Nyah chanted.

"You're going to have a little brother, Nyah," Doctor Silva said.

"No, my mommy's gonna have a baby," Nyah said.

"That's what I said," the doctor said, trying to explain and then gave up.

"It's okay. We'll explain it to her later," Shelby said.

"Thanks," the doctor said, relieved to have the help.

"I'm finally gonna get my boy," Phillip said.

"Gonna Phillip?" Shelby asked.

"Gonna, going to, goin'-ta,' whatever. It's a boy. I'm just happy," Phillip said not caring what or how he said it.

"Turn here."

"Where are we going?" Phillip asked.

"I want to stop by the baby boutique. It's been a while. Let's see what they have. I guess we can pack up all of Nyah's old clothes, since we're having a boy. We'll have to start from fresh."

"Yeah, I can see if they have any stuffed footballs and basketballs. I wonder if they have a little catcher's mitt."

"So soon, Phillip?"

"You've got to start them out young. That way

it's second nature. I know my son will be a great football player."

"Daddy, I want a football," Nyah said from the back seat of the Navigator.

"Baby girl, Mommy can get you a little baker oven or something," Phillip said, smiling at his daughter who quickly smiled back.

Shelby narrowed her eyes. "What's that suppose to mean?"

"What?"

"That little comment about Mommy getting her a little kitchen set?"

"That's girl stuff. You know I don't do stuff like that. You can help her pick out the right one."

Shelby put her hands on her hip. "I meant why can't you get her a football or basketball?"

"My little princess is not going to play football."

"So you're being a male chauvinist?" Shelby said.

"Those are strong words," Phillip said in defense.

"That's what it seems like you're doing."

"No, sweetheart. You know Nyah doesn't even like anything even closely related to sports."

"Maybe that's because we don't give her a chance. If my baby wants a football, then I'll get her a football."

"Mommy, I want to cook in my oven," Nyah said referring to her father's comment about the baker oven.

"See, I told you," Phillip said.

Shelby rolled her eyes and smiled.

"Why are you being difficult with me anyway?" Phillip asked.

"I'm not trying to be difficult. I just don't want my daughter to think she has to be confined to a box in which she can only do certain things because she's female."

"I wasn't doing that. Like I said, she doesn't like to play sports anyway. The only reason she wanted a football is because she heard me mention it. You know how impressionable she can be," Phillip said.

"I'd like to think she is observant, not impressionable."

"Our daughter doesn't miss much." Phillip looked in his rearview mirror at his daughter who was listening intently. "Isn't that right sweetheart?"

"Yes, Daddy," Nyah agreed without knowing what she was really agreeing to.

"I guess we should get his room together. My due date will be here before we know it."

"We need to call our parents and let them know what we're having so they can stop badgering us."

"Do you want me to call them now?" Shelby asked.

"No, we're almost at the store now. We can call them when we get home."

Phillip parked the SUV and opened the doors for his wife and daughter.

"It's been so long since we've done this. I wouldn't feel right using Nyah's old baby things especially all the pink items. I mean, the high chair and swing are still doable, but the pink stroller has to go."

"You got that right. My little man will not be riding in a pink stroller. But, you know you don't even have to worry. Both our families will have a ball shopping for the first grandson," Phillip said.

"It will be the first grand boy won't it?" Shelby nodded her head.

"I want a ball, Daddy," Nyah said.

"Huh?"

"You know your daughter; she doesn't miss a thing. You said our families would have a ball shopping for the baby. I think she heard the word ball and now she thinks she's going to get one," Shelby said.

"First stop, the toy section," Phillip said, scooping Nyah up into his arms.

"Yipee! I'm gonna get a ball," Nyah squealed with happiness.

"She's got you wrapped around her little finger, Phillip."

"Good. I like it like that."

"Come on before I'm too pooped to do anymore walking," Shelby said laughing.

Phillip put his other arm around Shelby's as they walked together into the store.

They looked like the American dream family. They were happily living in the suburbs with a perfect little dog. *The only thing missing was the white picket fence.* But, as with anything, looks can be deceiving.

Chapter 2

Shelby Tomlinson

Trust

Shelby checked her hair in the mirror again. Specifically, looking at her eyes to make sure there weren't any bags under them. She worked a twelve-hour shift the day before. Even though she had her hours cut at the hospital, she was still exhausted on her days off. The twelve-hour shift was a favor for a friend. She normally only worked from seven to three.

Ever since she had rededicated her life to Christ, she promised herself not to miss church services unless there was a valid reason. Being exhausted wasn't a good enough reason to skip church.

She always felt rejuvenated after church. From her first few visits to church, she realized New Hope was the place for her. Whenever she attended regular services or the Wednesday night Bible study, she would always get words from

God, which enabled her to cope with her daily life.

She looked forward to church every Sunday and Wednesday. Wednesday nights were reserved for Bible study. She wished Phillip would go with her more often than every few months. In the early years of their marriage, he wouldn't go at all.

"Nyah, did you brush your teeth?" Shelby called out to her daughter.

"Yes, Mommy. Look, see my teeth. They're nice and clean," Nyah said, showing her mother her pearly whites.

"Very good. Mommy will be ready in a minute. Get your purse. And, make sure you put some tissue in it for that runny nose."

"Okay, Mommy."

Shelby checked her own teeth, making sure she didn't have any lipstick on them.

Satisfied, she picked up her purse and headed downstairs.

Passing the game room, she looked in and saw Phillip lounging on the love seat. He was watching a game on the big screen television.

"Phillip."

"Yeah, baby?"

"Are you coming to church?"

"No, baby. You know the big game is coming on today. If I go to church, I'll miss the beginning of it."

"You can always tape it, honey," Shelby countered.

"It won't be the same. Besides, Rick and Will are coming over."

"Excuses, excuses," Shelby said.

Phillip turned his attention back to the television, "Huh, baby? Did you say something?" He was already consumed with the pre-recorded game he was already watching.

"No, honey. Don't worry about it."

"Okay. You and Nyah have a good time and pray for me while you're there."

"Don't worry, I will," Shelby said, meaning every word.

"Okay, baby. Love you," Phillip said loudly.

"I love you too, Phillip," Shelby said, even though she knew he probably hadn't heard her.

Shelby turned her attention back to her daughter. "Nyah, where are you?"

"I'm in the kitchen, Mommy," Nyah called from downstairs.

"Okay, Mommy's coming." Shelby carefully descended down the stairs, holding the bottom of her stomach with one hand, and the rail with the other. She was unable to see her feet.

Coming around the kitchen corner, her eyes fell upon a vase with a bouquet of three dozen red roses and an envelope from her favorite spa leaning against it. Nyah was standing next to the flowers, grinning like a Cheshire cat.

"Surprise, Mommy! Happy Mother's Day!" Nyah ran over to Shelby's legs and hugged her tightly as she opened the envelope. There was a certificate for the Diamond treatment at the Spa.

"Thank you, Nyah baby. The roses are beautiful."

Just as Nyah let go of her leg, Phillip rounded

the kitchen corner. "Happy Mother's Day, baby." He embraced her with a hug and kiss.

"Thank you, sweetheart. I thought you'd forgotten."

"Me? Never."

"Mommy, I helped Daddy buy the roses. I paid for them at the store."

Phillip nodded his head. "She sure did. And she didn't forget to get my change either. And never gave it back to me."

Nyah smiled, knowingly.

Shelby sniffed the plump roses. "They smell good. And thank you for the Spa certificate. The Diamond treatment, huh?"

"Only the best for you, baby." Phillip kissed Shelby again.

"And I kept it a surprise too, Mommy. I didn't even tell you, did I Daddy?"

Phillip picked up his daughter and gave her a nose-to-nose kiss, "You did a very good job, Nyah. Daddy is very proud of you."

Shelby looked at the time. "Guess we'd better head on out before we're late for church."

"Okay, baby. I'll be right here when you get back," Phillip said.

Shelby liked the roses, but wished Phillip would have come with her to church. That would have been a wonderful Mother's Day present also.

As Shelby drove to church, she listened to her Marvin Sapp CD. Her cell phone rang and she answered the call.

"Hello," Shelby answered.

"Good morning," her mother said from the other end.

"Happy Mother's Day!" Shelby said.

"And a very Happy Mother's Day to you also, sweetheart."

"What did you get for Mother's Day this year?" Shelby asked.

"Besides the Spa gift certificate you all got me, your Dad gave me a pearl jewelry set I've been eyeing over the past few months. Your brother sent me a gift certificate for the Mall. What about you? What did Nyah get you?"

"I got three dozen roses and my own certificate for the Spa."

"Nice. Those are two of your favorite things. What are you doing?" Her mother asked.

"I'm on my way to church."

"You're going to the early service?" Shelby's mother asked.

"Yeah, I've been going to both services for about six weeks now," Shelby told her mother.

"I knew you'd love New Hope once you started going there. I can't wait until I have an excuse to visit your church again."

"Hi, Grandma," Nyah yelled from the back seat.

"Is that my grand baby?"

"Yes, that's your little grand baby," Shelby answered.

"She doesn't miss a thing, does she?" Her mother chuckled.

"No, she doesn't," Shelby agreed.

"Tell her I said, 'Hi'."

"Grandma said, 'Hi'." Shelby followed her mother's request.

"Grandma, I made you a picture," Nyah yelled.

"What did she say?"

"She said she made a picture for you. I think she forgot it's supposed to be a surprise for your birthday. I think she's excited. She ran up to me at her learning center one afternoon this week, and told me she painted a picture for you."

"That's so sweet. She remembered my birthday."

"I hate to burst your bubble, but your granddaughter was eavesdropping and heard Phillip and I talking about what we should get you for your birthday that same morning," Shelby said.

"At least she thought about it the entire day." Shelby's mother chuckled.

"Yeah, she did."

"I won't hold you long. I need to let you get to church. You shouldn't be talking and driving anyway."

"Okay, Mom."

"Shelby, how are you feeling?"

"A little better, but not much."

"Alright, sweetheart. Give Phillip my love."

"I will, Mom. I love you."

"I love you, grandma." Nyah yelled.

Shelby's mother chuckled again. "Tell her I love her too."

"I will, Mom. Talk with you later," Shelby said and turned the phone off.

"Grand Mommy told me to tell you that she loves you."

Nyah smiled happily at her mother, showing her teeth.

Shelby and Nyah arrived in time for praise and worship. Shelby found a seat near the front and joined the congregation as they praised the Lord.

It took her a while to get used to New Hope at first. Her mother urged her to go to New Hope, saying that it was filled with the Holy Spirit. Shelby didn't know what to make of the church the first time she visited. She had never been to a church that started out the service praising the Lord.

She thought the congregation would never sit down either. They stood for what seemed like an eternity calling out Jesus' name, shouting hallelujah, and singing songs of worship to the Lord.

She considered not returning, and finding a church more subdued and that wouldn't keep her on her feet so long. But, the sermon that Sunday, and the Sundays after that, made her want to continue coming back.

Shelby experienced something she had never felt before. New Hope taught her about the scriptures. She was learning and could now apply the Bible to her daily life. When she left each Sunday, Shelby felt like she wasn't being preached to.

The Wednesday night Bible studies were better, because everyone was in a relaxed and casual mood and expected to learn the word. On Bible study nights, no one cared about who had on the biggest hat or fur coat. The real Bible seekers were there to study.

When Pastor Victor Jordan stood to give the sermon, Shelby opened her study Bible and followed along with him as he gave the scriptures to support his sermon. She highlighted the scriptures which interested her the most.

When the service ended, Shelby felt good knowing she learned something new. When the pastor invited unsaved people to receive the gift of life from God, she closed her eyes and prayed that they would follow their hearts and not the flesh to go to the altar.

She did as she promised and prayed her husband would come with her to church more often to learn more about the Word, so he would be as excited as she was about the Lord. She prayed he would accept the gift of life God had for him.

When she opened her eyes, there were three people at the altar. It was a young woman and two older men. She felt joy in her heart for the souls that were about to be saved.

She listened as the pastor led them to Christ. The congregation rejoiced once they were finished with the prayer.

After the first service was over, Shelby spoke to people as she went to the church daycare. She volunteered in the daycare for parents during the second service.

"Nyah, Nyah!" Nyah's friend from her preschool called.

"J.J.!" Nyah responded back.

"Hi, Shelby," Crystal Shaw, J.J.'s mother said.

"Hi, Crystal. Happy Mother's Day," Shelby said.

Crystal was the owner of the learning center where Nyah went to pre-school. Shelby and Crystal became good friends over the years after they met at the doctor's office where Shelby previously worked.

"Happy Mother's Day to you." Crystal said.

"Happy Mother's Day," both children said simultaneously.

"Isn't it funny how Nyah's with me during the week and J.J.'s with you on Sundays?" Crystal said.

"Yeah, I wonder if Nyah and J.J. will ever get tired of seeing each other."

"I hope not. They've known each other since birth. Even longer, if you count the time when I met you at Dr. Evans's office during the pregnancy."

"Poor kids. They'll probably know each other until they are old and gray," Shelby said.

"How are you feeling?" Crystal asked with concern.

"Still a little sick, believe it or not."

"Isn't this your third trimester?"

"Yes, as of yesterday I am twenty-seven weeks."

"Wow. I'll pray for you," Crystal said. "I remember my first couple of months. I was sick as a dog."

"Please pray for me. I need it."

"Don't worry, I will. How was first service?" Crystal asked.

"It was good. Pastor Jordan preached from Mark chapter four, verses thirty-five through forty-one. The title of the message was, "Don't worry, Don't fear."

"Sounds good."

"It was. Maybe he'll preach the same message.

Then again, you know pastor. He might change up and do another passage or change it entirely."

"I know. If he does, then I'll make sure I take good notes for you."

"Thanks, Crystal." Shelby smiled warmly at her friend.

"Well, let me get back here to my post."

"They'll have to find someone to take that post pretty soon." Crystal said.

"Yeah, I still get pretty tired when I'm on my feet for a long time. I'm glad they've got me sitting and just checking the children in. Speaking of, let me go ahead and check J.J. in."

"That'll work, especially since he and Nyah are already playing in the back."

"His number is one." Shelby handed Crystal a laminated tag with the number one on it.

"Thanks. If he gives you all any trouble, flash his nursery number."

"You know we will." Shelby was glad the church started a number system for the parents. If she needed a particular parent, Shelby would punch in the child's number and it would flash on a digital board in the sanctuary. This would notify the parent to come check on their child.

"See you later," Crystal said placing her child's number in her purse as she walked away.

"Enjoy the service," Shelby said.

When the second service was over, Shelby assisted the other volunteers in cleaning up the daycare area before going home.

"Nyah and J.J., can you put up all the blocks and balls for me?" Shelby asked.

"Yes, Mommy," Nyah answered.

"Yes, Miss Shelby," J.J. replied.

Shelby gathered the rest of the toys, wiped down the counters, and emptied the trash.

"J.J., are you ready to go?" Crystal asked coming to retrieve her son.

"Yes, Mommy. Can Nyah go home with us?"

"Mommy, can I go home with J.J.?" Nyah asked, quickly following J.J.'s lead.

"No, baby, maybe another day. Miss Crystal needs a break from you, honey. Besides, you'll see them both tomorrow," Shelby said.

Nyah poked out her lips and started to pout.

"Alright, young lady. You need to stop pouting. So, take that look off of your face. Pull those lips back in," Shelby said firmly.

Nyah did as she was told.

"I don't mind, Shelby. She can come," Crystal told her.

"Crystal, I don't want to put you through that. Nyah is always coming over and she hasn't had a nap yet. She's already starting to get a little cranky."

"You know she is always welcome."

"I know. We can do something another time. Maybe J.J. can come over next weekend and it will give you an extra break."

"That would be good, too. Either way, just let me know," Crystal said.

"I will."

"Let's go, J.J. We've got to go home and check on your dad."

"Is something wrong?" Shelby asked with concern.

"He's got a little bug. I'll probably stop at Mama Lula's to pick up some of her old fashion chicken soup."

"Mama Lula's sounds good. I think I'll go by there too. I don't feel like cooking today."

"Mama Lula's home-style dinners, always come in great during a pinch."

"You're telling me. Tell Warren I hope he feels better," Shelby said.

"I will. See you later."

"Bye. Bye J.J."

"Bye, Miss Shelby," J.J. said. "Bye, Nyah."

"Bye, J.J.," Nyah said, beginning to pout again.

Shelby heard her name being called, when she was at her car.

"Sister Tomlinson."

She turned, looking in the direction of the voice. "Hi, Pastor Jordan. How are you?"

"Blessed and highly favored. How are you and Nyah doing this fine Mother's Day?"

"We are doing fine, Pastor."

"That's wonderful, just wonderful. God is so good, isn't He?"

"He most certainly is," Shelby agreed.

"Shelby, I won't hold you long. I just wanted to stop you to say hello and see how you were."

"I'm doing well. Just ready for this baby to come."

"When are you due?"

"Three months."

"Are you sure? You sure are out there."

"According to the doctor, he won't be here until August 10th."

"He?" The pastor asked raising his eyebrows. "You know what you are having?"

"We found out the week before last. The ultrasound says it's a boy," Shelby smiled.

The pastor smiled also, "Oh how wonderful, just wonderful- a man child."

"Phillip is so excited to be having a son. I think he is more excited than me. There have only been girls on both sides of our families lately, and this will be our parent's first grandson. They can't wait."

"How is Phillip doing?"

She nodded her head. "He's doing good."

"I haven't seen him in church lately."

"I know. I've been praying that he'll start coming more."

"I'll pray with you. He'll come around one day. Maybe when you least expect it. Don't badger him though. You don't want him resenting the church, because of nagging. God is good and He'll work it all for the best. You just keep praying like you have been."

"I will, Pastor. Thank you for the advice and keeping it real."

"Hey, I've got to keep it real." Pastor Jordan laughed. "God won't let me do it any other way." The pastor continued. "Shelby, I've been praying about someone to help with the Pee Wee football team. I have a good feeling Phillip would be a good person to help coach the team."

Shelby thought about it for a second. "He would probably like that. To tell you the truth, he's at home right now watching the football game."

"CSU versus State?"

"Yeah."

"I hope CSU wins. They've got such a good team this year. We do have some of the best football teams here in North Carolina. I tell my family up north that all the time."

"I'll tell him what you said and give him the number to the church so he can call you," Shelby said.

"That would be wonderful." Pastor Jordan smiled warmly. "Well, I'd better let you two ladies go. Take care and be blessed."

"Thank you, Pastor. You too."

Shelby stopped at Mama Lula's on her way home to pick up dinner. As soon as she entered the house, she heard her husband and his friends yelling about the game. She placed the food on the counter and went to greet Phillip and the guys.

"Hey, baby," Shelby said and gave Phillip a kiss.

"Hey, sweetheart," Phillip said as he looked at Shelby then quickly back at the game. "Oh, man! I know he's got to be hurting. Number twenty-four keeps knocking everybody down."

"Whew, man, I'd hate to be on State's team right now. Number twenty-four is fast and relentless. He don't care who he hits," Phillip's friend, Will, said.

"State knew what was coming before they got

on the bus to come here. Ain't no surprise," Phillip's other best friend and fraternity brother, Rick, said.

"Hello, Will and Rick," Shelby said.

"Oh, I'm sorry, Shelby. I didn't mean to be so rude. How are you feeling?" Will asked.

Shelby rubbed her belly. "Real tired. But other than that, I'm good."

"I hear that." Will said.

"Shelby, you look like you're about to deliver any day now," Rick said.

"Thanks, Rick. I've still got three more months."

"Oh, sorry. You don't look all that big. Really you don't," Rick tried to counter the comment he'd made.

"Try to cover it up, Rick. Try to slip out of this one. I can't believe you just called my wife big," Phillip said, turning his attention fully to Rick.

"I didn't P.T. I don't know anything about pregnant women. I don't know when a woman is ready to deliver," Rick said, trying to cover up for his statement.

She heard the alarm in his voice. "You think I'm big, huh?" Shelby asked jokingly as she poked her stomach out for emphasis.

Rick shook his head with fervor. "No, Shelby, you know I would never say that."

"But you think it, huh?" Shelby raised her eyebrows while asking the question.

Will jumped into the conversation in hopes to help his friend. "Rick, you had better stop while you are ahead."

"Shelby I . . ."

"Mommy," Nyah said as she tugged on Shelby's dress.

"Yes, baby?"

"Can I have a cookie?"

"No, Nyah. You need to eat first. Change into the outfit on your bed and I'll get you something to eat," Shelby said. She turned back to face Rick. "You're lucky Nyah is saving you from the rest of this conversation."

"Yeah, man! Oooohhh yeah! That's what I'm talking about! CSU can't be stopped," Phillip said, shouting, he was already back into the game.

"Phillip, you sounded just like Deacon Green when he is shouting in church," Shelby said.

Without taking his eyes from the screen Phillip said, "Oh really, baby? But I was shouting for joy. CSU is about to win this game!"

"Deacon Green shouts for joy also. The joy of Christ and everlasting life."

"Okay, Shelby, honey I hear you. Baby, I'm trying to watch the end of this game," Phillip said, trying to concentrate.

"Alright, but you all missed a good service today," Shelby said.

Will interjected. "I went to 8:00 a.m. service, but I didn't see you there. I would have felt bad missing church all together," Will said.

"You did?" Shelby was impressed.

"What about you, Rick? Did you go to church this morning?"

"No, I uh . . ." he stammered.

"Don't even start, Rick. I wouldn't want you to add another lie to the list."

"Funny, Shelby. I go to church sometimes," Rick reasoned.

"Mommy!" Nyah said again.

"Okay, Nyah. I'm coming. Let me leave you men alone to finish watching this *awesome* game."

"Thanks, baby. What's for dinner?" Phillip asked.

"It's in the kitchen. I stopped by Mama Lula's."

"Mmm, Mama Lula's sounds good," Rick said.

"It sure does, doesn't it?" Shelby said.

"It's got my stomach growling," Will said.

"You know I always look out for you guys. Today is no different. There is enough for everyone."

"P.T., man, don't ever get rid of Shelby. She is a gem. I'll be glad when I can find a woman half as good as you," Will said complimenting Shelby.

"Me too," Rick said. "Shelby is the kindest, sweetest, most thoughtful woman I know."

Shelby laughed. "You two don't have to kiss up. I already got the food. We can eat when the game is over."

Shelby changed clothes and set the food out for dinner. She was going to set the plates when the phone rang. She wondered if it was going to be another hang-up call.

"Hello?"

"Hey."

"Hey, Kara."

"Happy Mother's Day," said Kara, Shelby's best friend.

"Thank you. Happy Mother's Day to you. What are you up to?" Shelby asked.

"Nathaniel and the kids are taking me out for dinner and a movie. It's my Mother's Day present."

"What about you?" Kara asked. "You sound a little annoyed."

"Oh, nothing. I just thought you might be the hang up caller again."

"Are you still getting those hang-up calls?" Kara asked

"Yeah, almost once a day now. It is really getting annoying."

"Don't you have caller ID?" Kara asked.

"Yeah but it comes up as a blocked call."

"If it continues, you need to have it traced and find out who is calling your house."

"I will. Hopefully it will just stop," Shelby said.

"So, other than that, how is everything else?"

"Fine. I'm still tired. I worked last night, and went to both services today. I stopped by Mama Lula's for dinner. There was no way I was going to cook. Will and Rick are here watching the CSU game with Phillip. I know they expect a meal when they come."

"Those guys aren't tired of each other yet? You'd think going to college together, pledging together, and now working together would be enough." Kara grunted. "I love you Shelby, but best friend or not, I couldn't spend that much time with you."

Shelby laughed.

"You've got those guys spoiled," Kara said.

"I know. I don't mind. They're good guys. If they don't get a good meal here, they'll be eating fast food somewhere."

"They should learn how to cook. It's Mother's Day for God's sake. They should be getting you dinner. Better yet, they should be cooking dinner while you put your feet up."

"Okay, Kara," Shelby said, trying to get her friend off of her soap box about what men should and shouldn't do.

"I'm serious. They can't expect you to feed them every time they come over. You are pregnant and tired."

"It isn't a big deal, Kara. All I did was stop and pick the food up. I called it in and it was ready when I got there."

"Girl, don't make me have to come over there and get Will and Rick straight. 'Cause you know I will. You, Phillip and Nyah are one thing. But Will and Rick know what they are doing," Kara preached on.

"Kara, you know you need to go ahead and get your license to preach," Shelby said, trying to change the subject, knowing Kara wouldn't want to talk about her calling to preach.

"There you go. You know I don't want to talk about that."

"I know. And I don't know why you keep running. You'll have to slow down one of these days. You can't run faster than God."

"Okay, point taken. I'll stop preaching about Will and Rick." Kara quickly changed the subject. "How's Nyah?"

"She's tired too. I told her to change her clothes for dinner and when I went into her room, she was asleep on her bed. Poor baby. She and J.J. played hard in the daycare today."

"So you're still really tired?" Kara asked.

"Yeah, maybe that's the difference in having a boy and a girl."

"You're having a boy? You didn't tell me. When did you find this out?"

"Yeah. Oops. I'm sorry I forgot to call you," Shelby said apologetically.

"You forgot to tell your best friend and the soon to be godmother?"

"Kara, I'm sorry. Charge it to my head and not my heart," Shelby said again.

"Okay you're forgiven. So you're going to have a big head boy, huh?" Kara laughed.

"Yeah. We're having a boy."

"I know Phillip is ecstatic."

"You know he is, girl. He wanted to buy the baby a mini baseball mitt. He's so happy he's finally going to get his boy."

"I'm glad; he needs a boy. You know Nyah is nowhere near tomboy. She's all girl."

"Both our families are excited too. There are only girls on both sides of the family. Everyone is ready for this little boy, but not as much as me. I am so ready for my little man to come." Shelby rubbed her stomach as she spoke.

"In due time, honey. When are we going shopping? We need to get all of that pink stuff out of the way and replace it with blue."

"Just say the word. You know I'm ready to shop," Shelby said.

"Thought you were tired?" Kara joked.

"Never too tired to shop. You know me."

"Yeah, I know."

"So, Nate and the kids are doing good?" Shelby asked.

"They're fine. Nate Jr. is coming to visit next week."

"How's that going?"

"It's going. Slowly. I'm praying for this whole situation with my stepson. If we could work with his mother, things would go much more smoothly for him." Kara huffed. "That woman is like a baby's mama, from you know where."

"Let me guess, she's got more antics up her sleeves?"

With sarcasm dripping from her voice, Kara said, "But of course. How on earth did you know?"

"What now?" Shelby asked.

"Every time she sends Nate Jr. to visit us, he only has the clothes on his back and a few toiletries. She knows we'll buy him clothes. I think that's how she gets out of buying him new clothing.

"Last time, we kept all the clothes we bought him and sent him back like he came. We can't afford to keep buying him clothes every time he visits. At least this way, we know he has something to wear when he comes back."

"What did she say?" Shelby asked.

"She was livid. She laid into my husband like there was no tomorrow. She called him everything but a child of God. She threatened to take him back to court for more child support."

"Do you think she'll do it?" Shelby asked.

"Who knows with that crazy woman? She might. If she does, we'll pull all our receipts for the clothing, and I'm sure once the judge sees the amounts, the case will be dismissed."

"You're spending a lot on clothing huh?" Shelby asked.

"Clothing, food and don't forget the phone bills." Kara huffed into the phone again. "He waits until Nathaniel and I are not home or at work to call his mom. We've spent hundreds on phone bills.

"You'd think she could call him every once in a while, but then she'd have to pay for those calls, wouldn't she? And we wouldn't want that now would we? Why should she have to pay for calls to interrogate her son about the happenings at our house?" Kara said.

"You don't think she's talking about what goes on in your house, do you?"

"I know so. Even when we are home she's asking him questions. She asks about what I'm cooking and if he likes it. I can tell from the answers he gives her. I am so sick of it."

"Wow." Shelby said. "How do you think Nate Jr. is handling all this?"

"I think he is just confused," Kara said.

"He's eleven years-old, old enough to see some things for himself, Kara," Shelby said.

"I know, but I know he feels torn. He loves his Dad and his Mother. He wants to like me, but because his mother doesn't, I think he feels like he would be betraying her. Girl, just pray for me and this whole situation."

"I'll pray for you." Shelby shook her head. "I take my hat off to you. I don't know how you do it. I don't know if I'd be able to handle dealing with a step-child and the baby's mama."

"Let me tell you, some days I don't know how I handle it myself. I'm glad you're not in my shoes. I don't wish any of this drama on anyone," Kara said.

"That's funny. I was just thinking that I am glad I'm not in your shoes." Shelby chuckled.

Kara sighed heavily.

"But you know I've got your back, right?" Shelby said.

Kara chuckled on her end of the phone. "I know you got my back, girl. And, I know you're praying for me."

"You got that right," Shelby said.

Kara replied, "I've put it in God's hands. Sometimes that's all you can do. I'm not worried."

Phillip descended the stairs. "Man, that game was good!"

"Alright, Kara. The men are finished with their game. We're getting ready to eat. I'll call and check on you a little later."

"Okay, but don't call me unless you've had a nap. You need to rest."

"Yes, Mommy Kara," Shelby said in a toddler sounding voice.

"I'm serious," Kara said.

"Bye, girl."

"Bye!" Kara said quickly clicking the phone off.

Chapter 3

Phillip Tomlinson

Mercy

"Phillip, congratulations, on your promotion."
"Thanks, Dan," Phillip said.

"You're the right man for the job."

Phillip agreed. "The competition was fierce."

"Yeah, it was. I'm glad the process is over. Those interviews were getting to me."

"It's worth it now, right man?"

"It most certainly is. Now I've got a new position and a new office; it can't get better than this," Phillip said with pride.

"Salary hike, right?" Dan added.

"True," Phillip admitted.

"New headaches," Dan added further.

"Very true. Thanks, for all the little reminders. Can a man bask in his happiness for one day?"

"Sure, I just wanted to come by and congratulate you. I'll get out of your way so you can finish packing this office up."

"Thanks, Dan."

"No problem."

"And, Dan?"

"Yeah, man?"

"I know you will be scared being on this floor all by yourself without me to fight your battles. I'll be right upstairs if the boogie man comes for you," Phillip said jokingly.

"Phillip, man. I knew there was a reason I was glad you got that position. Pack quickly and get out of here." Dan slapped Phillip on the shoulder. "I'll see you later."

"Bye, man," Phillip said.

Phillip emptied all of the desk drawers, placing the contents in a box. He cleaned off his desk and carefully placed the picture of him and Shelby in the box. He picked up the picture of Nyah as a newborn and thought about how beautiful she was as a baby. She had his hazel eyes and curly jet-black hair. Nyah looked just like him when he was a baby. Except for the slight discoloration of his baby picture, Phillip and his daughter's pictures could have passed for twins.

He placed the picture in the box. Then, he looked at the most recent picture Nyah took at her pre-school. Except for her hazel eyes, Nyah looked like her mother. Her hair started to lighten. Nyah was a mini Shelby through and through. She had the same hourglass shape, slender fingers, and long eyelashes. Nyah was also smart just like her mother, never missing much.

Phillip smiled when he put the pre-school picture into the box, along with everything else. He leaned back in his chair thinking about the baby boy he was finally going to get. He couldn't wait until he'd have a chance to hold his son in his arms. He had so many plans about what he and his son would do.

Phillip had many valuable memories with his own father. He thought back to the first day of school. His father took him, because his mother couldn't bear to see him off. He remembered his first football game with his father on the sidelines cheering him on. Even though the team lost that day, his father took the family out for a celebration dinner.

Phillip had many wonderful moments with his father as a child, teenager, and even now as an adult. He could call his father to talk about anything. Phillip wanted the same kind of relationship with his son, and he looked forward to it. He wanted to be there for his son in everything.

Phillip pulled out another empty box to clear out his file cabinet. Drawer by drawer, he emptied the cabinet's contents. In the back of the bottom drawer, he pulled out the last of the remaining files. Phillip froze seeing the name Jeana Sands on the top of a lingering sheet. He'd thought he had destroyed everything with Jeana's name on it. However, this sheet of paper still remained.

He must have placed it in the wrong folder. He was glad no one else was in his cabinet looking for a particular file. Phillip shook his head again, and wondered why he kept the information in the first place. The memory of first getting the letter was still vivid in his mind.

Phillip woke up early one Saturday morning to fix Shelby breakfast. He knew she was tired from working hard, and recording her temperature each morning during the time they were trying to rule out possible fertility problems.

That morning, he had fixed Belgian waffles with blueberries, whipped cream and hot maple syrup. Shelby was pleasantly surprised, when she woke up smelling the sweet breakfast. Phillip treated Shelby like a queen, because she was his queen.

After the breakfast was over, Phillip insisted Shelby relax and he would do the dishes. The doorbell rang while he was in the kitchen. The mailman brought a certified letter addressed to him. When he read the letter, he couldn't believe what he saw.

The letter was a summons for him to appear in court for back child support. The plaintiff on the letter was Jeana Sands, one of his ex-girlfriends from college. Confused about what was going on, he hid the letter from Shelby. He wanted to do an investigation to find out why he got the letter.

After days of calling and getting the runaround, Phillip was told he had to go to court to clear up the situation. He called his father's lawyer to assist in getting to the bottom of what was a mishap.

Phillip had to go to court, where he saw the ex-girlfriend that he hadn't seen in years. Jeana Sands was a freshman when he met her. Phillip remembered her southern drawl the most. She was from a little town in Eastern North Carolina, but he couldn't recall the name of it. He never dated her long enough to actually go home and meet her parents. But, it wasn't like Jeana was going to invite him.

Phillip remembered Jeana as a sweet country girl. His teammates called her that anyway. He admitted that he really liked Jeana. She was very naive. She wasn't like the urban girls who always accused him of being up to something. Always accusing him of infidelity. Phillip found a way to weasle himself out of compromising situations.

Jeana was a breath of fresh air in that regard. He would tell Jeana something and that was that. She believed everything he said. She never asked for clarification, when he knew his stories weren't true. She always smiled, and was understanding when emergencies would come up and he couldn't see her. These so called *emergencies* involved damage control with one of his other women.

Jeana was a good girl. If he said he was going to call her at a certain time, she was always there waiting by the phone. If she said she was going to meet him somewhere, she was always there. If he needed an errand run, she always helped him.

Things were going well, until the day Jeana told Phillip she was pregnant. He couldn't believe it. He always wore protection when with a girl, but he remembered a couple of times when he didn't use condoms with Jeana.

Phillip knew she didn't have sexually transmitted diseases, since she was a country virgin. It was a matter of running out of condoms and not picking any up before seeing her. He would never do that with the other girls, but he took it for granted with Jeana.

She was no longer the naive looking freshman he remembered. She was dressed in a tailored suit that fit her body to a tee. When she took the suit jacket off, he could see her muscular arms in the sleeveless vest. Glancing at her long legs, he saw they were also muscular. He imagined her entire body was sculpted. She looked like a body-builder. His mind drifted back to the days, when they would sneak away to be together. For a fleeting moment, he wondered how her body would have felt right then. When she looked over at him, he quickly avoided her eyes. He wanted to get the whole ordeal over with.

The judge ordered a DNA test to determine paternity. When the results came back, Phillip was found to be the father. Still in denial, Phillip told his lawyer to do whatever he needed to do to get everything resolved. He told the lawyer he didn't want to see Jeana again or his supposed child. He was glad the child had not been brought into the courtroom.

His lawyer set up a secret account for the delinquent child support payments, and the future payments so they would automatically be taken out every month. Phillip gave his lawyer explicit instructions that he did not want to be bothered by Jeana Sands. He didn't want to meet the child and wanted to make sure Jeana Sands didn't have any of his personal information. His most explicit instruction was that Shelby could never know about the account and the child.

Phillip never told Shelby the truth about the lie he told in regard to the abortion. He didn't plan on telling her about the child he knew was actually alive.

"Phillip."

Startled, Phillip looked up and saw Will standing in the doorway. Will was only an inch shorter than Phillip, but one wouldn't know it with the high top fade he still sported. Will wore black wire-rim glasses, which made him look as smart as he actually was. He held an MBA in Finance and was working on his doctoral degree.

"What, man?"

"What's on your mind? You seem preoccupied," Will said.

"Nothing, man," Phillip said as he quickly stuffed the sheet of paper inside the box. "Is that hazel nut coffee I smell?"

"Yeah, I just made a pot. Want some?" Will offered.

"Yeah."

"Then go get it. I'm not your secretary, man," Will said. "Maybe that's what they do on the fifth floor, but down on four it's *Y.O.Y.O.*—you're on your own."

"Ol'—Will, always making jokes," Phillip said, picking his coffee cup up off his desk. "Moving up isn't going to change me. Menial work doesn't bother me either."

"Movin' on up to the eastside. You sure you aren't part of the Jefferson family?"

"Move out of my way so I can get some coffee." Phillip brushed past Will towards the door. He went to the kitchen, and poured himself a cup of coffee. He added cream and sugar.

"Drink a man's cup. I drink mine without all the frills," Will said.

"I like mine smooth and creamy. I can't help it if you prefer yours to be hard and dull," Phillip countered.

"You need any help moving the rest of your things?"

"Nah. I'm on the last file cabinet now. By this evening I should have everything in order upstairs."

"I'm glad for you. You deserved the promotion. Especially since they passed you over the last time."

"I guess they learned the hard way how much it cost the company. I'm happy they realize it now."

"Things are going well for you. Can you give a brother some tips?" Will asked.

"Tips on how to work your way up in management?"

"The whole shebang; the job, wife, kids, all of it. You are really blessed. You realize that don't you?"

"Yeah, I know," Phillip said nonchalantly.

"I'll be glad when I find the right woman to settle down with one day. And, I look forward to having my own children too. Nyah is adorable and you've got a son on the way. All you need is a white picket fence."

"Don't forget the dog. The American dream has a dog in it somewhere, doesn't it?"

"Yeah. I want that, man."

"You can have it, Will—if you stop being so picky," Phillip told him.

"Me, picky?"

"Yeah, that cutie from Dewayne's bachelor's

party gave you her number and you threw it away. Then that fine girl with the big . . ."

"Whoa, man. Let me set you straight again. There should be more to a woman than her looks and how big her physical assets are. When I asked your so called cutie what she wanted to do with her life, she told me she was living for the day. And, when I asked the other fine thing you like so much if she was going to church the next day, she said flat out that she didn't believe in the whole Father, Son, Holy Spirit thing. Those were definitely signs for me to leave those two and all of the other women alone. I believe the woman I am looking for was at home thinking about her future, getting ready for church the next day and definitely believes in the Trinity."

"Good luck, Will," Phillip said, shaking his head. "You will spend many a night on your couch alone watching TV by yourself with that wait and see attitude. I'm sure there were some church girls in the club that night."

"I just don't want a Church girl, Phillip. You're missing the whole point. I want a woman who is saved; a woman who has a purpose in life. I want a soul mate."

"Shelby is my soul mate, man, and I didn't meet her in church. When we first met she wasn't even saved. I mean, now she is and it's all good, but I didn't meet her that way and everything turned out fine like you said earlier. We are living the American dream," Phillip said proudly.

"I know it may sound funny to you, but I know God is going to send me a woman who is already saved because I am saved. I want a woman that I am equally yoked with," Will said.

"I do admire the things you and Shelby have. And I do mean admire. But I'm not the least bit jealous. I know God will bless me with all those things too. The only difference is that my wife and I will be saved. When we have trials and tribulations to endure, we'll know exactly why we are going through them and we'll know how to get through them together."

"What's that suppose to mean, man?"

"Phillip, do you know that we all have a purpose in this life? That purpose is not to find out how much money we can make and what kind of car to drive. The purpose is so much bigger than you or me."

"You're losing me, Will." Phillip poured a little more cream in his coffee, and stirred it. "I know you like to get philosophical, but sometimes you go over my head with what you say," Phillip said. He hoped his friend would lay off whatever subject he was about to broach on.

"Simple. We all have obstacles in life—times when we face hard times and only God can help us. When those times come, it can be comforting to know the Lord is there to help you."

"I believe in God, Will. And, I got it going on right now. So, I don't see any trials or storms or whatever you are talking about," Phillip said.

"Phillip, I needed to tell you that. God put it on my heart to plant that seed."

"Okay, it's planted. Like I said before, you are just too deep for me. If I ever need to talk to God, I'll call you since He doesn't talk to me. Wish I had a direct line to Him sometimes. Then, I'd know which teams are going to win the games and maybe I could win a few bets," Phillip said, laughing.

"That's not funny."

"I know. I was trying to lighten this conversation up. You sound so serious, as if its life or death or something."

"Like I said, I needed to plant that seed," Will said, in a serious manner.

Phillip wanted out of the conversation. "I guess I better get back to my office and finish packing. I'll catch you later."

"Alright man, catch you later. Let me know if you need anything," Will said.

"Thanks." Phillip returned to his office. The sheet of paper with Jeana's name on it was peeking out of the box. He felt like it was taunting him. He snatched it out of the box. As he did, he heard a knock at his door. It was Rick, who let himself inside the office.

"Hey, Phil." Rick entered the office and closed the door behind him.

"What's up, man?" Phillip asked hiding the paper behind his back.

"Whew," Rick said, wiping his brow with his hand as if to remove some imaginary sweat.

"What now?" Phillip said, knowing Rick had gotten himself into some sort of escapade the night before.

"Joy, Joy, Joy."

"Joy?" Phillip asked.

"Yeah, man. Joy was her name, and let me tell you, that is just what she was."

"Your newest conquest?" Phillip asked.

"I don't know if you could call it that. She has more game than me. I tried my usual lines on her, and she stopped me dead in my tracks. I felt like she could read my mind or something."

"She got game, huh?" Phillip asked with curiosity.

"Yeah, I may have to take lessons from her. I tried to run my lines on her, and she cut me off cold. She gave me a run down on what I was going to say and do next. She told me to quit while I was ahead."

"Finally met your match, huh?" Phillip laughed.

"Did I? Yes! She said she knew my goal was to get her back to the apartment so I could score. I couldn't believe it! Phil, you know how smooth my game is. Women look at this baby face and melt."

"So what did you say to her after she told you all this?"

"I said nothing. It wasn't what she said, but how she said it. She told me she would save me the trouble and breath. I knew then, I needed to be on the look out for another honey. She wasn't playing around," Rick said.

"What happened? Why are you wiping your forehead?" Phillip asked.

"She got game, man. I thanked her for the conversation, and started to turn away. She pulled me back to her and asked where I was going. Next thing I know, we were in our cars headed to her place."

"No, Rick? You're pulling my leg. You got

shorty to take you to her place?" Phillip asked in disbelief.

"No, shorty got me to come to her place. She told me we didn't need to waste time with all the small talk, and we were both adults knowing what the ultimate goal was anyway." Rick paused.

"Go ahead, man, go on. What happened next?" Phillip asked in suspense.

"I got to her apartment, and as soon as she closed the door, she pushed me on her couch. She started undressing and I followed her lead."

"Stop, Rick, you're pulling my leg. Ain't no way that happened. That is the playa's dream."

"Dreams come true. I am here to tell you!" Rick slapped his leg.

"So you hit it, man?" Phillip asked already knowing the answer to the question.

"I hit it, she hit it, we hit it. There was a lot of hitting going on, *all night long*!" Rick said, stressing the last part of his statement.

"All night?" Phillip asked in disbelief.

"All night," Rick confirmed.

"I woke up this morning in her bed and she was gone. She left me a note telling me to call her. That is why I'm just getting here. She didn't even wake me up."

"Did you expect her to wake you up?"

"It would have been the nice thing to do," Rick said, a little perturbed.

"Rick, you don't know her from Adam. Just because she was good in bed doesn't mean she has any manners."

Rick reminisced, "She was good not only in bed, but on the couch, in the bathroom . . ."

"Okay, believe it or not, I don't want to hear the minute by minute details," Phillip said. "I've got to finish packing up this office. I start tomorrow on the fifth floor."

"Oh sorry, man. You need any help?" Rick offered.

Phillip looked around. "No, I got it."

"We can finish talking about this later. She did this thing with her..."

"Rick, later!"

"Alright man," Rick conceded. He stood up to leave.

"Rick," Phillip said, "We'll talk later. But, be careful in the meantime. I know it sounds like you had a good time, but you really don't know this woman. Do you even know if that is her real name?"

"Don't know and I don't really care. I probably won't even call her. She is a little out there for me. And, if her game is tighter than mine, I really don't need to mess with her."

"Good. I am glad you are thinking straight."

"Always. You know me," Rick said.

"Well, since you are thinking so straight, let me ask you one thing," Phillip said.

"Yeah what?"

"Did you use a condom with this woman?"

"Of course. I ain't crazy, man."

"Just making sure. Now get out of here so I can finish packing up all this stuff," Phillip said.

"I am, and if anyone asks, you saw me come in when you came in this morning," Rick winked.

"I got your back. See ya."

Phillip shook his head after he left. He hoped

Rick would slow down some day. Rick reminded him of how he was during his college days. He thought about what he was hiding behind his back.

Jeana Sands was one of his many conquests during his playa days. She was the only one who ended up pregnant. Phillip recalled his other conquests. There was Dawn from Michigan. She was an around the way girl, or so she thought. Phillip had her fooled into thinking she was his only girl friend.

It wasn't pretty when she found out about a couple of the other girls he was seeing in the other dorms. She keyed his car and broke the windshield. He didn't see her do it, but he knew it was her. Phillip told his father someone from a rival school vandalized his car before one of the games. Within one week, the car was fixed as good as new.

There was Bethany, a girl from Dallas, Jaden from Charlotte, Veronique who was from Durham, and Kanedra who was from St. Louis. He dated some other girls but couldn't remember where they were from. He tried to remember all the names, but couldn't. There was Portia, Adrian, Ingrid, Jhonetta, Tracy and Traci.

He had to be careful when buying gifts for the last two, because of the different spellings. Sometimes it was hard to distinguish the two on his answering machine since their voices sounded very similar. If he couldn't figure out which Tracy it was, he didn't bother to try returning the call. He'd just wait until she called back.

There were girls he had one-night stands with,

especially if he was out of town for an away game. He didn't even try to recall any of their names. He didn't even want to remember their faces. He got what he wanted with them, and he forgot them when it was over.

Looking back now, Phillip wasn't proud of his lifestyle. Especially, when he looked into the eyes of his daughter. He hoped she wouldn't come into contact with any men like him or Rick.

After his football accident, Phillip lost a couple of his so-called girlfriends. It was clear to him they were with him for the sake of saying they dated the quarterback of the team. By the time he met Shelby, he was only down to two steady girlfriends, which he quickly dropped once he knew Shelby was indeed the one.

Everything from that past life was gone and forgotten until the day he received the certified letter from the Pender County courthouse. His past had caught up with him in a surprising way.

The memory of the night Jeana told him about the pregnancy was still clear in his mind. She called him, saying she had some very good news to share. She wanted to tell him in person. She had come over to his dorm room with plastic champagne glasses and sparkling white juice. The grape juice threw him for a loop, especially since he was used to drinking Alize with her and she knew it.

He had asked her what the reason for the grape juice was and she told him to celebrate, but she couldn't drink any alcohol because of her condition. Then she laid it on him like a ton of bricks. Smiling, she told him she was pregnant. Immediately, his heart began to race. He couldn't have heard her right. He didn't say anything, and hoped it was a bad dream. When she touched his arms and tried to hug him, he snapped out of his trance.

The next part was a blur. He remembered asking her how it could have happened and there was no way he was ready to have a baby. He told her it was a mistake that needed to be taken care of in some way. He guessed she understood, because she left his room almost quickly. The more he had a chance to think about it, he came to the conclusion that Jeana had to get an abortion. He wasn't ready to have a baby. It wasn't in his plans.

The next time he met with Jeana, he told her she needed to get an abortion. He pulled a couple thousand dollars out of his savings account, and gave it to her. He knew it would cover the procedure and would give Jeana a little extra cash for her pain and suffering. It was the least he could do, he felt.

Phillip knew Jeana did not agree with the idea, but told her she didn't have any choice. That was the last time he saw her. The next thing he knew, she had dropped out of school. Phillip figured after the abortion and their break up she probably wanted to start a new life. He never bothered to call her to check on her to see how she was doing. And, she had never tried to contact him either. As far as he was concerned, they ended on *good terms*. He moved on with his life and she moved on with hers.

Phillip wondered why Jeana changed her mind and not had the abortion. For years, she had let him go on thinking that she had gone along with the plan. He wondered why she never contacted him about it. How she could keep the information from him? If it was his son, he had a right to know. But, she never gave him that chance. She just sprung it on him with a court summons.

After finding out about the boy, Phillip wondered what the child looked like. He wondered if he looked like him at all, and if he had the Tomlinson physical traits. Most of the men on Phillip's side of the family had thick black eyebrows and pronounced dimples in their cheeks when they smiled. In his hometown people could tell who the males were in the Tomlinson family. They would look at them and say, "You must be one of the Tomlinson clan."

He wondered early on if the boy had any of the same character traits as him. Phillip also wondered if he was athletic or liked any of the same sports.

But, the more he thought about it, the more upset he got about Jeana keeping something so important from him for all those years. It wasn't his fault she had done what she had done. She never gave him an opportunity to get to know his son. Never sent him a picture or anything. Plus, he felt with all the years that had passed, the boy must have been doing fine without him in his life.

He washed his hands of it, thinking about the boy less and less to detach himself. He decided the best thing to do was to pay the money Jeana wanted and leave it at that. He and Shelby were already on shaky ground, while she was still trying to get pregnant. Divulging the partial information about Jeana existing in the first place had been a mistake. He didn't want Shelby to be further upset by the new information about a child Phillip really had had nothing to do with.

He kept the information from Shelby. She was pregnant soon after that and Nyah was born. Their marriage became stronger, and Phillip stopped thinking about Jeana and the boy.

The piece of paper was the only thing that lingered as a reminder. Phillip was glad he'd found it. He shook his head while locating his shredder in the corner of his office. Within three seconds, the last remaining tangible reminder in his office was shredded. "I'll never have to be reminded of it again. I've moved up in the world and I don't need any of those old memories holding me down."

He smiled as he looked at Shelby and Nyah's picture, on his custom-made desk calendar. "I am a lucky man." He stared at his beautiful wife and daughter with love. They were two of the best things that had happened to him in his life. And soon he was going to have the son he had been waiting so long for.

Later Phillip sat in his new office with just about everything unpacked. It was nearly 4:00 and he would be ready for his next day at work. He admired his new surroundings. The fifth floor was a stepping-stone to his goal of one day becoming the VP of finance for the company. Even though his new job was just a move one floor up he could immediately tell the difference in how the higher echelon lived.

His new office was equipped with the best that money could buy: a refrigerator, microwave, and coffeepot. His company spared no expense when it came to its valued employees. He'd never have to go down the hall and around the corner. He'd miss chatting with some of the other employees in the lounge, but knew the higher executives rarely ever congregated there so he too would have to follow suit.

Phillip's new office sat in the corner of the building giving him a spectacular view of the city. He looked forward to coming into work the next morning and welcoming the bright rays from the sun, which were sure to permeate the room.

His office was even equipped with a television and VCR. The new mahogany desk was twice the size of his old oak desk, to match the size of the office, which was twice the size of his old one. On one of the walls was a massive bookshelf made of the same mahogany wood as his desk and file cabinets.

By 4:30 p.m. he had everything unpacked. He had even had time to hang his African Art on the walls along with the various awards he had earned over the past years with the company. On the book shelves he placed African sculptures he had acquired during one of his business trips to South Africa.

Phillip sat in his buttery-soft leather seat at his new desk, pleased with himself. He did have it all; a loving wife and daughter, a new son on the way. Plus he had a great job taking him up on his ladder of success. And to top it off, his pro and college football teams were winning. He knew his future could only get brighter and brighter.

Chapter 4

Shelby Tomlinson

Trust

Shelby looked up at the clock on the hospital wall. "Mrs. Santini, your contractions are now coming about five minutes apart. We'll meet this little girl pretty soon.

"I'm ready," Mrs. Santini said.

"Have you all decided on a name yet?" Shelby asked Mr. Santini.

The Santini's looked at each other and laughed. "Yes, we finally decided."

"What's so funny?" Shelby asked.

"We've been back and forth on a name for our baby. It was between Mallory and Isabella," Mr. Santini said. "We asked our families to vote on the names. We even sent e-mails out to ask people to vote."

"Big mistake," Mrs. Santini said.

"Why?" Shelby asked.

"We got numerous answers to our e-mails. Most people voted for the name Mallory."

"So you've decided on Mallory?" Shelby asked.

"No, we are going with Isabella," Mr. Santini said.

"Okay?" Shelby said quizzically.

"Some of them liked it so much we got a couple of e-mails saying they were going to use the name. One person actually said they were due soon and had not picked out a name yet and they decided to use Mallory," Mrs. Santini said.

"Well, Isabella is a very pretty name also," Shelby said.

"Next time we have a baby, we'll keep it to ourselves."

"I don't blame you," Shelby said laughing.

"When are you due?" Mrs. Santini asked.

"In about two and a half months," Shelby replied.

"Are you sure? You look further along than that," Mr. Santini said. "I'm sorry I don't mean to sound like you are big are anything," he said apologetically.

"It's okay. You are not the first person to make comments about my size in this pregnancy. But no, I'm not due for another two and a half months."

"Do you know what you are having?" Mrs. Santini asked.

"Yes, we're having a boy," Shelby said proudly.

"Is this your first?"

"No, we have a little girl named Nyah." Shelby smiled.

"That's a pretty name," Mrs. Santini commented.

"She is such a blessing. My husband and I

waited a while for her and for this little bundle of joy I'm now carrying."

"So did we. We tried for eight years and could never get pregnant. We decided that maybe it was not meant for us to have a child naturally so we started talking about adoption. Then a month later we were pregnant. God works in mysterious ways."

Shelby shook her head. "My husband and I didn't have to wait that long. I don't know if I could have waited eight years. We decided to try in-vitro fertilization after about two years and it worked."

"In-vitro fertilization, now that's something I don't think I could have done. We never even considered it once."

"Well, it's not for everyone. God knows what we can handle and what we can't. For me, I guess it was having to wait more than two years and for you I guess it was not having to go through the sometimes grueling process of IVF."

"You're right. Everyone has their limits," Mrs. Santini said. "Whoa, here comes another one."

"Okay, just breathe like we practiced again, honey," Mr. Santini said.

"Let me get the doctor. That was only three minutes," Shelby said, leaving the couple in the delivery room to get Dr. Evans. He was her former boss from Silvermont OB/GYN.

She saw the doctor coming towards her from the nurse's station. "Dr. Evans, Mrs. Santini is only three minutes apart. The baby just started crowning," Shelby said.

"Thanks, Shelby. I am on my way in there right now," Dr. Evans replied.

Shelby returned with the doctor. Within 45 minutes, Mr. and Mrs. Santini were holding their seven pound, twelve ounce daughter, Isabella Rose Santini. Isabella made the appearance, just before it was time for Shelby to get off work. She was glad the baby came before her shift was over. There were times when she hated leaving before a baby was born, especially if she had already spent her whole shift with an expecting mom. But, babies come when they are ready and not usually a minute before with natural deliveries.

Shelby wished them well as she left their room. She returned to the nurse's station to retrieve her things to go home. She opened her locker and pulled out her purse and keys. Then, went back to the nurse's station and said good bye to her co-workers.

As she was leaving the ward, she heard a familiar voice behind one of the hospital room doors. Even with the door closed Shelby could hear the woman clearly.

"I don't need no pain medication. I do it better by myself. All that medicine does is make me groggy afterwards."

It only took Shelby a split second to realize who the person behind the door was.

"You must be new here. Look, I said I don't want no pain medicine. I am going to breastfeed my baby and I don't want any of that medication in my system."

"Miss, I am just trying to check your baby's heartbeat," the nurse said.

Shelby could tell the nurse was agitated. "Poor nurse," Shelby said under her breath.

"Oh! Oooo! Another contraction. They're coming pretty quick. You need to get my doctor cause this baby will be here soon. I should know, this is my seventh child!"

"Okay, I'll go get the doctor for you," the nurse said.

"Hurry up or else I'll have to have this baby in here by myself," the woman replied.

Shelby turned around and headed back to the nurse's station.

"Shelby, you're back," Erin, one of the other nurses, said. "Did you forget something?"

"No. I heard a voice I thought I recognized in room 213. Does there happen to be a Ms. Lewis in that room?" Shelby smiled at Erin. She was a nice girl who had just started working at the hospital six months prior right out of college. Erin was a sweet girl but a little dingy at times.

Erin looked to see who was checked into room 213. "No, it's a Mrs. Sidbury."

"That's funny she sounds just like a patient I used to have at Dr. Evan's office named Melva," Shelby said beginning to dismiss the familiarity.

Erin giggled. "That is funny. This lady, Mrs. Sidbury's, first name is Melva also. Isn't that a coincidence?"

This girl is so dingy, Shelby thought. For further clarification she asked, "Erin, does Mrs. Sidbury have a middle initial?"

"Yeah it's L. Hey, I wonder if that's for Lewis."

"Probably," Shelby said. "Who is her nurse?"

"Jessica."

Jessica was new also. She had just graduated

from college two months prior. She wasn't dingy but she did let the patients intimidate her.

"Thanks, Erin. I'm going to peek in on Jessica and Ms. Sidbury."

Shelby turned back around from the desk. She wondered how people with book sense and no common sense made it through life. She also wondered why the heck she was going to peek in on Melva Lewis Sidbury. "I guess I'm a glutton for punishment." Shelby sighed.

Shelby had known Melva Sidbury for years. Melva had been one of Shelby's most dreaded patients when she worked at her previous job. Melva Lewis, as she knew her then, was always loud and spoke whatever came to her mind weather it was rude or not.

When Shelby first met her, Melva was on her third pregnancy. By the time she stopped working at Dr. Evan's office, Melva had her sixth child. That was over four years ago. Shelby recalled what Melva had said to the nurse, about this being her seventh pregnancy, and thought maybe Melva was trying to follow the advice she had given her during the fifth one. Shelby stressed the importance of birth control. At the time, Melva didn't want to hear anything about birth control, and didn't want to discuss the possibility of abstaining from sex. Shelby thought it would be a good idea, since Melva was single and already had five children. Shelby told her she might want to think about slowing down. But, a year after the fifth child, Melva had come to the office shamefaced with the news that she might be pregnant.

Shelby also remembered that Melva told her

about a new man she'd met. She ranted and raved about how this new guy was so sweet and didn't press her to get rid of the baby. Melva thought the guy might be a keeper. Shelby thought the new guy would end up being the *one*, but maybe she was wrong.

She took a deep breath before she tapped lightly on the door of room 213.

"Knock, knock," Shelby said as she finally tapped on the door.

"Who is it?" She heard Melva's distinctive voice-loud and demanding. "Come in whoever it is. It better be the doctor."

Shelby heard Melva say. She opened the door and shut it behind her. The curtain in the room was pulled midway.

"Well, who is it?" she heard Melva say again.

"Hi, Melva," Shelby said as she stepped further in. Then she peeked her head around the curtain.

"Oh, Shelby!" Melva squealed. "Hey, girl! Come on in here. Are you going to be my new nurse?" Melva asked as she looked at Shelby's work clothes.

"No, Melva. I was just getting off and I heard your voice outside in the hall. I asked the nurse if you were in here and she confirmed it for me," Shelby explained.

"Shoot. I wish you could be my nurse. These young little girls don't know what they're doing." Melva eyed the nurse who was still standing in the room.

"Hi, Jessica," Shelby said, offering the new girl a smile.

"Hi," Jessica said. Her voice was timid even though she tried to cover it.

"How far is she dilated?" Shelby asked.

"Seven centimeters. She is one-hundred percent effaced."

"Who's her doctor?" Shelby asked.

Melva cut in. "Dr. Evans. You know that. You left Dr. Evans, I didn't."

"Okay, Jessica, go get Dr. Evans. I last saw her in room 206. I'll stay here until you get back," Shelby told the new nurse, who gladly took the cue to leave.

Shelby found a place to set her purse and keys and removed her sweater.

"Shelby! What in the world? What have you been up to?" Melva stared at Shelby's stomach. "You pregnant again?"

"Yes, six and a half," Shelby replied.

"You sure? You sure are big for six and a half months."

"Thanks, Melva," Shelby said, rolling her eyes directly at her.

"Sorry, Shelby. That wasn't nice. You look really good though. Pregnancy does agree with you."

"Thank you, Melva." Shelby couldn't believe she'd actually received a complement from Melva. She had to mark this date on her calendar.

"What did you have before? I remember when you left, they told me you were pregnant."

"I had a little girl. Her name is Nyah."

"Nyah. That's a pretty name. Sounds sorta like my daughter Nyeimah's name?"

"What are you having this time?" Shelby asked.

"A boy; the last one too. Freddy wants a little boy, and he's finally going to get it." Melva sucked her teeth. "After this I am going to have my tubes tied."

Shelby couldn't believe her ears. Melva was actually going to take herself out of the baby making business.

"You remember Freddy don't you? He's the guy I told you about the last time I was pregnant. I knew he would be the right one. I guess I just had to go through all those other guys to find my diamond."

"Freddy? Was that his name?" Shelby asked trying to remember.

"Yes. He is my last baby's daddy. And, Shelby, he made an honest woman out of me, see." Melva held up the necklace around her neck. On it was a gold wedding band. "I had to take it off on account of all this weight I gained. I'll be glad when I can put it back on."

"That's wonderful, Melva. I am happy for you."

"I am happy too. I wonder where he is." Melva looked worried as she looked out of the window. "He said he would be here in thirty minutes and he just works around the corner."

"I'm sure he'll be here soon. Everything will be fine. You've done this before. You are a pro, but just remember your nurse is only trying to help you. And don't discount her for just coming out of college. Some of these new girls are actually very good. Better than some of these old nurses around here who have not been back to school for any refresher courses," Shelby said.

"I know, Shelby. I don't mean to be so hard on the little girl. I am just ready for this baby to come on out."

"I understand."

The door opened and closed. Then a lanky man, who looked to be of Asian and African American decent, emerged from around the curtain. He wore a pair of faded black pants and a work shirt with a patch that said Winchester Plastics.

"Hey, baby," he said to Melva.

"Hey baby," Melva replied. "What took you so long?"

"Traffic. They are always doing construction around here. I thought I was gonna have to get out of the car and run here."

"I'm sorry, Shelby. Freddy this is Shelby. She used to be my nurse a few years ago."

"Nice to meet you," Freddy said, extending his hand. "I'm Melva's husband.

"Nice to meet you too," Shelby said as she shook his hand.

"Ohhh! Where is that doctor?" Melva asked. As she spoke the door opened again and Jessica returned with the doctor.

"Melva, I hear you're ready," Dr. Evans said.

"I sure am, Dr. Evans," Melva sighed.

"Shelby, you're still here? I thought you got off at three," the doctor said.

"Yeah, but I heard Melva was here and thought I'd stick my head in to say hello. Now that you're here, I'm getting ready to go."

"Shelby, you don't have to leave. You can stay," Melva said.

"Melva, I'd love to but I need to pick my daughter up from day care. I'll check back on you tomorrow, okay," Shelby offered.

"Okay. You make sure you come by tomorrow," Melva said.

"I will." Shelby turned to retrieve her things. "It was nice to finally meet you, Freddy, and congratulations on the marriage and the baby."

"Thank you," Freddy replied.

Just before leaving the hospital, Shelby pulled Jessica out into the hall. "Jessica, hang in there. Don't let Mrs. Sidbury or any of the other patients intimidate you. You're the professional. Mrs. Sidbury is really a sweetheart deep down. And, her bark is a lot worse than her bite."

"Thank you, Shelby," Jessica said, "I hope one day I will be as confident and proficient as you are."

"You will. Now go back in there and do what you love to do. Everything will be fine." Shelby patted the young nurse on the shoulder.

"I will." The nurse turned and smiled for the first time since Shelby had first entered the room.

Shelby left smiling also. She was happy for Melva. Melva came a long way. She had a very nice husband and wasn't as unpleasant as she used to be. She actually seemed more sympathetic to other people's feelings.

Shelby was glad Melva found happiness. She was happy Melva finally decided to use a permanent form of birth control.

When Shelby finally made it to her car, she turned her cell phone on. It beeped indicating there was a message waiting. When she punched in her access code she found there were two messages. The first message was from her mother.

She could tell her mother called from her convertible with the top down. The sound of her mom yelling into the receiver over the wind made it hard for her to understand the message.

She did understand a few words between the gusts of wind. Her mother said something about looking forward to seeing them that weekend, and for Shelby to call her when she got the message.

Shelby's parents were coming for the Memorial Day weekend as well as Phillip's parents. They had planned to have a baby shower for Shelby as well as a cookout. Shelby still had to finish getting the house clean for all the company.

She made a mental note to call her mother later in the evening. The second message was from Phillip. His message was crisp and clear.

"Hey, baby, I just wanted to say I love you. I was just looking at you and Nyah's pictures. Call me when you get this message. I'll let you know how my day is going . . . I guess I better go before your voice mail cuts me off. Love you, sweetheart."

Shelby smiled. She loved her husband so much. They had hit if off immediately. She had known from the first time she'd met him her freshman year in college that he would be the one. She had first seen him at the library. At the time she was studying for an Anatomy exam. Phillip was one of the finest men she had seen in a long time. He stood 6' 3" inches with hazel eyes and jet-black wavy hair. His skin was the color of mocha. It had complemented her tawny complexion.

After an exchange of phone numbers, and a couple of rounds of phone tag, Shelby and Phillip went out on their first date to Mama Lula's. Years later, she and Phillip still eat at Mama Lula's Restaurant. That first night, they talked for hours getting to know each other. They went out on more dates and talked on the phone for countless hours as their relationship progressed.

After only a few weeks, Phillip had asked Shelby to be his girlfriend. She accepted without hesitation. She knew she fell in love with him. She accepted his invitation without knowing some key things about Phillip's life. He never told her about being in a fraternity and his history of being the star quarterback of the college football team. He conveniently left out information during their dating about his family being well off.

He wanted her to know him for him, not for the fraternity, football or money and prestige his family possessed. She was surprised to find out all of the information, but it didn't change her feeling about him one way or another.

Phillip had become Shelby's soul mate. He was also her confidant. When she was struggling with the idea of changing her major to nursing, Phillip stood right by her in her decision and literally stood by when she told her parents. They had always been able to talk about anything. That is until she started wanting children.

Shelby's fond thoughts suddenly turned sour. In remembering all the good times she and Phillip had together she'd almost blocked out the secret he'd kept from her for years. Reluctantly, her thoughts drifted to the day Phillip told her about an ex-girlfriend from college.

Phillip asked her to join him in the living room,

so he could sit down and talk to her. Bells of alarm immediately sounded in Shelby's head. She didn't know what to think.

When they were seated, he took her hands and told her there was something from his past that he'd been keeping from her. He told her about an ex-girlfriend in which he had gotten pregnant in college. Shelby was confused. She wondered what was wrong and why he waited until that moment to tell her about the ex.

Phillip apologized for his actions, and keeping the secret from her. He said he would do anything it took to get her forgiveness. He agreed to go through any procedures the doctor requested during their infertility treatments.

Even though it was 80 degrees outside, Shelby shivered as she thought about that time in her life. The afternoon Phillip came clean had been a dark time in their marriage and she never wanted to relive anything like it again. She never liked the way she felt as emotions she never knew existed within her came out in full force.

Shelby was thankful nothing like that had ever happened again. She felt blessed. She had friends who had gone through a whole lot more throughout their marriages. She especially thought about her best friend, Kara, and all the problems she was going through with her stepson's mother. She definitely didn't think she could put up with all the crap Kara had been putting up with for the past seven years. She also thought about her earlier conversation with Mr. and Mrs. Santini waiting eight years for a child. Shelby knew God wouldn't put more on a person than they could handle.

Shelby pushed all of the bad memories out of her head. As she pulled up to Nyah's learning center, she thought about the upcoming cookout and baby shower with all her family and friends. She knew there was no reason to dwell on the past anyway.

Shelby entered the front doors of The Learning Center, called T.L.C. by the parents and children. Through the opaque glass of the director's office, she could see that Crystal was in. She also saw Nyah playing blocks with J.J.

"Mommy!" Nyah squealed as soon as she saw her mother. She dropped the blocks she was playing with and ran up to hug her.

"Hey, sweetheart," Shelby said, bending over to give her daughter a hug. Nyah, in turn, tried to hold on to her mother's neck.

"Hold me, Mommy. Hold me!"

"Sweetie, Mommy can't hold you right now. Let go," Shelby said gently.

Nyah did what was requested of her. "Mommy's tired?" Nyah asked.

"Yes, Mommy's tired."

Shelby stood up as straight as possible and held her back. She was actually more tired than she'd realized. "Get your back pack so we can get ready to go."

"But, Mommy, J.J. and I are playing."

"Nyah," Shelby said with authority, "It is time to

go. Get your things. You'll see J.J. tomorrow. And you'll see him again this weekend on Saturday."

"I don't go to school on Saturday, Mommy." Nyah poked her lip out.

"Nyah, J.J. and Mrs. Crystal are coming to our house for the cookout, remember."

Nyah thought about it for a second, remembering the cookout on Saturday. "Yipee!" she said, turning to J.J. "J.J., you can come to my house Saturday!" Nyah was happy—her face one huge smile.

"Yipee," J.J. said, "We can play with my dinosaurs."

"I don't wanna play with your dinosaurs. I wanna play with my dolls," Nyah replied.

"Dolls are for girls. I don't wanna play with no dolls," J.J. countered.

"Mommy," Nyah said, starting to cry, "J.J. don't wanna play with my dolls."

"Miss Shelby, dolls are for girls," J.J. said, trying to plead his own case.

"Children, it will be alright. We will find something you can both play with. Now calm down, and Nyah, go get your book bag. I need to talk to Mrs. Crystal for a minute.

Nyah did as she was told and Shelby walked over to Crystal's office. "Knock, knock," Shelby said as she knocked on the door.

"Come in," Crystal answered from inside.

Shelby opened the door further and entered, trying not to waddle her gait.

"Shelby, hey. I was hoping you'd peek in. I tried to pull up your registry online a few minutes ago but was unable to retrieve it. I know I shouldn't have waited until the last minute to get you something, but it has just been so busy around here. You know with the new wing being added," Crystal explained.

"I understand," Shelby said.

"So just tell me what you really think you'll need. I want to get you something you can use right away."

"I don't know, to tell you the truth. I registered just as a formality really. I think we have everything we need; more than enough really. Our families have been sending us stuff left and right. This being the first grandson everyone is so excited. You'd think the baby was African royalty or something. He already has twice as much as what we had for Nyah when she was born, and that isn't even including the hand me down items from Nyah.

"I know he won't be able to wear all the clothing they've gotten him, not unless I change him three times a day," Shelby laughed.

"Hopefully he won't be like J.J. was. He spit up so much I had to change him three or four times a day. You never know, those clothes may come in handy."

"You're right. I hadn't even thought about that. It has been a couple of years since I've had to do this."

"It'll all come back to you and you know if it doesn't, you can always call me."

"I know. Don't worry about rushing to get anything either. Just come Saturday and have a good time, okay?" Shelby said.

"Okay, I'll just have to be creative. Have you all come up with a name yet?"

"Of course." Shelby looked at Crystal as if she should have known what the name was going to be.

"Let me guess, Phillip Jr.," Crystal stated.

"You got it. We never even considered anything else."

"You can call him P.J." Crystal said.

"I guess so."

"After a while, no one will know him by his first name. Just like J.J."

"What is J.J.'s first name?" Shelby asked.

"Warren James Shaw II. W.J. didn't have a ring to it, so we started calling him J.J."

There was a knock at the door. Shelby and Crystal looked at the door.

"Hello, ladies," Vivian Parker said.

"Vivian! Hey, how have you been?" Shelby asked.

"Wonderful. How have you been? Crystal told me you were expecting again." Vivian gave Shelby a warm hug, when she came inside.

Shelby placed her hands on her stomach. "I'm due in two months."

Vivian looked at her questioningly.

"I know it looks like I'm about to go any day now. You wouldn't be the first to say so," Shelby said.

"I wasn't going to say anything." Vivian laughed, realizing the look on her face had said everything already.

"Hey, Crystal, I just wanted to stop by and check the progress of our workers in the new wing. It looks as if everything is right on schedule. My husband will be happy to hear that," Vivian said.

"How is Roland doing?" Shelby asked.

"He's fine."

"And the kids?"

"They're good also. Kyle looks up to his big brother William, and Kylia enjoys being a big sister."

"How is little Zaria doing?"

"She's growing like a weed. She loves her big brothers and sister. She acts like she's their mother sometimes."

"That is so good to hear," Shelby said, pleased to know her friend was doing well.

Shelby met Vivian and Crystal when she was a nurse at Silvermont OB/GYN. All three women were facing various infertility problems. Shelby deemed them the "Secret Sisterhood." Like so many women who have issues with infertility, Shelby felt the sisterhood was a secret because so many women who face these problems feel like they are alone. This is a secret they keep to themselves, not realizing there is a sisterhood of women going through the very same thing.

Various circumstances allowed these three to become good friends. Crystal and Shelby were closer because their children were the same age. Shelby didn't see Vivian that often, especially since she quit her job at the OB/GYN office and decided to work at the hospital.

"How are your husband and daughter doing?" Vivian asked Shelby.

"They are wonderful. You probably saw Nyah out there playing with J.J.," Shelby said.

"No, I saw J.J., but he was by himself."

"That's funny. She should have gotten her bag by now," Shelby said with a weary look. "Let me go see where that girl is. Crystal, I'll see you later. It was really good to see you again Vivian." She gave her a hug.

"It was good to see you too," Vivian replied.

"Vivian, when are you going to come back to New Hope?" Crystal asked.

"We've been going to another church on the west side of the city. But, we are thinking about coming back to New Hope. I really like it there, and it seems as though I'm not getting what I need at this other church," Vivian admitted.

"Well, I hope you come back. We really miss you," Shelby said.

"I might come this Sunday," Vivian said. "I'm sure the kids will enjoy coming back also. They loved the youth program New Hope has."

"That would be good. Maybe we can all go out to eat afterwards," Crystal said.

"Sounds like a plan to me," Vivian said.

"Oh yeah, and Vivian, if you're not doing anything this Saturday, you are welcome to come over to my house. We are having a cookout to celebrate the baby coming. They are calling it a baby shower, but I think it's only a formality," Shelby said.

"I wish I could," Vivian said sadly, "but Roland and I are taking the kids to Myrtle Beach for a day trip. They have been looking forward to it."

"Okay, well, hopefully we'll see you at church Sunday," Shelby said. "Let me go find Nyah and get home. You both take care." Shelby hugged them both as she left.

Shelby cut the engine of her Navigator off and closed the door of her garage. In the backseat Nyah had fallen to sleep. She looked peaceful, and Shelby hated to wake her up.

As she opened Nyah's passenger door, her cell phone rang. Quickly hitting the answer button, she softly said, "Hello."

"Shelby." She heard her best friend's strained voice on the other end of the line. Shelby knew something wasn't right.

"Kara? What's wrong?" She asked cutting to the point.

"That woman was in my house!"

Shelby could hear fury in Kara's voice. Fury she hadn't heard since the two were in middle school and one of their classmates wrote all over Kara's textbooks. Kara fought the girl, and was suspended from school. The fury also caused Kara to get a case of the chicken pox. She was sick with it during her entire suspension.

"Kara, where are you?" Shelby asked.

"I'm sitting in my car, in the parking lot at work." Kara said, through what sounded like clenched teeth.

"Are you on your way home?" Shelby asked.

"No. I can't drive. I've been sitting in this car for the past 45 minutes trying to calm down."

Shelby thought, *if this is calm, I'd hate to have heard her 45 minutes ago.* "What happened?" Shelby figured it must have something to do with Kara's stepson's mother.

"That woman had the nerve to come into my house. She came a day early to pick up Nate Jr. and she knew Nathaniel and I wouldn't be home until after five. And that—" Kara took a long deep breath, "shady woman came into my house."

Shelby's mouth dropped open.

"She knows I don't want her in my house. I've never even let her past the front door." Kara said. "So I guess she figured a way to get in. It wasn't like Nate Jr. was going to tell his mom she couldn't come in."

"How'd you find out?"

"Nate called me and said Miss Thing left a little note on our message board, saying she'd picked up Nate Jr. and that we had a lovely home." Kara screamed.

Shelby held the phone away from her ear.

"I could strangle her. She crossed the line this time," Kara said.

"Okay, Kara, calm down please."

Kara's heavy breathing filled the phone. She didn't utter a word.

Shelby returned to the driver's side of her SUV and got back in. She cranked the SUV back up and opened the garage to back out. "Kara, honey, you've got to calm down. Did Nate say anything was missing or askew?"

"He said he didn't see where anything was out of place. But you know how men can be sometimes. They don't notice the little things that we notice. And, I'd better not find anything misplaced."

"Don't let this woman get the best of you. She is just trying to get your goat. I mean, what can she really do to you? She has no power. And obviously doesn't have a life, the way she's always trying to find things to do to get on you and Nate's nerves." Shelby said. "Don't do anything crazy. All this woman wants is some attention."

"Shelby, I'm just so mad right now, I don't know what to do. I'm shaking so bad I can't even drive."

"Don't worry; I'm on my way to your job now. I'll drive you home," Shelby said. "I'm not trying to get in you and Nate's business. I'll drop you off and the kids can hang out with Nyah and me for a little while, so you two can talk."

Kara was silent for a moment. "It just makes me mad, Shelby. I don't know what time she came. Who knows how many hours she was in my house walking around looking through our stuff? That is a complete invasion of our privacy. Who does she think she is?"

"I don't know. But at least you know some of what this woman is capable of. When you get home, look around and check things out. But, don't worry yourself. She can't touch you. You're protected by the blood of Jesus. No weapon that is formed against you will prosper. Stand on God's word." Shelby said.

Shelby's phone beeped indicating her battery was low. "Kara, my phone is about to go out. I'll be there in about five minutes. I'll see you in a few."

Shelby's phone shut off before she could get a response from Kara.

Chapter 5

Phillip Tomlinson

Mercy

Phillip walked towards the front door to answer it. The doorbell rang again. "I'm coming," Phillip said as he approached the door. His house shoes slapped against the marble floor as he walked.

He was expecting his parents to arrive early, so without bothering to look first, he opened the door. The first thing he saw was a huge blue bow and on top of an enormous box.

"Hey, son," Phillip's father, Gordon Tomlinson said.

"Hey, Pop," Phillip said as he gave his father a hug. Phillip was the spitting image of his father, except for the sprinkles of gray throughout his father's head and the pouch in his father's stomach from years of not eating well. Gordon Tomlinson stood at 6' 4", just one inch taller than his son.

"Hey, baby," his mother, Glenda Tomlinson said.

"Mama," Phillip said giving his mother a hug. Glenda was the shortest of the Tomlinson clan. She was only 5' 5". She had what people would call a small frame. At the age of 53 she only weighed 125 lbs. And that was the heaviest she had ever been in her life, even with both of her pregnancies. In her younger days, her weight fluctuated between 105 and 110.

"What is this?" Phillip asked as he eyed the enormous gift.

"It's a surprise. You and Shelby will see when she opens the gift later," his mother said.

"Come on in." Phillip moved to the side. "I'll take the gift in, Dad."

His parents stepped into the foyer. "Whew it feels good in here. I can't believe they are forecasting the temperature to be 90 today. It would be a great day to go to the beach," Glenda said.

"Not on Memorial Day weekend. I'll bet the beaches are jam-packed with people. I'll be just fine sitting by Shelby and Phillip's pool," Gordon said.

"I'm glad I went ahead and got it ready last weekend. Come on in to the den," Phillip said behind the box he was holding. "This thing is pretty heavy."

"Well, don't shake it trying to guess what it is. You'll never guess," Glenda told him.

Phillip did as he was told and put the box next to the table for the shower gifts. Phillip's father took a seat on the couch, picked up the remote control and started flipping through channels looking for the sports on ESPN.

"Where are Shelby and Nyah?" Glenda asked.

"They're upstairs. Nyah spilled grape juice on her dress about ten minutes before you all got here," Phillip replied.

"Grape juice? That stain will never come out. What color was the dress?" his mother asked.

"Pink. A very pale pink."

"Oh, I hope she got some good wear out of it before today."

"She did. It was actually her favorite dress."

"Poor little Nyah. I wonder if Shelby needs me to help her do anything. Something sure smells good already." Glenda inhaled.

"I don't know, Mom. Go on up; she'll let you know. Dad, you can help me with the grill."

Phillip's mother headed for the stairs, while the men went to the back deck.

Phillip poured the charcoals into the grill and poured lighter fluid on them so they could soak. He grabbed the broom to finish sweeping the deck off.

"Have a seat over here, Dad." Phillip pulled a chair over to the side where he has already finished sweeping. I'll finish cleaning this deck off in a few minutes. Then, we can go out to the garage and look at the Chevy."

"How is the restoration coming?"

"It's coming along great. I have just a couple more things to do and I'll take it out for its first real spin." Phillip swept as he spoke.

"What color did you decide on?"

"Do you even have to ask? Candy apple red."

"So it'll match your fraternity tag, huh?" his father chuckled.

"You know it. You know every since I was a little boy that's been my dream. I wanted to pledge the same fraternity as you and drive a Chevy pick-up truck like grandpa's. When I saw this truck for sale, I imagined it would have fraternity colors. It's a dream come true!"

"Your grandfather would have been proud of you. I wish he could see you now. Too bad we weren't able to keep the truck he had years ago," Gordon said.

"It's funny now that I think about it. You've got all these dealerships and all these cars. You could easily buy Grandpa's truck a hundred times over."

"I can now, but that was a long time ago. Your grandparents did the best they could to raise me and my other nine brothers and sisters. They worked hard and made us appreciate working also. They couldn't send us to college, so they made sure we knew how to work to send ourselves through college.

"All their work has made a better man out of me. I appreciate all they did. That's why I didn't pledge the fraternity until my senior year, when I knew I was going to graduate for sure. I didn't have the luxury of loafing off, and wasting my parents' money. I was spending my money. I made good on it."

"You had it pretty hard back then, didn't you, Dad?"

"You don't know the half of it. There were many nights when I wondered if I was even going to make it. I worked at night and went to school all day. I not only paid for school and living expenses, but I always sent something home to help my parents with my brothers and sisters.

"My parents never asked me to, but it was just something I felt I had to do, especially after Mother got sick with diabetes. I made a personal vow to help as much as I could. I learned a great deal, and that's why I ended up majoring in business. I knew people who had their own businesses were thriving and those who were working for someone else were getting by for the most part.

"I wanted to have my own business one day. I wanted to be my own boss. That was my goal and I achieved it," Phillip's father said.

"Wow. You never told me that. I know you had it pretty hard, but I never knew it was that hard for you. I guess that's where I get all my hard work and determination from."

"You remind me a lot of myself, especially as you tried to make your own statement in life. You could have slacked off in school too. Even though you knew your mom and I were well off, you still studied hard and received your degree.

"Look at you now. You are working your way up on the ladder of success by your own rights. You have a lovely wife and a beautiful daughter. Your baby boy is on his way—my first grandson.

"This house of yours could make three of the houses we had when I was your age. And, you just don't quit. You have so much determination. I know it would be easy for you to work for me. You know the business will be yours one day. I can't leave it to your brother," Gordon Tomlinson snickered. "He'd have it run into the ground before my body got cold."

Phillip agreed. "You're right about that. I am a

lucky man. I have the American dream. Shelby is wonderful. I couldn't have asked for any one better. I love Nyah with all my heart. And I can't believe I have a son on the way! Sometimes I want to pinch myself. I just received the position I've been wanting in the company for the past three years. It was hard work, but the success is so sweet."

"And you do this even though I could give you our family business on a silver platter right now. You don't hang on our coat tails."

"I've always wanted to make you proud of me, Dad."

"You have, son. Your mother and I are so very proud of you. We love you and that crazy brother of yours."

"How's he doing anyway? I haven't heard from him in a while."

"He's okay. He calls every now and then for money, saying he has a sure deal, which will make him some big dough. I tell him only hard work is going to give him the kind of dough that lasts, but he is so stubborn. He's my son and I love him, so I can't say no."

"I don't mean any harm, Dad, but you can say no. He's just using you and Mom. The last time he called and asked me for money, I told him no. That's probably why he hasn't called me in a while. He acted like he was hurt at first, then he got down right angry, telling me I was no kind of brother and that I should help him out."

"I know son but . . ."

"Dad, that's just it. You surprise me when it

comes to him. I know you work hard for your money and so do I. Gordon Jr. doesn't. It's just like he has a career of trying to see who he can take advantage of. I'd help him if he was actually helping himself, but it's time out for handouts."

"You're right. I guess when it comes to Gordon Jr. I just have a soft spot. I don't want to see him fail or anything."

"If I know anything about Gordon Jr., it's that he's resilient. If he had to swim or drown, be sure he would swim. He might only be able to back float into shore, but he'd get there. I have just two words for you, Dad," Phillip said with all seriousness.

"What's that?" his father asked.

"Tough love."

"That's what my big brother needs from you and Mom. He'll come around, you'll see."

"You're right, son. And I respect your opinion. I'll have to take into consideration what you are saying. I don't want Gordon Jr. to fail because I wasn't stern enough with him. Maybe I have been going about this the wrong way."

Phillip scooped all the dirt into the dustpan and threw it in the trashcan. "Think about it, Dad."

"I will," his father replied.

"Now let's get off that subject. How about we go look at my truck," Phillip said.

"Sounds good to me."

Phillip and his father walked out to the unattached garage. Phillip had the garage built soon after buying his used Chevy. He needed a place of his own to work on it and store it. Instead of adding on to his attached two-car garage, he built another one in the back of his house.

The garage was made for three vehicles. In addition to his dream of restoring the Chevy, he wanted to restore two more. The candy-apple red one was just the first. It was a hobby he had taken on and literally loved.

Phillip pulled the hidden key from above the door, unlocked it, and flipped on the light. A cool rush of wind hit them as they stepped in. Phillip installed a heater and air-conditioning unit. He didn't want to freeze or burn up while working on the cars.

He installed a stereo system and television. There was a refrigerator for cold drinks as well as a coffee maker. That way, he wouldn't have to trek in and out of his house in the middle of his work.

The garage was a place of solace, especially after a hard day at work. He had pictures of old Chevy's on the wall. One was a 1967 just like the one he was remodeling. Phillip had also acquired a couple of old Chevrolet Dealership signs with some assistance from his dad. He'd mounted them on the walls. It was a car lover's dream.

"Son, you've done a good job with this garage." Gordon admired the pictures and signs he had helped his son get. "This car," he ran his hand over the chrome rearview mirror, "looks like it's in mint condition. What else do you have left to do?"

"I need to fix the steering wheel. I hired someone who will custom make it out of mahogany wood and varnish it. It will be beautiful!"

"It's beautiful." His father continued to admire all the work his son had done. "Look at those bumpers and these wheels. They are gleaming and not a scratch to be seen. It brings back so many memories."

"Look here, Dad. The truck bed is wooden also. I remember how you used to say Grandpa would pile you all up in the back of the truck. And how he had put wood back there, so it wouldn't be as cold in the winter, or too hot from the sun in the summer."

His father looked at the bed of the pickup truck. Tears welled in his eyes. "This is absolutely beautiful, son. I can't wait to take a ride in it."

"I ordered that steering wheel over four weeks ago. It should be in any day now. I'll call the guy when we go back to the house and see if it's here yet. If it comes in we can take it for a spin before you leave."

"Look at this engine, Dad," Phillip said as he popped the hood.

"Umph, now that's some power. Are you sure those people from that show *Overhaulin'* didn't do all this work?"

Phillip rolled his eyes, "Yeah, right. They have nothing on me. Look at this engine; it has a 400 high-compression automatic shift. I used high compression pistons with head and added a 285-lift cam. I added a four-barrel carburetor. I've got 60 tires on the front and 411 positive traction tires on the rear. They are N-50-15 street tires."

His father was speechless with admiration.

"Feel how smooth this dashboard is, Dad. I sanded and primed it."

His father felt the smoothness of the dashboard. "I hope that steering wheel is in. I'm ready to take a spin."

"Let's go back up to the house and call." Phillip turned off the lights and locked the door of the garage.

Gordon Tomlinson looked around. "I'm surprised you don't have a phone line installed in there."

"Nah, usually I just bring my cell phone out here, but I left it on the charger."

Upon their entering the sliding glass door, Shelby said, "Welcome back, strangers."

"Hey, baby," Phillip said. "We were outside looking at the truck."

"Mom and Dad are here," Shelby said as soon as Phillip walked into the back door.

"Good, where are they?" Phillip asked looking around.

"They just pulled up. Can you help them unload the car? They brought some more food for the shower."

"Sure, baby." Phillip closed the sliding glass door and walked to the front to greet his in-laws.

"Hey, Mom and Dad," Phillip said to Lloyd and Vanessa Adams. He had been calling Shelby's parents Mom and Dad since he and Shelby got married. The whole time he'd known Shelby's parents, they'd treated him as if he was their own child.

"Hey, Phillip," Vanessa said. She placed the Watergate Salad she was holding on the hood of the car and gave him a quick hug and kiss on the cheek.

Phillip then shook his father-in-law's hand.

"Mom, let me get that for you." Phillip took the salad from his mother-in-law. "Is there anything else you need me to get?"

Vanessa said, "Yeah, there's a blue bag in the back seat. Can you get it? And be careful, it's got hot wings in it."

"I sure will." Phillip reached into the back seat of the Cadillac and retrieved the bag. "How was the drive down?"

"It was good. We hit a little bit of rain, but that was it," Lloyd said.

Shelby's parents grabbed the rest of their belongings and followed Phillip into the house.

"My parents got here about 45 minutes ago. The women are in the kitchen, if you want to join them," Phillip said once they were inside. "Dad, my Dad is in the living room. He's probably found a game to watch by now."

Phillip put everything on the kitchen bar, and joined his father and father-in-law. "Let's see if the steering wheel is ready." Phillip picked up the cordless phone to call. The shop owner said the wheel was ready for pick up. "Good news! It's ready," Phillip grinned.

"How's the restoration coming?" Lloyd asked.

"Great. I just showed my Dad the truck. The steering wheel was the last part I was waiting for. If I can get it on this evening then we can take it for a spin."

"You should see it. Phillip did an extraordinary job. It reminds me so much of my Dad's 57' Chevy pick up truck. Of course my father's truck was blue, not candy apple red."

"I bet it's nice," Lloyd commented.

"Nice isn't a sufficient enough word. After the shower, we can pick up the steering wheel and go out to the garage and put it on. Then we can all take it for a spin," Phillip told his father-in-law.

Phillip looked down at his watch, "I guess we had better get back out on the deck and start the meats."

The men congregated outside to bar-b-que the ribs, chicken, steaks, and sausages, and the women prepared all the other hors d'oeuvres inside. The guests arrived at 2:00 p.m. as planned. Shelby and Phillip invited close friends and family for the intimate celebration. By 5:00 that evening, everyone was full and ready for Shelby to open up the gifts.

Phillip stepped out onto the deck to call everyone outside, in. "Come on in, everyone. Let's go into the living room so Shelby can open the gifts."

The people who were enjoying the spring warmth outside relocated in the cool spacious living room. All the gifts for the baby were located on a table in the corner of the room. Since Shelby and Phillip had already gotten most of what the baby would need, their family and friends knew they'd have to be creative in their gift giving.

"First of all, Shelby, Nyah, Little Phillip and I would like to thank you all for coming. You are all our closest family and friends and you mean so much to us." Phillip looked lovingly at Shelby as he spoke.

"Yes, we love you all. And thank you for all the

support over the first six and a half months of this pregnancy. I've needed it. My pregnancy with Nyah was nothing like this," Shelby said.

"Oh, Phillip and Shelby, you know we love you too," Phillip's mother said.

"Yes, and we will always be here for you," Vanessa said.

"You know you can call me at any time," Crystal added. "I remember the first three months with J.J.'s pregnancy. That is why I have taken so long in considering if I even want to go through it again," Crystal laughed.

"Yeah right, Crystal," Shelby said.

"You're right. If God blessed us with another child and I had to go through that sickness again, I would," Crystal admitted.

"Come on, Shelby, you're going to make me cry in a minute with all this melodrama. When are the violins going to start playing? We all love you. We know you all love us, now let's get on with the opening of the presents. I can't wait for you to see mine," Kara, said.

"Okay, okay. I just need to run to the bathroom for a quick second," Shelby said. "You'll have to wait a couple more minutes." Shelby stood and waddled to the bathroom.

"Ugh, I wanna see the presents now!" J.J. said.

"Me too, me too," Nyah added.

"J.J., Nyah. Where are your manners? I know I've taught you both better than that. Now sit down and be patient," Crystal said.

"Does anyone else need anything?" Phillip asked.

"Yeah, son, could you get me some more cola?" Phillip's dad asked.

"Sure."

"I'd like some more punch," Shelby's mother said.

"Okay, one cola and punch coming up. Anyone else?" Phillip waited for a reply.

No one else said anything. Phillip took the cups and headed to the kitchen. While he poured the soda and dipped the punch he hummed lightly. He could picture riding on the beltline in his candy apple red pickup truck. "Life is so good!" he said to himself.

He picked up both cups and headed back into the living room. As he passed the cordless phone on the kitchen wall, it rang. He then put both cups in one hand in order to answer it. "I'll get it!" he said loudly.

He picked up the receiver. "Hello," he said in a singsong voice similar to what he had been humming just a couple of seconds before. He heard nothing. "Hello," he said again. Still hearing nothing he said, "Is anybody there?" He listened again. It sounded as though he heard shallow breathing so he knew someone had to have been on the other end. "Look, who ever this is, you need to stop calling my house. It's rude to play games on the phone. Call again and we'll have your number traced."

Nyah came in to the kitchen and tugged at his pants leg. "Daddy, Daddy come on. Mommy is about to open the presents!"

"Daddy's coming, go on, tell Mommy to start," Phillip told his daughter. He listened again. He heard a bearish growl before the phone was slammed down on the other end. "Good riddance. I hope that teaches them to stop playing games on the phone," Phillip said with exasperation. He was tired of whoever was calling his house and job.

"I'm back." He handed the drinks back after reentering the living room. "What did I miss?"

"Nothing, this is the first gift," Shelby said.

"Why don't we open the big box, with the enormous blue bow first?" Phillip asked.

"Because your parents said we have to open it last," Shelby told him.

"Patience, my son," Phillip's mother said.

Everyone laughed.

"First present." Shelby opened the card. "Okay this is from Kara and the family." She tore the blue and green wrapping off the box, which revealed the gift. "Oh, a hand and footprint kit. Thanks, Kara. I can put it right next to the one we had framed for Nyah. You got us hers didn't you?"

"Sure did. I couldn't leave little Phillip out. Now all our kids will have the same memories."

"Thank you. Kara is into sentimental things," Shelby told everyone. "She's so creative when it comes to gift ideas also."

"Look under the kit. There's something else," Kara said.

Shelby lifted the kit and saw a gift certificate to the Baby Boutique. Her eyes widened when she saw the amount. "Thanks, it's a gift certificate to the Baby Boutique. Wow, Kara. Did you add an extra zero by accident?"

"That's for after the baby is born in case you forgot to get something," Kara said.

Phillip looked at the amount also. "Forgot something like what, a mini race car?"

"Nothing's too good for my new godson," Kara said.

"I should have known," Shelby laughed.

Shelby continued opening the gifts. They received a Bible from Crystal, and her family with promises to have it engraved with the baby's name once he was here and they were sure he would be a boy.

They received an ivory sculpture from her parents. It was of a family with a father, mother, a little girl and a baby. Every one admired its intricate detail. They had gotten numerous specialty gifts from the people who were present and others who could not attend but sent their gifts anyway.

Finally they were down to the last gift.

Phillip asked for permission in a childlike tone. "Mom, Dad. Can we open it now?"

His mother answered back in a similar tone, "Yes."

As Shelby removed the massive bow, Nyah started crying.

Shelby stopped. "Nyah, what's wrong?"

"I didn't get any presents," Nyah wailed.

"Nyah," Shelby said fully understanding. She had wondered why Nyah had been so good during the opening of all the other gifts. She'd been waiting patiently for a gift.

Phillip's mother spoke up. "Nyah, sweetheart. It's okay. Grandpa Gordon and I have something in this box for you too."

Nyah wiped her tears and Phillip and Shelby looked at his parents with relief and thanks.

"Now I'm really curious," Phillip said.

"Me too," Shelby said. "Nyah do you want to help Mommy open this gift?"

Nyah sniffled and wiped her face again. "Un huh," she said, shaking her head with confirmation.

"Can I help too?" J.J. piped in.

"No, J.J., sit back and watch," Crystal said.

J.J poked his lips out and crossed his arms.

"Watch it, young man." Crystal said with her finger wagging.

J.J. pulled his lips in slightly and turned his attention to the gift.

Nyah stood next to her mother and timidly tore the wrapping off the box. Once the paper was off, the outside of the box still gave no indication as to what the contents were. Shelby stood and removed the lid.

She removed the balled up paper, which had been stuffed in the box to prevent its contents from moving around too much. Then she pulled out one of the items.

"Chains?" She asked quizzically. Then she pulled out another item. "Plastic rings, long pieces of rubber and a home sweet home sign? What on earth?"

"Is that what I think it is, Mom and Dad?" Phillip asked.

"Sure is." His mom and dad smiled gleefully.

"But Nyah already has a swing set," Phillip said.

"But not one with a little house, the infant swings and a kiddie pool all in one. I promise you all have never seen one like it." Phillip's father said.

"Where is all the other stuff?" Phillip asked. "I know it can't be in this one box."

"No, the people at the Home Warehouse will deliver the rest and set it all up. You won't have to even lift a finger," Phillip's father said.

"Yipee! I'm getting a play house!" Nyah said.

"Can I play in it, Nyah?" J.J. asked.

"Yeah, J.J. We are gonna have fun!" Nyah replied.

"Thanks, Mom and Dad," Phillip said.

"This one will be just what we need for both children. I never would've guessed what was in the box," Shelby said. "And thank you for thinking about Nyah too."

After the last present was opened, the women sat around and talked while the men drove to pick up the steering wheel for the truck. When they returned, Phillip affixed it in the proper place. Once he was done he smiled with pleasure.

"Done! After ten months of hard work, it is finally finished."

"Looks good, son," Phillip's father said.

"I remember when you first got this old heap. You surely saw something I didn't. Are you sure you didn't just go back out and buy one someone else had remodeled?" Phillip's father-in-law chuckled while he asked.

"No sir. Everything you see is genuine. I did most of the work by myself. My fraternity brothers, Will and Rick, helped me some I must admit though."

Lloyd Adams patted Phillip on the back. "I know, I'm just kidding. You should be proud of yourself."

Phillip smiled with pride. "I am."

Phillip heard the door open and slam shut.

"Hey, Daddy," Nyah said.

"Nyah, baby? What are you doing out here? I thought you were inside playing with J.J." Phillip said.

"J.J. went to sleep. What you doing, Daddy?" Nyah asked, changing the subject.

"Daddy is looking at his truck with your grandfathers."

Nyah placed her face in front of the trucks shiny reflective door. "Pretty Daddy, I can see my face." She giggled. "Look, Daddy my face looks funny." She moved her head up and down watching the distorted face turn from normal to wide then skinny. She giggled again. Then she took her hands and rubbed the place where she saw her reflection.

"No, Nyah!" Phillip said sternly.

Nyah pulled her hand back quickly, startled by the elevated volume in his voice.

"Nyah, don't do that sweetheart," Phillip tried to soften his tone realizing he had scared his daughter.

Nyah started crying. "Oh, sweetie, it's okay; don't cry." Phillip started towards his daughter. She shrunk back and ran to her grandfather.

"I've got her son," Gordon said.

"I didn't mean to scare her. It's just that she ate some more ribs. Look at that smeared rib sauce on the side of the truck," Phillip explained.

Nyah started crying harder.

"It's okay baby. Daddy didn't mean to scream." Gordon Tomlinson picked his granddaughter up. "Let's go in the bathroom and wash your little hands."

Phillip turned to his father-in-law. "Really, Dad, I didn't mean to scare her," he said with embarrassment.

"I know, son. She'll be alright."

"Let me clean this sauce off the truck." Phillip grabbed a rag and some water, then commenced to cleaning the spot.

His father returned with Nyah a couple of minutes later. Nyah avoided looking at her father.

"Nyah, baby, come here." Phillip picked his daughter up. She didn't resist. "Daddy loves you. I didn't mean to yell. Are you okay?"

Nyah shook her head to let her father know she was going to be okay.

"Tell you what. Tomorrow I'll take you and J.J. to get some ice cream in the new truck. Would you like that?"

Nyah smiled.

"Now don't cry anymore. Your face is too pretty for all those tears."

Nyah smiled again. "Daddy, is Mommy going to be mad at me?"

"No, sweetheart. We won't tell Mommy what happened. It is all over now. So you just keep smiling."

Nyah gave Phillip a hug.

Phillip's father-in-law shook his head. "What in the world are you and Shelby going to do when the baby gets here? Nyah's so used to getting all this attention from you being the only child. You'll have to start splitting it."

Phillip shook his head too. "I don't know. I really don't know."

Phillip didn't know why, but when his father-in-law made mention of Nyah being an only child, a thought of Jeana's son, crossed his mind.

Chapter 6

Jeana Sands

Vengeance

Jeana growled and slammed the phone down. "The nerve of him!" Rage bellowed from within. "Daddy, Daddy, Mommy's gonna open her gifts," she said mocking the little girl's voice she heard over the receiver.

She didn't know why she kept making crank calls to Phillip's house and job. But after calling the first few times, it was like she had some sort of addiction. She knew she was wrong, and she vowed it would be her last call. But, every time she hung up, it left her with a growing sense of rage that hovered deep within.

"Mom, what's wrong?" Jeana's thirteen year-old son, Taren, asked.

Jeana hadn't realized her son was standing behind her, and hoped he hadn't witnessed what had just happened. "Oh nothing, honey. It's just those darn telemarketers. They make me so mad sometimes. They call at the most inopportune times. I know I should've put my name on that do not call list," Jeana said, trying to cover up the rage she was feeling. She hoped her son hadn't sensed she was lying.

"Oh. Granny hates it when they call too."

"Yeah, what brings you in here? Have you finished unpacking your boxes?"

"Not yet. I'm almost finished though," Taren answered.

"Well, go ahead. I need to finish unpacking all this kitchen stuff." Jeana pulled the colander out of the box marked utensils.

"Okay, Mom," Taren said with reluctance in his voice.

Noticing the hesitation in her son's movements, Jeana asked, "What's wrong?"

"Mom, you know my birthday is coming up soon."

"I'm your Mama, boy; of course I know your birthday is coming up." Lovingly Jeana stroked her son's curly jet-black hair.

"Mom," Taren said in a stop that tone. "You're always doing that. Promise me at my new school you won't do that in front of the other boys. I'm too old for you to be treating me like a little five-year old with all the hugging and kissing. People are gonna think I'm a Mama's boy or something."

"You are a Mama's boy. Don't listen to everything your granny tells you either. There are some little boys who would love to have their mothers hug them every once in a while." *Or their father's,* Jeana thought.

"It's just embarrassing that's all."

"Okay, I tell you what, I promise not to embarrass you in front of your friends, but at home I don't want to hear you talking about how embarrassing it is for a mom to love her son. You're my baby, sweetheart, and no matter how old you get, you will always be my baby." Jeana pulled her son close and gave him a bear hug. She held on and didn't let go until he spoke.

"Okay, Mom." He pulled away. "Will that hug hold you for the next couple of days?"

"No, smart alec, but it will probably hold me until mid-night. Now stop being so funny." Taren smiled at his mom. "Now what was it you were saying about someone having a birthday in the near future?"

"Me, Mom."

"What about it? What do you want?" Taren looked down at his shoes. "Son, why are you looking down? Did you drop something?"

"No."

"Don't you want to tell me what you want for your birthday?"

"Yeah, but now that I think about it, don't worry about it. A cake and my favorite dinner will be good," Taren said.

"Just a cake and a special dinner? Are you sure that's all you want?" Jeana knew what her son really wanted. "I thought all the kids were into the game player 3000 these days. But, I guess you're different from those young boys who still want hugs from their mothers out in public."

Taren's eyes lit up. "Mom! How'd you know I wanted a game player 3000?"

"I know. I think you'll be pleased with your birthday present this year," Jeana said.

"Wow, Mom. I can't believe I'm getting a game player 3000. All the kids are into it." The cheer in Taren's voice subsided. "But, Mom, I know you can't afford it."

"Don't worry about money. In the past, no we couldn't afford it because I was in school, and we were trying to make ends meet. But, with this new job, things are really looking up for us."

"Does that mean I can have a pair of Kelsey Jackson high top sneakers?" Taren pressed.

Jeana smiled. "Yes son. You can."

"Are you serious, Mom? I can?" Taren asked in disbelief.

"Yes," Jeana said with all seriousness.

"Mom, you're the greatest. This will be the best birthday ever! I can't wait to go back home and show my friends. This is so cool!" Taren hugged his mom, and then he pulled back. "When are we going back home, Mom?"

"This is it. We'll go back and visit Granny and Grandpa but this is our home now."

"What if I don't like it here?" Taren asked with concern.

"You'll like it. I promise. There is so much to do in Silvermont. And the Middle school you'll be going to is one of the best in the nation. There are so many more opportunities for us here."

"If you say so," Taren conceded.

"Now run along and finish unpacking your boxes. We're going out for dinner tonight. I don't feel like cooking and for the first time in a long time we can afford to go."

"Burgers or chicken?" Taren asked.

"How about smothered pork chops or Salisbury steak?" Jeana asked.

"That sounds better than having burgers and greasy fried chicken again," Taren admitted.

"We're going to a restaurant called Mama Lula's. You'll love it. I used to go there when I was in college. She has some of the best food; real good southern cooking."

"Like Granny's cooking on a Sunday?"

"Better than Granny's," Jeana said.

"Sounds good. I'll go finish unpacking right now." Taren turned, running to his room.

"Be ready by 6:30, okay," Jeana said as he entered the hallway.

"I'll be ready."

Jeana watched her son as he dashed to his room. He was the spitting image of his father. He had the same hazel eyes as Phillip as well as the same curly jet-black hair and mocha skin tone. Soon he'd be as tall as his father, she figured in about three years or so. The only major difference in Taren and his father was that Taren had a cleft in his chin. Jeana knew Taren would turn out even more handsome than his father.

Her son asked her where his father was. Jeana couldn't tell him the truth, so she told him his grandfather was going to be his father. But, he kept asking about what happened to his real father. Jeana told him his father had gone away and would never come back. She made the insinuation seem as if his father had died.

For years, Taren wished his father would come back as his birthday present. He gave up on this happening two years ago. Jeana was glad that with her new job, salary, and degree, she could finally give her son something he wanted. The fact that Taren still wanted deep down for his father to return laid heavy on her mind. This year her son would get all three wishes. He'd get his game player 3000, the Kelsey Jackson high top sneakers, and if things worked according to her plans, he'd finally get to meet his father.

Her parents were from a little community called Edgecomb and had lived there all their lives. As far as Jeana was concerned, she knew they would probably die there. They hadn't seen much of a reason to take Jeana or her five brothers and sisters anywhere. Jeana was the youngest and had been deemed the black sheep of the family for having aspirations and "lofty dreams" as her dad often said.

Jeana had dreams and aspirations. She knew they'd be met someday. She knew there was more to life than just living in Edgecombe and working at the local Hardee's restaurant. She would show her family she could make it without them.

Silvermont was the best thing to happen to her. Jeana was a smart girl, and knew her parents weren't going to help her go to college. With the help of her counselor at school, she got all the classes she needed and studied hard, graduating as the class valedictorian at Topsail High School.

Before going to Silvermont to attend Central State University, Jeana traveled a 100 mile radius from the home she had lived in since birth. The few trips she took were with her school to the aquarium or to museums—all educational trips.

Silvermont had been a metropolis she was not used to.

She first met her college roommate at freshman orientation. She was also from a small town in North Carolina just like Jeana's; they only had one traffic light. So, they meshed immediately.

She received offers for full scholarships from colleges across the country, and ended up choosing CSU because of its prestige. She wanted to obtain her Bachelor of Business Administration in Marketing, and she knew CSU had the best business school in the nation.

Jeana looked for the business building during her freshman orientation and ended up asking a handsome guy she saw if he knew where it was. He was very friendly and walked her there. They made some small talk as he showed her around.

He said his name was Phillip and asked what her name was.

Jeana knew if she had been a red bone, her face would have been beet red. She was glad she was what most people would call a dark almond color. She became self-conscious about what she was wearing and how her hair had looked. She had worn a mint colored mini skirt with a cream blouse. Her shoes were cream sling backs with one-inch pumps. She wore her shoulder length hair down with soft curls. The jewelry she had worn was all silver, since she hadn't been able to budget in real gold.

Jeana stuttered out her name. "Jee-aana." She was embarrassed. She was stuttering and knew her Southern drawl was even more prevalent when she did so.

"J' Anna, what a pretty name for a pretty girl," Phillip said.

Jeana quickly collected herself and cleared her throat as if she had something caught in it. "No, it's Jeana." She tried to make it not sound so southern.

"Still a pretty name."

The guy didn't notice her stuttering. She allowed herself to relax some.

Jeana wanted to pinch herself. It felt like she was dreaming.

"So where are you from?" he asked.

"Edgecomb."

"Where's that?"

"In Eastern North Carolina. It is between Wilmington and Jacksonville," Jeana said. "It's closer to Hampstead."

Phillip shook his head. "I've never heard of it."

"It's tiny compared to Silvermont. Where are you from?"

"Born and raised in Raleigh."

Jeana had never been to Raleigh. "What's your major?" she ventured asking.

"Business."

"Me too!" Jeana said excitedly. "I'm concentrating in marketing."

"I'm concentrating in finance."

"What a small world." Jeana smiled.

The topic of their majors had spiked Jeana's sociability. She talked non-stop, until they reached the business building. He gave her his pager number.

Not long after that, she learned the guy she'd been talking to was CSU's star player. She felt lucky to get his pager number. She found herself thinking of him often. She went to one of the home football games and saw Phillip, also known as P.T., in action. This made her think of an excuse to call him.

She paged him to ask some questions about their majors. He asked to meet her by the student union, then he drove them to the park where they talked. She finally gave him her number and he started calling her. They dated for a couple of months. Jeana felt like she was dreaming during that time. She read about love stories in the books she had checked out of the library, and it felt as if she was a character in one of them.

During the time they dated, Phillip made her feel like a queen. He gave her flowers and candy. He took her to lunch and dinner. Her fondest memories were when they had gone to Mama Lula's for lunch or dinner. The food and conversation together were always good.

Not wanting to wake up from the fairytale, Jeana had made sure not to ask Phillip to come home and meet her family. She knew they would only embarrass her. They'd think Phillip was uppity with his clothes and manner of speaking. They'd probably call him proper to his face. She didn't want Phillip to feel uncomfortable.

Jeana thought when it was time for her to give up her virginity, it would be to the man she was married to. Phillip had changed her thinking. He told her he loved her and that was all that mattered. As far as Jeana was concerned, he was right. She knew they had a love that was special, and it would only be a matter of time until Phillip would ask her to marry him.

They had so much in common, especially with having the same majors. When Phillip made his move to sleep with her, she didn't resist the first time or the numerous times after that. She gave in to him willingly. Any requests Phillip made of her were met. She made sure she was available whenever he wanted to see her, also to the point of her grades starting to slip. But when they did, she didn't worry about it because he'd one day make the pros and everything would turn out fine.

Jeana hadn't originally seen herself as a housewife, but if that was what Phillip would have wanted, she would oblige. Her dreams of obtaining her own degree slipped to the back burner and thoughts of her future with Phillip became stronger and stronger.

In November of that year, Jeana started feeling sick. She had daily nausea and was vomiting regularly. Her roommate told her to buy a pregnancy test to see if she was pregnant. She bought one and it came out positive. Then, made an appointment at the school infirmary to confirm the test further. The nurse gave her the same results.

She was in shock. She couldn't believe she was pregnant even though she knew it was very probable. Phillip didn't use protection. And, she'd never been on any kind of contraceptives. It scared her at first, but the more she thought about it, Phillip's undying love for her was consolation.

Jeana had wanted to tell Phillip at the perfect

time and in the perfect place. She thought about how and where she'd tell him the news. She ended up buying a bottle of sparkling grape juice and some plastic champagne glasses to celebrate in his dorm room.

Her heart began to race as she thought about the next sequence of events. Then her blood started running cold.

Phillip snuck her up to his room that fateful night. As soon as she was safely inside, she hugged him and kissed him. Then she pulled the chilled bottle from her overnight bag and poured them each a glass.

She asked him to hold the glass up for a toast. He eyed her curiously. Smiling, she then told him she was pregnant.

He hadn't extended his glass for a toast, nor had he even cracked a smile or hugged her with joy. He stared as if he were looking right through her. He then became agitated and turned away from her. With a towel, he started wiping the sweat beads, which were forming on his forehead. It was nothing like the reaction she'd hoped for.

He asked questions to confirm that she was indeed pregnant. She told him about the two tests and that she was probably eight weeks pregnant. Then he started rambling about how he wasn't ready to have a baby and told her she wasn't ready either. He told her she needed to terminate the pregnancy.

She couldn't believe her ears. He kept on talking about the need to end the pregnancy as soon as possible; not to let it go on too long. Jeana had been dumbfounded, feeling it was all a terrible nightmare. It wasn't supposed to happen like this. He was supposed to take her in his arms and be happy about their baby.

She ran from his room, leaving everything, even her jacket. The temperature had dropped that night to 40 degrees and she shivered all the way back to her dorm. Her roommate was fast asleep when she got there. She was glad. She didn't want to face anyone right then. She climbed into her bed and curled up into a ball. She wanted the pain and coldness she felt, not only from the weather outside, to go away, but she also wanted the coldness she had felt from Phillip to go away.

The next day, he met her in the lobby of her dormitory and handed her an envelope with money in it, telling her she knew what to do with it. She couldn't believe he still wanted her to end the pregnancy.

He left her standing in the lobby, with her mouth open in disbelief. Feelings of the previous night flooded her, and she ran to her dorm room for solitude.

She tried for the next few days to catch up with Phillip. She left numerous messages on his answering machine, and blew up his pager. He wouldn't call her back. She saw him on campus a couple of times, but he avoided her and walked in the other direction. The pride she had wouldn't allow her to run after him or cause a scene.

She was devastated. She loved him with all her heart, and thought the feelings were mutual. She was ashamed of herself for falling for what she now knew must have been an act, especially for him to act so callous at the drop of a dime.

Except for Jeana's roommate, no one knew about her pregnancy. She hadn't wanted to tell anyone else. She couldn't face her friends with the information. Knowing she'd start showing soon, Jeana decided to drop out of school and return home, even though she knew what the poor reception there would be like.

She gave up on Phillip and went back home. She decided to keep the baby and not to tell him either. Jeana knew she couldn't live with herself if she terminated the pregnancy. She loved the baby growing inside her and it was a small part of Phillip that she would have forever. She hated to think what his reaction would be when he found out what her ultimate decision was.

The pregnancy was extremely hard on her. She hadn't had any emotional support from Phillip or her family, least of all her parents. They reminded her daily that she was never going to amount to anything, especially after getting knocked up by some college boy.

They had given her minimal financial support. Her pride wouldn't allow her to take any kind of charity and she didn't apply for welfare or food stamps. Instead she got a job at a local factory. She was determined to make it on her own.

Many nights she cried herself to sleep wondering how she and a new baby were going to survive. She prayed God would change Phillip's heart and he would take care of his responsibilities. She hoped he would apologize for treating her so badly. She felt as if the prayers had gone to deaf ears, because God never answered them for her. Slowly she stopped attending church services and altogether depending on the Lord for answers.

She ended up working right up until two weeks before the baby was born. After she had him, she went back to work four weeks later; that was the longest she could afford to stay off. Jeana's parents and family refused to baby-sit for her. She had been lucky enough to find an elderly woman who watched her little Taren for next to nothing. The woman said Jeana reminded her of her own daughter.

Her family's cruelty only fueled her determination to succeed on her own. After her son was in kindergarten, she started taking night classes at the local community college, and then transferred the classes to University of North Carolina at Wilmington.

Tired of struggling, Jeana realized Phillip was never going to come back to her. She took matters into her own hands. The cost of raising her child alone was too much to handle. Jeana obtained a lawyer and took Phillip to court for child support. She won her case, once it was determined that Phillip was the father, and was able to start receiving payments. The monthly child support payments were enough to help sustain her and Taren. The added money also assisted in paying for her last years in college.

She was able to get a part-time job at a local realty company. When it was slow in the office, she studied for her courses. Twelve years after first becoming a freshman at CSU, Jeana had finally gotten her degree in marketing.

She wondered what Phillip's reaction would be now if he realized that he had basically paid for her education with the money from the child support.

The day she'd seen him in court, he wouldn't look directly at her. She thought with the passage of so many years that maybe he'd be more compassionate. Jeana had brought a brand new suit for the occasion and had also had her hair and nails professionally done. She'd wanted to look her best; exuding the appearance of a mature, confident woman who had it going on, not the stupid little country freshman he had once taken advantage of.

She kept her composure during the proceedings, even though every time she looked over at him, he ignored her. Rage grew inside her, with every passing glance. Phillip had a smug look on his face the whole time. She wanted to jump over and slap it off his face, then tell him how much pain he caused her and his son. She couldn't bring herself to do it. Like a stupid little freshman, she let him win again.

Now 14 years later, she was more than ready to confront him. And, she'd finally make him acknowledge the fact that he had a son. This time she wouldn't back down or shy away.

"Mom, where do you want me to put my winter clothes?" Taren yelled from his room, breaking Jeana's train of thought.

"Put them in the living room for now. We'll

place them in our storage unit tomorrow," she answered.

She looked down and realized she'd balled up one of the aluminum baking pans she was holding. There was blood. She'd cut herself. And on top of that, one of her migraine headaches was starting. Memories of how she had been wronged always brought out the worst in her, especially when it came to Phillip Tomlinson.

She stopped and took a deep breath, looking upwards. "Dear God, why do I let the these thoughts get the best of me."

Looking back down at the pan, she threw it away and rinsed her hand with cold water. The cuts were small when she examined the hand closer. She applied pressure and the bleeding stopped. She couldn't let her son see what had happened.

Again, Phillip had done something to hurt her by the blood being drawn.

"Phillip, you will pay for this and so much more!"

She was on her way to confronting him. The first part of her plan was working so far. She'd landed a job at Silvermont Realty as a Realtor a few months prior. The first months at the company had been very lucrative for her. She'd sold four houses and another contract was being signed on Monday. To save money for those few months she'd rented a boarding room. And now that Taren was out of school, they'd moved everything to their new apartment.

The realty company was only a couple of

blocks away from where Phillip worked. Jeana did her homework before coming to Silvermont, acquiring the name of the company Phillip worked for, and some other helpful tidbits of information. She searched for his phone number via the Internet, and found out he had a wife named Shelby. Because she worked for a realty company, it was easy for her to obtain his home address. Phillip and his wife lived in a gated community, but she was easily able to get in and out because of her realtor status.

She called his home number out of curiosity the first time. A woman answered the phone, so she figured it must have been the little wifey. Her voice sounded so loving and cheery, it made Jeana want to gag. She wondered what Phillip's wife looked like and if she was anything like her.

She called the house again several times, and each time, Phillip's little wife seemed to get more and more agitated. For some reason, this pleased Jeana. She wanted this Shelby woman to feel some discomfort in her life.

Jeana had never thought about the fact that Phillip might have other children, until one time she heard the voice of a little girl. She wondered how many children there were. The Internet couldn't tell her all that. So, she followed Phillip and his wife around. She knew some people might call it stalking. She called it curiosity.

Jealousy flowed through Jeana's body whenever she thought about Phillip and his perfect wife and kids. She figured they'd never had to want for anything. The little girl whose voice she heard surely never went to bed hungry or ever had to wonder who her father was or even where he was. It just wasn't fair that her son had missed out on everything Phillip could have easily offered.

She had driven by his house on numerous occasions. One day, she hoped to be able to afford a house in his neighborhood. She laughed. "I can make his life a living hell."

Jeana remembered the day she sat at the traffic light waiting for it to turn green. Like a gift sent down from God, she looked over and saw Phillip in his shiny black SUV, bopping his head to music like he didn't have a care in the world. The entire time they sat at the light waiting, he never looked down at her insignificant Toyota Tercel. This made her mad. She wanted to ram her car into his SUV, but the light turned green and she couldn't catch up in her little car with the "May Pop" wheels. She feared if she pushed the car too hard and fast, the tires might actually pop.

She had to devise a plan for their reunion. She knew she wanted to do it at his job or just show up at his house. Maybe she'd corner him in the parking deck. Whatever the plan was, it had to be good and she had to be smart about it. Phillip would soon know the pain he had caused her for over a decade.

Chapter 7

Phillip Tomlinson

Mercy

Phillip looked over the figures for the report submitted to him by one of his subordinates. The numbers for June 7th looked good, but the numbers of June 14th didn't. Overall, he was pleased with all of the money the company was generating from his department, knowing it was only under his direction. But, if the numbers continued to decline, then so could his favorability with his boss.

"Mr. Tomlinson." Phillip heard over his phone intercom.

"Yes?" he replied.

"You have a call on line two," Phillip's secretary said.

"Thanks." He heard the phone beep indicating the call had been successfully transferred.

"Hello, Phillip Tomlinson speaking."

"Hey, baby," Shelby said.

"Hey, sweetheart. What's going on? Is everything okay?"

"Yes, everything is fine. I'm a little tired, but my shift is almost over. I just want to go home and get some rest."

"Why don't you do that? When you get off work go ahead home, I'll pick up Nyah."

"Are you sure, Phillip?"

"Yes. I want you to get some rest. Nyah and I will probably ride to the park or something. I'm sure we can find something to do."

"Now that you mention it . . ."

"What?" The way Shelby was stalling, Phillip knew she had something in mind for him.

"Nyah does need to have her hair washed. I've been meaning to take her to Kiddie Kuts, but I just haven't felt like it. They take walk-ins."

"No problem," Phillip said. It was no sweat off of his back.

"Are you serious?" Shelby asked in disbelief.

"Yep. You just get some rest when you get home. Nyah and I will be fine."

"Thanks baby. I really need it."

"I know you do, honey. Now that I've settled into my new position, I'll have more free time at home to help you."

"Oh yeah, I've been meaning to tell you something and it keeps slipping my mind."

"What's up?"

"Pastor Jordan wanted me to ask if you might be able to assist with the Pee Wee football team. He knows about your sports background and thought you would be the perfect person to help the young boys."

"I don't know, Shelby."

"What do you mean?"

"The pastor will probably want me to become a regular church attendee."

"It would be nice." Shelby laughed. "I don't think he'll beat you over the head or anything."

Phillip didn't laugh and said nothing.

Shelby continued. "Pastor doesn't just want people filling the pews. He wants members who want to be there. He wants members who are there for the word of God."

"Why doesn't he choose someone else from church?"

"He must see something in you."

"I'm not feeling it, Shelby. I'll think about it and I'll let you know. But, don't count on it."

"You know, Phillip, the church really isn't bad. If you gave it a chance you'd probably like it. And I know if you gave the Lord a chance, accepting him as your Lord and Savior, you won't regret it. There is nothing like being spirit filled," Shelby said.

"Here we go again. Shelby, sweetheart, I'm just not feeling that right now. I don't think I fit the role of a holy roller. And, it's not like I have to be a fanatic or anything. Don't get me wrong; I believe in God but not all that other stuff right now, okay."

"Okay, Phillip, I don't want to push you; just let me know what you've decided about the Pee Wee team."

"I will." Phillip paused feeling bad. "Are you mad at me?"

"No, I'm not mad," Shelby replied.

"Disappointed though, right?"

"To everything there is a season. Everything happens in its own time. I won't badger you about the subject."

"Thanks. Who knows, maybe one day I'll be a great preacher," Phillip laughed.

"Funny."

"Just kidding. Look, I've got to go. Rick and I are having a late lunch. I'll pick Nyah up this evening. So don't worry about her.

"Love you, bye," Shelby said.

"Love you too," Phillip answered before hanging up.

Phillip picked up his keys and headed for the door. The phone rung. He returned to the desk to answer the call. It was on line four meaning it was an internal phone call.

"Hello, Phillip Tomlinson speaking."

"Hello, Phillip," a woman's voice said.

"How can I help you?" Phillip asked, not recognizing the voice.

"You already helped me," the woman said.

"Excuse me? I don't understand what you mean. Who is this?"

"You don't know? Why, Phillip, I'm hurt," the mystery voice said.

Phillip looked down at line four blinking. He knew whoever it was must work for the company. He tried to think if he had done any favors for anyone he may have forgotten about.

"Look, I'm sorry, but I don't know what you are talking about and I am never going to guess, so put me out of my misery. What is this all about?"

The tone of the woman's voice changed. She

sounded angry. "You haven't seen misery yet. You just wait. You're going to get what's coming to you."

"Excuse me?" Phillip said again, taken back by the change of tone in her voice.

"There is no excuse for you, Phillip Tomlinson. You are scum and I will make sure you know it. Your word isn't worth anything. You are a liar and a cheat. And, you'll be exposed for what you are."

"Look, I don't know who this is, but you . . ." His voice trailed off. He had heard a click on the other end. "Hello? Hello!" He hung the phone up. "What in the world?" He shook his head and headed for the door again. He didn't know what to make of the call.

Phillip pulled his candy apple red pickup truck out of the parking garage.

"This is nice, Phil." Rick ran his hands over the leather interior of the pickup truck. "How long have you had it running?"

"It's been running for a while, but I took it out for its first spin Memorial Day weekend when my parents came down for the baby shower. My Pops loves it. It reminds him so much of my grand-father's old pick up truck."

"I bet you get a lot of honeys looking at you in this baby."

Phillip cut his eye at his friend, "Honeys, Rick?"

"Don't look at me like that. You know what I mean."

"Yes, there have been a few women I've caught looking at me from time to time."

"You should let me borrow it for a couple of days. I'll be able to fill my black book up. I'd drive it to just the right places."

"Sorry, you'll have to find your own chick mobile. I can't contribute," he said as he turned onto the beltline. "Where do you want to go for lunch?" In his rearview mirror he noticed a car, which had been following him since he'd left the parking garage. It looked like the same car that had followed him a few days prior. The windows were tinted so that he couldn't tell who was driving.

"How about Ginny's." Rick said.

"Sounds good to me," Phillip replied.

Changing the subject, Rick said. "I'm really tired of Joy. All she wants to do is have sex."

"What? You're complaining about a woman wanting to have sex all the time?" Phillip asked while eyeing the car in his rearview mirror. Every time he signaled to change lanes, it signaled and changed also. Whenever he sped up, the car sped up and did like wise when he slowed down.

It gave him an eerie feeling.

"She calls me all the time at work. She left messages at my house. One weekend, I was gone out of town and I came back to find that she had left fifteen messages on my voice mail. I left my cell phone home by mistake and she'd left twenty messages on it."

"Told you to watch out, man."

Rick nodded his head in agreement. "I should've listened."

Phillip turned on his signal to exit.

"Where you going? I thought we were going to Ginny's for lunch?" Rick asked.

"We are, but I think there's a car following us. I'm pretty sure I saw it following me the other day too," Phillip replied.

Rick ducked down slightly. "Is it a red late model BMW?"

"No, it looks like a Toyota Tercel."

"Whew," Rick said, sitting back up with relief. "Joy drives a BMW. I hope she doesn't start getting any ideas about trying to follow me. I might have to change my cell phone number and lay low for a few days."

Phillip sped through the light, which had turned yellow. "Good; whoever it is will have to stop at the light." He crossed over the intersection to re-enter the beltline.

Rick turned around to look out of the back window. "It worked. Who ever it is stopped."

"Who do you think it is?" Rick asked with curiosity.

"I have no idea. At first I thought I was being silly, but every time I made a move so did the car."

"It could be someone from the club. I saw those honeys pushing up on you at Dewayne's bachelor party."

"I don't think a couple of dances with a couple of women would warrant me getting followed."

Rick turned back around to look behind them. "That is strange. You'd better be careful."

Phillip thought about the phone call he had gotten just before he left for lunch. "No, let me tell you what's strange. Just before I met you for lunch, I got a phone call from some woman whose voice I didn't recognize."

"What did she say?" Rick gave Phillip his full attention.

"She was pleasant at first, but then her whole attitude changed. It was like she hated me, or something. She told me I would get what's coming to me."

"Freaky, man. Some weirdo off the street calling you at work," Rick shook his head.

"The funny thing is, the call was on line four."

"One of the internal lines?"

"Yeah. Then the next thing I know, this car is following us from the parking deck."

"Whoever it is, must work here. You really better watch your back."

Back at work, Phillip stepped out of the elevator and into his office. He continually looked over his back. He had been paranoid since he realized he was being followed.

He entered his office and closed the door behind him, thinking more about the phone call he'd gotten earlier. The voice was vaguely familiar and it seemed like he should have known who it was.

He thought about the women he had worked closely with at the company, but didn't think the voice matched any of theirs. The woman sounded like she was trying to disguise her voice in some way. It was the way she said some of the words. They sounded southern, then sort of mid-western, like it wasn't her usual way of speaking.

Phillip sat at his desk and drummed his fingers

on the report he had reviewed earlier. He couldn't focus. The call and car following him continued to weigh on his mind. He hoped he would figure out what was going on soon.

"Mr. Tomlinson." Phillip heard his secretary over the intercom.

"Yeah?"

"There's someone here to see you. She doesn't have an appointment but says she only wants a couple minutes of your time."

"Okay, just a minute," Phillip said. He heard the edge in his voice. He wondered who wanted to speak with him. He looked at his watch.

He did his best to regain his composure before opening his office door to see who was interrupting his time. Sitting in the waiting area was a woman reading a magazine. He couldn't see her face.

"Miss, I'm Phillip Tomlinson. How may I help you?"

The woman slowly pulled the magazine down, revealing her face. Immediate recognition registered. His mouth and head dropped simultaneously. He couldn't believe his eyes.

She stood staring at him with fire in her eyes. "I know who you are, Phillip."

As she stepped towards him, he stood frozen and disbelieving.

She walked past him into his office. "Phillip, I'd like to speak with you about a couple of matters.

Phillip's state of ice held him. He hadn't known how long he'd been there until his secretary asked him if he was all right.

Finally closing his mouth, he said, "Yes, I'm fine."

His secretary looked at him quizzically. "Are you sure? You don't look very well?"

Embarrassed by his recent composure, Phillip turned abruptly towards his office. "I'm fine. Please hold all my calls and I don't want to be disturbed."

"What if your wife calls?"

"I said, I don't want to be disturbed," Phillip said in a voice reminiscent of a tyrant kind of boss. He left the secretary sitting with her mouth agape. Somehow, he knew as soon as he closed his office door the secretary would be on her phone gossiping to her other friends in the building about the display she'd just witnessed.

He closed the office door and stood by it. He didn't know what to think and wondered why she was there to see him. The voice on the phone made since now. She didn't have the *Gone with the Wind* southern drawl anymore. He wondered what was going on.

She was standing by his desk with her back to him. When she turned around she was holding the picture of his daughter Nyah.

Swiftly he walked over and snatched the picture from her hand, forcefully placing it back on his desk.

"Phillip, you seem surprised to see me. What, no hug to say hello? You're being so rude?"

Phillip glared at Jeana from the business side of his desk. She was dressed in a taupe suit and brown pumps. Her hair was pulled back in a neat bun. She resembled the freshman he dated years ago, but a fully-grown up version. Her voice was different and there was something else about her he couldn't quite put his finger on.

She'd changed from the last time he'd seen her at court a few years prior. The softness in her demeanor was nowhere to be found. She had a hard edge to her now; an edge which seemed to border on deranged. Even though her clothing and hair were immaculate, her lipstick was uneven and smeared.

All of it just didn't sit right with him. Intuition told him to be careful.

"What, cat got your tongue?" Jeana continued to taunt Phillip. She walked over to his wall of success and started reading the plaques and certificates. "I see the great P.T. is still making a name for himself."

"Hello, Jeana. What do you want?" Phillip said. "And why are you here? You were given explicit instructions not to contact or come near me."

Jeana turned around swiftly. "What do I want? Now that's a good question." She nodded her head and started pacing. "I want so many things. Your son, you know the one you've ignored for all these years, wants a lot too."

Phillip took into account the way Jeana was avoiding his statement about not contacting him.

"It's been a long time. In all these years, Phillip, did you even think about me once? Probably not," Jeana said without waiting for a reply. "I've thought about you. Every day for the past fourteen years I've thought about you, Phillip. How could I help it? I was carrying your baby—our baby. And you didn't even care." Jeana continued to walk slowly around the room as she spoke.

"I thought about you while returning home to face my parents. I cried night after night hoping you'd call, realizing how wrong you were—and that you wanted me back." She paused. "You never called, Phillip."

She turned towards the window. "I thought about you when I was working in that factory day after day. It was so hot in there. I worked my fingers raw some days trying to get overtime hours so I'd have enough money to get by. Yes, I thought about you then."

She paused, picking up the paperweight off his desk, gripping it tightly in her hand. "Still like the stupid school girl I was, I hoped you'd come one day like some knight in shining armor and rescue me." She paused again slamming the weight on his desk.

He jolted in astonishment.

"You never came, Phillip!"

Phillip slowly and meticulously moved back towards his office door where his golf bag was located. He didn't know what this new Jeana was capable of. If she tried anything crazy, he'd hit her with the nine-iron. "Jeana, that was so long ago. Why don't you . . ."

Jeana cut him off. "Why don't I what? Just crawl under some rock for you, like I did years ago? Not this time, Phillip. I'm not that little girl anymore."

"Jeana, I'm not the same person I was years ago either. We all change. I'm sorry you had to go through all of what you went through."

"You don't know the half of it, Phillip. Your

son, and by the way his name is Taren, thinks you're dead. Year after year he asked me where his father was. I got so tired of making up lies that I just told him you were dead. Until I told him that, the only birthday present he asked for was to see his daddy.

"Do you know how hard that was? Do you? Of course you don't."

Phillip decided to let Jeana vent out whatever she needed to say. It seemed as though she had a great deal on her mind.

"Your son has had a hard life, Phillip. A life he didn't deserve. If only you had given him half the chance. He deserved it. Darn it, he still deserves it! And I am going to see that he gets all he deserves and more.

"Our son's birthday is coming up soon. This year he asked for two things; a game player 3000 and a pair of Kelsey Jackson high top sneakers. As a bonus, I am going to make sure he gets his third wish. The wish he had years ago. My son will get to meet his father."

"Look, Jeana, I can see you need to get a lot off your chest, but I am going to have to draw the line right now. The boy . . ."

"His name is TAREN!" Jeana screamed. Her well kempt bun was starting to show ware.

"Okay, okay," Phillip said. "He doesn't need to see me. I've moved on with my life and you need to move on with yours. Let it go, Jeana. It's over and has been for years. You were the one who was deceptive. For years I thought you terminated the pregnancy until I got that summons for court for back child support. Now I ask you, was that fair? Be reasonable, you never even told me you went ahead and had the baby. So as far as I'm concerned, what has been buried needs to stay buried."

Jeana roared, "You pompous son of a . . ."

Phillip cut her off. "Jeana, I'm trying to be patient with you. I should've called security as soon as I saw you, but I guess I'm too nice."

"I can't believe you . . ."

"Shut up, Jeana. Listen to me. I don't want you to miss a thing. I've been sending you child support payments for years. The amount you receive is more than generous. I don't know what you've been doing with the money, but maybe you should manage it a little better. If the boy wants the game and shoes, get them. But I will not, under any circumstances, be meeting him. Too much time has passed. There's no use now anyway!"

For a brief moment, Phillip saw what looked like the old Jeana—the kind and unassuming one. "How can you be so cold? Today I see how truly callous you are. You don't have a heart. How could I have ever loved you?"

"It's all in the past, move on," Phillip said, his voice softening also.

Then within a split second, old Jeana resurfaced with her evil personality. "Move on? Like you did? I see you've got a pretty little wife and daughter," Jeana said with a sneer. "I'll bet wifey lives in the lap of luxury. And, that little daughter of yours with the floppy ponytails doesn't have to want for a thing." Jeana picked up the picture of Phillip's daughter again. "You know she looks just like Taren did when he was little."

"You don't know anything about my wife and daughter! You leave them out of this!" Phillip went to snatch the picture, but Jeana moved it out of his reach.

"I've seen your wife and daughter. By the way, I like that pretty candy apple red truck you have. Still love those fraternity colors don't you?" Jeana laughed.

"That was you following me, wasn't it?"

Jeana smiled and pointed her finger in a circular motion. "Let's just say we travel in the same circles." Then she changed the subject. "I have to hand it to you; you've got some pretty good driving skills, loosing me at that light."

Phillip's temper flared. Dismissing the change of subject he said, "And you'd better not bother my wife or daughter! You hear me? You leave them alone!" Phillip snatched the picture from Jeana's hand and held it this time.

Jeana inched herself closer and closer to Phillip. "Ahhh, Phillip, so you do have a couple of compassionate bones somewhere in that buff body of yours. But, I guess not when it comes to me and your son, huh?"

"Look, I don't know what your problem is, but I am telling you right now to leave me and my family alone. If you don't, I promise you you'll be sorry."

"Ha! You can't hurt me anymore, Phillip. I won't let you."

"I'm not trying to hurt you, but touch one hair on my wife or daughter's head and so help me God I will—"

"You don't scare me with your empty promises.

You made promises years ago and didn't come through."

Phillip drew near to her, putting his index finger in her face. "I can promise you this, come near me again and you will regret it." Phillip felt like choking Jeana. "I suggest you leave right now before I call security." Jeana was inching herself closer.

Before he knew it, she had him in an embrace. She had wrapped her hands around his waist. "Tired of me again already, Phillip? And, I thought we were having so much fun reminiscing." Jeana had a tight hold on him. "Don't you still want me, Phillip? I can forgive you for everything. We can start off fresh. You know, with a clean slate."

"Get off of me! Get out, now!"

"I'll leave, but only because I want to. I will not be dismissed so easily again, I can promise you that. You'll hear from me again. My son has a certain birthday wish he needs filled."

"Don't bother, Jeana. If you know what's good for you, you'll go back to Hartsfield or where ever you came from. And, don't come back!"

Jeana left the office and slammed the door behind her. Phillip sat at his desk. He couldn't believe what had just happened. Jeana had been following him and now she was making threats. She'd also called him earlier. Then it dawned on him that she might be the person who'd been calling their house and hanging up.

When had the calls started? It had been over three months ago, Phillip thought. "What's this woman up to?" He asked himself.

"Mr. Tomlinson," Phillip's secretary said over the intercom.

He took a deep breath before answering, "Yes?"

"Is . . . everything . . . okay?" He heard the hesitation in her voice.

"Yes, everything's fine," Phillip replied. "Disgruntled customers," Phillip chuckled lightly. "You know how they can be."

"Okay, I just wanted to make sure. I was about to call security."

"No, everything is under control." Phillip hoped the secretary hadn't heard any of the specifics during the argument. "Did I have any calls while I was in my meeting?"

"No, sir."

"Thank you. That will be all."

Phillip walked over to the window. On the street below him he saw the Toyota Tercel turning onto the next block. She was out of the building. Without realizing he was doing so, he exhaled a deep breath.

He turned back towards his desk, picked up the phone, and called his lawyer. "Hey, it's Phillip Tomlinson. We need to talk!"

Chapter 8

Jeana Sands

Vengeance

Jeana stormed out of Phillip's office, slamming the door behind her. She wanted to laugh as she saw the stunned look on the secretary's face. She walked pass without saying a word.

At the elevator she punched the down button continuously in hopes that it would make it come faster. She wanted to get off the floor with Phillip. In all her years of anticipating a reunion with him, it had not gone as planned. She'd hoped when he saw her he'd realize the error of his ways and take her in his arms, tell her everything was going to be alright.

She jabbed at the elevator button with her thumb. "Come on!" she said to the elevator. She figured Phillip's nosey secretary was probably looking at her.

She turned her head slightly and looked over her shoulder. Sure enough, the secretary had been looking at her. When the woman realized Jeana was looking back, she quickly put her head down.

Jeana huffed under her breath. Her head began hurting. The elevator opened and a tall handsome man stepped out.

"Good afternoon," the man said.

Jeana brushed by him. *First it's good afternoon, then it's what's your name and can I get your phone number. Then before I know it, I'll be pregnant again*, Jeana thought. She had no time for good-looking, slick-talking men. They were all alike as far as she was concerned.

She punched G for the ground floor where she'd parked. It seemed to take forever for the elevator to descend its way to the ground floor. A burst of hot air hit her from the lower level of the garage as soon as the doors opened.

She stepped out and took a deep breath. She'd finally done it. She'd confronted Phillip. Jeana wished she'd had a camera to capture the look on his face the moment he saw her sitting in the waiting area. "Ha, Ha, Ha," she laughed and continued laughing as she walked to her car.

She passed Philip's pick up truck parked vulnerably in its space. There were so many things she wanted to do to it. Her keys felt as if they were magnetized to its perfect red finish. Words danced around in her head, which longed to be scratched thorough the surface.

Or she could get some lye and pour it all over the truck. "Phillip would just love that," Jeana said and laughed to herself again. Her tire iron was also handy; all she had to do was pull it out of her trunk. That way she could bash in every piece of glass.

She was itching to do something. The grasp she had on her keys was causing her hand to hurt. Looking down she realized there was blood once again. "I've really got to be more careful," Jeana said. She looked around to see if anyone was watching her and noticed the security cameras trained in her direction.

"That's okay, Phillip. You'll get yours." She left the truck alone and returned to her Toyota Tercel. "I can't let anyone see me destroying Phillip's car. I've got to be smarter than that." She wiped her hands with a napkin from KFC that was tucked in her glove compartment.

After she finished wiping her hands as best she could, Jeana pulled out her cell phone. She punched buttons to reveal her missed calls. "Bingo!" she said. "I've got your number now!"

As soon as Jeana entered Phillip's office she saw his cell phone sitting on the corner of his desk. With quick thinking she dialed her cell phone, which was on vibrate in her purse.

She'd learned the trick watching a movie. The girl in the movie had made a call from a guy's home phone to her home phone. When the girl got home, his home number was on the caller ID. Jeana thought it was an ingenious idea but never knew she'd one day get the chance to use it.

"555-8091." She hit save on her cell phone. "Thanks for the number, Phillip. I'll talk to you later."

Jeana rummaged thorough her purse looking

for some medication for her head. She then popped two pills in her mouth and cranked her car, which sputtered at first. She put it in reverse to pull out of the garage. She looked at her watch. It was already 3:00. She needed to pick Taren up from his summer camp program at the YMCA. She was already thirty minutes late.

After paying the attendant, she pressed the accelerator and sped out of the parking garage. The car backfired as she turned the corner. It was so embarrassing. "Now that I am going to be making the big bucks, I think Taren and I need a new car." Jeana nodded her head, deciding to stop by some of the car dealerships to look for a new car.

"Hi, Mom," Taren said as he opened the car door. He threw his book bag in the back seat and crammed his long legs under the dashboard of the front seat.

"Hi, how was your day?"

"It was great, Mom. The kids played the staff in basketball and we beat them 37 to 26. The staff can't play at all. They're so old. Mr. Ford can barely walk from class to class. I don't even know why he played."

"That's good. Congratulations."

"The staff even had their own cheerleaders. Some of the teachers used to be cheerleaders when they were in school. A couple of them put on their old uniforms to help cheer on the staff. It didn't work though. As Granny would say, the only thing that would have helped them was Jesus."

"Sounds just like your granny. According to her, everybody needs Jesus, even most of the people at her church."

Jeana pulled out of the YMCA parking lot. She saw three girls who were walking home. As they drove by the girls, Jeana noticed her son smiling. "Who are they?" Jeana asked.

"Who?" Taren turned his head in the other direction.

Jeana was no fool. "Those girls you were just looking at."

"Oh, them. They just go to the center too. One's name is Rochelle. I think she likes me or something."

"Or something, huh? You like her too, huh?"

"No, Mom. I don't like that girl," Taren said with repulsion.

"You could have fooled me. I saw the way you were just smiling." Jeana said, but didn't get a response back from her son. She knew he liked the girl. And, she knew the girls couldn't help but like her son.

He was probably going to be just like his father. The girls would keep flocking to him, as he got older.

Jeana changed the subject. She didn't like thinking about her son and girls. "Guess what?"

"What, Mom?"

"We are going to get a new car!"

"We are?" Taren asked.

"We sure are. The Lincoln dealership is having a Midnight Madness sale, and after we have dinner, we'll swing by and have a look." Jeana slapped the dashboard of the car. "We've had this old heap long enough. My job is going well, business is booming. I'm selling houses left and right and we can afford it now."

"Can I have this car? You know I'll be able to drive soon."

"Son, you are only thirteen."

"Almost fourteen," Taren added.

"Almost, but you still have a few more years before you're ready to drive. You're still growing and your legs are already about to out grow this car."

Taren sat quietly.

"When it's time for you to drive, you'll get a car, I promise."

"Really?" Excitement registered in her son's voice.

"Yes," Jeana replied. She made sure her son wouldn't have to go without again. Also, making sure he wouldn't want for anything, including his father. Phillip's empty threats had not deterred her. She was still going to make sure her son got all his birthday presents.

"I'm hungry. What's for dinner?" Taren asked.

"What do you want?"

"I don't know. That food we had from Mama Lula's was good."

"It was, but we can't eat that kind of food all the time. All that grease and pork isn't good for us."

"But we ate that way all the time at Granny's"

"We're not at Granny's anymore," Jeana said with irritation. She was tired of hearing about what her mother would or wouldn't say or what her mother would or wouldn't do.

"We really need to start eating better. I want you to get accustomed to other types of food. There will be a time in your life when you'll need to know there are foods other than fast food and pigs feet."

"We are going to Ginny's for dinner," Jeana proclaimed.

"Ginny's? What's that?"

"It is a high class restaurant. It's five star."

"What does five stars have to do with anything?" Taren asked.

"My young son, you have so much to learn. Keeping you in the country all these years has been a hindrance to your social awareness."

Taren shrugged his shoulders. "We didn't have to worry about all this stuff at home."

"Things change, son. And there are a lot of things that will be changing in the very near future." Jeana looked over at Taren. "Just remember change is good, okay."

"Okay, if you say so, Mom."

"Let's go home and change clothes."

"Change clothes? Why?" Taren looked down at what he was wearing.

"Because the restaurant we're going to doesn't accept sweats and sneakers as the proper attire."

"Wow, you are really sounding proper now. Granny . . ."

Jeana huffed. "Look, I don't care what your granny would say. Your granny hasn't been exposed to anything in her life. Anything she doesn't understand is proper to her. We are going home and I want you to take a shower and put on one of your dress shirts."

"Mom," Taren protested.

"And a pair of dress shoes."

Taren huffed this time.

"And that pair of black slacks I bought you to wear for my graduation."

"I sure hope we don't have to go to this place too often."

"Get use to it. Our lives are changing. This is the way we should have been living all the while." Jeana thought for a second. "Maybe I should take you by the barber shop."

"Mom!" Taren said in protest.

"You're right, we don't have time. After dinner we will go look at some cars."

"Now that sounds like fun," Taren said.

"Dinner will be fun too, you'll see."

"If you say so, Mom."

"I like this one, Mom. It's so cool," Taren said as they test-drove a vehicle from the dealership after enjoying dinner together.

Jeana took in the smell of the new leather. She gripped her hands around the leather steering wheel as she coasted down the exit ramp. She felt like she belonged in the Lincoln Navigator she was driving. It was just like the one Phillip's wife drove.

She had adjusted the seat to suit her so that it fit like a glove. Even though it was still humid outside, she and Taren were cool as they drove down the beltline.

Taren adjusted his seat all the way back. "Look, Mom, I can stretch my feet all the way out! We've got to get this one. I like it better than all the rest."

Jeana had to admit. "I like it too." In the rear view mirror she admired a corner of her face and the massive back seats of the Navigator. After years of driving her little car, the sight brought on a state of euphoria. She knew this was the automobile she wanted. It was what she and her son deserved. Now she knew what Phillip's wife must feel like when she drove hers.

Taren pressed the button to turn on the radio. He played with the dial until he found a local R& B station. He turned the volume up as loud as it would go and started dancing in his seat.

Jeana quickly turned it down. "That is too loud."

"What is the use of having it if you can't turn the music up?" Taren asked.

Jeana had to agree with her son, but didn't want to blow out their eardrums. I don't think the volume was meant for being played that high while driving.

"It sounds good. It's been so long since our radio worked in the car." Taren squinted his eyes as if trying to remember something. "Has the radio ever worked in the car?"

"Yeah, knucklehead," Jeana said playfully, hitting him upside the head.

"I know. It just seems like so long, that's all."

Jeana turned back into the parking lot of the Lincoln dealership. The salesman greeted them as they exited the SUV.

"How was the drive?" the salesman asked.

"Wonderful. We'll take it!" Jeana told him.

"Excuse me?" the salesman asked.

"I said we'll take it, everything. The fully loaded package. As a matter of fact, I want the one we just drove. My son and I loved it."

"Don't you want to know how much it is?" the salesman asked.

"It does not matter, I want it. Now what do we need to do now?"

The salesman led the way to his office. "Right this way. Have a seat. Can I get you anything to drink?"

"Yes, I'd like a diet cola," Jeana said.

"Can I have a Sprite?" Taren asked.

"One diet cola and a Sprite coming up. I'll be right back."

As soon as the salesman was out of sight, Taren said, "Mom, are we really going to get it?"

"We sure are, son. We'll probably even be able to drive it home tonight."

"Wow, great!"

"It sure is. I told you, things are looking up for us. Get use to it."

In the best sounding sophisticated voice he could imitate, Taren said, "I think I can get use to this kind of life."

"You will, I promise," Jeana said in an assuring tone.

An hour later Jeana and Taren were driving out of the parking lot in their new Lincoln Navigator.

"I feel sort of bad leaving our car, Mom. It looks so lonely," Taren said.

Without looking back towards the car Jeana said, "I don't." She pressed the accelerator even harder. She never wanted to look back.

* * *

Jeana pressed the remote unlocking the doors of her Navigator. She still felt like she was dreaming. Every time she drove the SUV she felt like it was right. After only a few short weeks of driving it, she finally felt like she belonged in it; like she deserved it.

Usually when she drove it, she thought about Phillip's wife. Sometimes, she pretended she was Phillip's wife. She had his first child. Phillip loved her, before he found this other woman.

Jeana could tell the woman was pregnant. It was hard to miss her waddling gait and swelling stomach. Every time she saw it, she wanted to scream bloody murder. She should have been pregnant with another one of Phillip's children. It seemed to Jeana that Phillip was having children left and right. He forgot about her and Taren. Jeana felt as if Phillip's wife had taken the spot, which was rightfully supposed to be hers. "Damn her!"

The more Jeana thought about it, the angrier she got. She gripped the steering wheel even harder. She could tell her blood pressure was rising. Without feeling her temples and forehead, she knew the veins were sticking out. She had to calm down. She was feeling dizzy and didn't want to pass out. She rummaged through her purse and found the blood pressure medication she'd failed to take that morning.

She wanted to confront Phillip's precious wife so badly. She would have to do it when Phillip wasn't around. After months of her own handy research, she knew Shelby's patterns. Jeana knew his wife worked at the hospital from seven to three. She picked Nyah up, and either ran errands or went straight home. On Wednesday nights, his wife went to Bible study, at a church called New Hope. Instead of just following and watching her from afar one night, Jeana had actually sat in one of the Bible studies, just two pews behind Shelby.

The pastor was talking about making a good confession and repenting for sins. The message had actually convicted Jeana's heart, so much that she'd excused herself before the session was over. Her heart was convicted, that was true, but she was in no way ready to repent to God, even though she knew it was long over due.

Jeana pulled behind the Lincoln Navigator. It was just like hers; same color and year. She read the North Carolina license plate to make sure it was Shelby's "KNL4979. Bingo!"

"What, Mom?" Taren said, looking up from the comic book he was reading.

Jeana moved forward looking for a parking space. "Nothing, son. I was talking to myself."

"Hey, there's a Navigator just like ours over there." Taren pointed to the SUV.

"Oh really? I hadn't noticed," Jeana lied. She looked for the first available parking space and parked.

"Why are we parking?" Taren asked. "Didn't we just go grocery shopping the other day?"

"I need to pick up something I forgot for the cook out tomorrow," Jeana lied again.

"Are we going to see the fourth of July fireworks this weekend?"

"Yeah, why?"

"Cool. I finally get to see some real fireworks." Taren said.

"They had fireworks back home," Jeana said.

"Not like the ones I've seen on TV. I wonder if the fireworks here will be as nice as the ones they show on TV?"

"Sure." Jeana had barely heard what her son had said. She was to busy looking around to see if Shelby was coming out of the store. So far she hadn't seen any signs of the woman.

They exited the vehicle and walked into the store. Jeana's heart raced with every step. She was finally going to get her chance to confront the woman who was stopping her from having the man of her dreams.

She had no idea what she was going to say. She thought so much about where and when to meet her, but hadn't decided what she would say. She figured she'd play it by ear.

"Can I get some Twinkies?" Taren asked, running towards the snack isle.

"Okay, just hurry back up here to meet me. I shouldn't be long." Jeana continued to scan the store as she spoke. Slowly she walked the length of the store, passing each isle. She pretended she was reading the signs on each isle as she looked for Phillip's wife.

Not seeing her, she turned around and she finally saw her. Shelby was close enough for her to touch. Close enough to grab.

She inched closer to the register where Shelby stood waiting to have her groceries checked out. The closer she got, she heard the voice of the same little girl she had heard over the phone.

"Mommy, mommy I want a gumball," the little girl pleaded.

"Nyah, no candy before dinner," the wife said.

"But, Mommy, it's just a little gumball," the little girl whined.

"Nyah, you know the rules. Stop whining."

Jeana was in the next isle. From behind the candy and gum separating them, she could hear everything. But Shelby couldn't see Jeana from where she was.

She thought quickly. What could she say? Then, she looked over at the gumball machine. She walked over to it, pulling a quarter out of her purse to get a gumball for the little girl.

She held it in her hand. Then, she went back to the checkout line and stood right behind Phillip's wife. She grabbed a magazine, so she'd have a reason for standing in line.

Jeana looked down at the little girl who was fingering the candy bars in front of her.

Slowly, she opened her hand and extended it to the little girl. When the girl noticed, she looked at the hand and then up at Jeana. Jeana could see Phillip in her eyes. She had Phillip's cheekbones and forehead just like her son. She really did look like Taren when he was about three years old, except for the long ponytails drooping from her head.

Apprehensively, the little girl took the gumball

and placed it in her mouth before her mother could notice.

"Thank you," the little girl said as if she had finally remembered her manners.

"You're welcome," Jeana said with the voice of an angel. She could still feel the roundness of the gum she had just recently gripped in her hand.

Behind her, Jeana heard her son as he walked up to her, "Hey, Mom, I got a box of oatmeal cakes also. Is that okay?"

"Yeah, son. That is fine."

Phillip's wife looked down at her daughter. "Nyah, what is that you have in your mouth?"

"Oh, I gave it to her. I heard her say something about wanting a gumball. She is so cute, I just couldn't resist," Jeana said in a syrupy voice.

Jeana was excited. She finally had the woman's attention.

Phillip's wife glanced at Jeana quickly as she spoke. "Well, thank you. My daughter knows the rules, but I guess one piece of gum won't hurt. Tell the lady thank you." Then she turned her attention back to the cashier.

"Oh you're welcome." Jeana had an open line of communication, but the wife cut it off by abruptly turning her back on her again.

She wanted more. She spoke again. "How far along are you?" Jeana looked at her stomach, which now seemed enormous close up.

She got no response from the wife who was talking to the cashier.

"My mommy's gonna have a baby," the little girl said. "I'm gonna get a baby brother." The little girl smiled with glee.

Phillip's wife was ignoring her. Jeana had given her daughter a gumball and all she got in return was to be ignored. This made Jeana angry. She started twisting the magazine in her hand. She felt as if she could tear it in half.

"Come on, Nyah, we need to pick up dinner before Daddy gets home," Phillip's wife said.

She hadn't turned around to say goodbye to Jeana. She ignored her and Taren. She hadn't even looked fully in their direction. It was obvious to Jeana that Phillip's ungrateful wife didn't have time for lowly people like her and her son.

"Bye, nice lady," the little girl said.

Jeana said goodbye while trying to keep her composure.

"Miss, Miss," the cashier said. "Would you like to buy that magazine?"

It was only when Phillip's wife and daughter were out of eyesight that she stopped staring at them.

"Mom, the lady is talking to you," Taren said.

"Yes, here." She thrust the magazine at the woman. "And these too." She slammed the boxes of Twinkies and oatmeal cakes on the conveyer belt.

"Mom, is something wrong?" Taren asked with apprehension.

Jeana smoothed invisible wrinkles out of her blouse and took a deep breath. "No, everything is fine. And, everything is going to be fine. I know what I need to do now."

"What, Mom? You're not making any sense. And they say us kids act crazy some times." Taren shook his head.

They returned to their SUV and Jeana headed towards Barrington Estates. She knew exactly what she needed to do. She wasn't going to let Phillip's wife dismiss her either. Shelby would talk to her whether she wanted to or not. It was Jeana's day and no one was going to spoil it for her.

"What's for dinner?" Taren asked.

"I don't know yet. We'll probably go out to celebrate later. Think where you want to go," Jeana said with a smirk only her rearview mirror could see.

"What are we celebrating?"

"Your birthday, honey. I have one last gift I need to get for you, and after tonight, you'll have it."

"A surprise?"

"A huge one," Jeana said smiling.

"What is it? Is it a new bike? Or is it another pair of roller blades?" Taren asked with excitement.

"No, it's much bigger than that. You'll never guess in a million years."

"Give me a hint."

"Just wait; you'll see," Jeana grinned.

"Pleaeeese, Mom."

"Okay, one hint. It is something you have wanted for a very long time."

Taren sat quietly for a second, tapping his finger on his chin. "That's not a good hint. Give me another one."

"Nope, that's all I'm giving you. You'll find out soon enough." Jeana turned to enter the front gate of the development.

"Hi, Ed," Jeana said to the security guard manning the gate.

"Hi, Ms. Sands."

"I am meeting a client to talk about their future home."

"Okay, Ms. Sands, you can go on through," the portly security guard said. He pushed the button to open the gate.

"Have you thought anymore about the houses I showed you in our magazine?" Jeana asked.

"No, I think the Misses and I are going to stay in our little ranch home. The kids are all grown up and we don't need to be moving again this late in our years. Thank you though for all the information you bought me," Ed replied.

"You're more than welcome. If you change your mind, just let me know. Or if you know of anyone else who needs a forever home, just call me. You still have my business card?"

"I sure do. I keep it right here in my wallet," the guard said.

"Oh, I'm sorry; I'm being so rude. You've never met my son have you?"

"No, I haven't."

"Taren, this is Mr. Ed . . ." Jeana hadn't remembered his last name.

"Ed Wilkens. Nice to meet you," he replied.

"Hi," Taren said.

Ed squinted his eyes. "You look so much like someone I know. Can't quite put my finger on it though."

"Well, Ed, I really need to be going," Jeana said quickly. "You have a nice day, and tell your wife I said hello." Jeana pressed her foot against the accelerator, leaving the guard in the middle of his next sentence.

"Can't I go home while you finish work? I don't want to sit around while you talk about boring stuff like plaster and toilets."

"That boring stuff is what has you riding in this nice SUV. That boring stuff is what has us in the nice apartment we have now. That boring stuff is what buys you the things you want like your game player 3000 and Kelsey Jackson sneakers," Jeana said.

"Okay, Mom. I get it. Sorry," Taren apologized to his mother. "Is the boring stuff paying for my other surprise?" Taren pressed.

"No. Your other surprise can't be bought with money. Your last surprise is priceless," Jeana said. "You'll see soon enough. Just be patient."

Jeana pulled up in front of 12768 Barrington Drive across the street from Phillip's house. From the conversation she heard earlier between his wife and daughter, she knew it wouldn't be long before they'd be home.

Jeana also knew their work habits well enough to know Phillip usually arrived home at 6:00. It was now 5:15. If she was lucky, she'd catch his wife before Phillip arrived home. She wanted to talk to the woman one on one without Phillip's interference.

She knew Phillip wouldn't allow her to talk to his wife. But, she wasn't under Phillip's rule, and he didn't intimidate her anymore. He'd learn soon enough, that she wasn't the same stupid schoolgirl he'd once known.

Jeana cut the engine off. "Looks like they're not here yet. We'll have to wait for a few minutes. I know they'll be here soon." She was pretty sure her son had not detected that anything was amiss. She didn't think he had paid any real attention to the guards comment about him reminding him of someone else. Jeana was glad the old man wasn't too quick to think. If she had sat there long enough, the man might have blurted out that Taren looked just like Phillip.

Anyone who knew Phillip and laid eyes on Taren would know he was his son. There was no mistaking it. If Phillip's wife, had seen Taren, *really* seen him, she would have stopped dead in her tracks.

Jeana had a remedy though. This time Shelby would see her son and there would be no way she could deny the relationship between the two. Taren looked more like Phillip and Phillip's father than Phillip's older brother. She remembered the pictures Phillip displayed proudly in his dorm room of his loving close-knit family.

She gripped the steering wheel again, twisting it until her hands were hot.

"Mom, Mom?"

"Yeah?" Jeana hadn't heard her son calling her at first. She released her grip of the steering wheel.

"I said they are having a dance at the YMCA for all the kids. Can I go?"

"When is it?" Jeana asked while watching the house and the garage.

"Next Saturday."

"Sure. We don't have anything planned." She looked in the rearview mirror and saw a car approaching. It wasn't them.

"What are you suppose to wear?" she asked.

"It's a sock hop. Just socks, shorts and a t-shirt."

"Oh, okay." Jeana continued to look for movement in her rearview mirror. Her hands hurt from the pressure she had put on the steering wheel. She looked down at them. There was sticky green dye in the palm of her hand. She tasted it. It was from the gumball she had given Phillip's daughter earlier.

"Yuck! What is that?" Taren exclaimed.

"Just dye and sugar from a gumball I had in my hand earlier. Be quiet boy and hand me a tissue out of the glove compartment," Jeana chuckled.

She took the tissue from his hand and dripped water from her water bottle on it. Then she proceeded to wipe. She extended her hand to her son. "You can barely see it now."

"Look, there's another truck just like ours. Wow, there sure are a lot of people who have our truck. It must be popular."

Jeana looked up. Pulling into Phillip's three-car garage was the SUV identical to hers. Phillip's wife had arrived home. She watched as the brake lights were turned off and the two people exited. She watched until she saw feet climbing the stairs to enter the home just before the garage door shut.

Jeana then turned the ignition again. "My appointment is here." She pulled her SUV into the driveway and cut it back off again.

"Stay here. I'll be back in a few minutes," Jeana descended out of the SUV. Her pumps clacked against the pavement as she strutted towards the front door. She took deep breaths as she walked.

Once she was at the door, she paused, looking back for a moment at her son who was sitting, unassuming, in the truck. After today he would know the truth about his father.

She stared at the doorbell. It called to her. She had to do this. It was the right thing to do, she told herself. Enough time had passed.

She pressed the doorbell a couple of seconds longer than she meant to. Her heart felt as if it was going to jump out of her chest. She had wanted this moment to happen, but now that it was happening, it felt like a dream, it was exhilarating.

"Just a minute."

She heard the cheery voice of Phillip's wife from the other side of the massive front door. Time ticked for what seemed like an eternity before she heard the lock being turned on the other side of the door.

The door opened and she was face to face with her nemesis.

Jeana looked directly into her eyes without wavering and said, "You left before we could finish our conversation."

Chapter 9

Shelby Tomlinson

Trust

Shelby looked at the woman standing at her front door. She looked vaguely familiar, but she couldn't remember where she had seen her. Something about the woman's demeanor made alarms go off in Shelby's head. Unconsciously, she placed her hands on her stomach.

"I'm sorry, Miss, you look familiar, but I can't quite place where I've seen you." Shelby spoke cautiously. Something wasn't right about the whole situation, she could just feel it.

Nyah pushed her way around her mother. "Mommy, it's the lady from the store," Nyah smiled with delight. "Look, nice lady, I can blow a bubble. Wanna see?" She proceeded to blow a bubble with her gum and then popped it. "See." Nyah smiled with glee.

"That was a very good bubble, Nyah," the woman said.

"How do you know my name?" Nyah asked with innocent curiosity.

"Yes, how do you know my daughter's name?" Shelby asked.

"Well, you said it almost ten times at the grocery store," the woman replied.

Shelby thought back. It was at the grocery store where she had seen the woman. She was the one who gave Nyah the bubble gum after she had already told her daughter she could not have one. It irritated her. She knew if the woman had heard Nyah ask for it, she should have just as clearly heard her tell Nyah no and that she couldn't have one.

Shelby wondered why the woman was now ringing her doorbell almost forty-five minutes later. She thought back again to the grocery store. Had she left something there? Maybe the woman was just being nice again and wanted to return something to her.

Shelby's intuition told her that was not the reason for the woman's visit. She thought about her method of payment at the store. Had she written a check? Maybe the woman was deranged and followed her home to rob her.

She didn't know what was going on, but she was sure going to find out.

"Nyah, go upstairs to the game room and watch TV" Shelby told her daughter.

"Daddy said don't touch that TV if he's not here," Nyah said.

"It's okay. Go ahead. Put in your Dora movie," Shelby said. She didn't want Nyah around for what ever was about to happen. Her gut told her it wouldn't be pretty.

"Yipee, I'm gonna watch my Dora movie!" Nyah ran to the stairs.

Shelby took her left hand and pulled the door closer to her. She didn't want the woman to see any further into her home. The woman gave her the creeps. She wore a tailored cream linen suit with burgundy pumps. Her hair was neatly done in a tight bun on her head. Her nails were freshly manicured with a wine colored polish. She looked very astute.

Shelby's discerning spirit still told her something was truly off kilter.

"Is there something I can help you with?" Shelby asked.

"I knew your daughter's name before I saw you in the grocery store, Shelby." The woman said.

How did she know my name? Shelby thought back and remembered paying cash for the groceries she bought. "How do you know my name?"

"I not only know your name, but where you work also. I know your husband's name is Phillip too," the woman continued. "I know where he works, where he went to school and even that he has a mole on his inner left thigh."

Shelby placed both her hands back on her stomach. Who was this woman and why was she standing at her door. Why did she know so much about her family? She wondered if it was some kind of crazy joke.

"What's this all about?" Shelby asked. "Why are you here? What do you want? Who the heck are you?" Shelby was agitated. She thought maybe she was in some kind of bad dream.

"Slow down; I'll answer all your questions. I've been waiting years to talk to you," the woman said.

Years? Shelby thought. Who was this woman?

"I am here to claim what is mine. Or shall I say, rightfully my son's."

The deranged woman at her door wasn't making any sense. Shelby wondered just how crazy the woman was. She wanted to slam the door in her face but she was too close. She'd never be able to move back quick enough for her stomach to clear the door closing. She was sure the woman would try to stop her.

She also didn't want to put her daughter in any danger. She tried to stay as calm as possible as not to set the woman off. She had seen enough movies and documentaries about crazy people, to know that if they were crazy enough to do anything to themselves, then they didn't give a damn about anyone else.

Shelby tried to take control of the situation. There was no way she was going to let some crazy woman get the best of her. "Okay, it's obvious you know my name. So, at least give me the courtesy of giving me your name."

"It's Jeana," the woman said.

Shelby thought. She didn't know anybody by the name Jeana. The woman had paused as if Shelby should have known who she was.

"I'm sorry, but I don't know who you are. Maybe you have me and my family mixed up with someone else," Shelby offered.

"No, I have the right family." The woman had stuttered when she said the word family.

"What do you want then?"

"I already told you. I want what is rightfully my son's. He should get what he deserves. And why not? You all have lived in the lap of luxury all these years. My son shouldn't be deprived."

Now this really was getting wild, Shelby thought. Was this Jeana woman there because she was a taxpayer who thought her family was reaping all the benefits of the money she was paying into the tax system? Heck, Shelby was a taxpayer also. The woman needed to go to a politician's house instead of hers.

"My son only wants three things for his birthday. Do you know what he wants?" The deranged woman asked.

Shelby wondered if the woman thought she was a psychic or something. "No, I don't know you or your son, so how could I possibly know what he wants?" This woman was really starting to get on her nerves now. She must want someone to talk to, Shelby thought.

"He wants a game player 3000, a pair of Kelsey Jackson High Top Sneakers and to see his dad," the woman said.

"I got him the game player and the sneakers. The last wish I am granting for him."

Shelby saw pain and anger mixed in the woman's eyes. She wondered if the boy's father, was incarcerated or something.

For a lack of any other words Shelby said, "I'm glad to hear your son is going to get his wishes."

"Good then, we're on the same page. This is

going to be easier than I thought it was going to be."

Shelby heard the teakettle starting to whistle. "Miss, I am really sorry but I need to go finish preparing my dinner. I don't see how my family has anything to do with your son's needs or his birthday presents."

"What do you think I am, stupid or something?" the woman asked with a sneer.

"Excuse me?" Shelby's eyes widened. What was up with this woman? She wondered if her neighbors would hear if she screamed. She wanted to look down at her watch to see what time it was, but didn't want to set the crazy woman off.

It should have been almost 6:00 pm. Phillip would be home soon, and he would be able to get rid of the woman.

"You are just as callous as your husband," the woman said. "I hoped you'd have some kind of heart, but I see you are just as cold as him. You don't want my son to have what is rightfully his either."

"I don't know what you are talking about. Why are you calling my husband and I callous? We've never done anything to you. We don't even know you!"

The crazy woman clapped her hands. "Bravo, bravo. You are such a good actress. You know who I am and who my son is. You and Phillip are going to go to hell for what you are doing to us."

"This ends right now! I am not going to continue to stand here and listen to you slander our names. You need to leave right now. I will call the police," Shelby threatened.

"Mom." Shelby looked towards the voice calling to the crazy woman on her front porch. Walking up behind the woman was a young boy.

The woman turned her attention to him and said abruptly, "What, son?"

"I called you from the truck but you couldn't her me. Can I have the keys so I can turn the CD player on?"

"Yes, here are the keys," she handed him the keys. He kissed her on the cheek.

"Oh, hello, Miss," the boy said, then ran back to the SUV.

Shelby's mouth dropped. The boy looked exactly like Phillip. If he had been taller, she would have mistaken him for Phillip in his college years.

"What's going on?" Shelby asked in awe.

"Now how can you deny that boy his father? He hasn't done anything to you. He has a right to meet his father."

Shelby stood stunned. Her mouth refused to move. *What is going on?* Was she in some bad nightmare? Surely she'd wake up soon. The events unfolding in front of her could only be a scene coming from a bad off Broadway play. She wondered when the hecklers would start throwing tomatoes. She wished she'd wake up soon.

"So, you're going to stand there and not say anything? You know when I went to see Phillip the other day at his office he tried to ignore me also. I told him like I'm telling you right now, I will not be dismissed so easily again.

"You tell him I'm not scared of the empty threats that he made to me the other day. I will not let him do me like he did years ago in college.

I was a stupid little school girl then, but not anymore. He can't tell me to just go away. It won't work."

Shelby didn't know what was going on? None of it made any sense. She continued to stand speechless.

"And you tell Phillip I will take him to court again. Now that I see how nice you all are living, I want him to increase the child support payments he's sending me monthly. There is a private school I want to send Taren to," the crazy woman said.

Shelby couldn't make any sense out of what the woman was telling her. She was saying something about child support payments and taking Phillip *back* to court. She found her voice. "Who is that boy?" she asked with all sincerity. If the woman answered that simple question, maybe it would all make sense.

"Taren. My son. Phillip's son! Don't play stupid with me!" the woman said.

Shelby thought back to the day Phillip had divulged a secret he had been keeping from her their whole marriage. Phillip had told her about an ex-girlfriend in college who'd gotten pregnant and had a miscarriage. Phillip had told her the girl's name. Was it Jeana? She couldn't remember. But Phillip said the girl had a miscarriage after he told her not to go through with an abortion. That was the end of it. Wasn't it? She'd never asked him anything else about the girl. She never asked what happened to the girl or anything. She hadn't wanted to know.

Could this be the girl, now a woman, standing

in front of her? Was Taren really Phillip's? Her head started throbbing. The baby inside leapt.

"Did you go to CSU with Phillip? Did you date him?" Shelby formed and asked questions as they came to her.

"Cut the act, Shelby. You know good and well Phillip was my boyfriend! Until he dumped me when he found out I was pregnant with his baby. Yeah, he thought he was so smart telling me to have an abortion and giving me the money to do so. It was like he was trying to pay me off or something. Now he knows I didn't listen to him. I had my baby anyway and used the money he gave me to help with the pregnancy," the crazy woman said.

"But you had a miscarriage," Shelby said.

"You're really going to play this thing out aren't you? I didn't have a miscarriage. My son is sitting right there in the car."

Shelby looked back over at the Lincoln Navigator sitting in her drive way. The woman must have been telling the truth. That is the only way everything would make sense. It would be the only explanation for the boy looking like a spitting image of Phillip.

"I didn't know," Shelby said. She started feeling dizzy and nauseous. Her head felt as if it was going to explode. "I can't talk right now." She held her stomach. "I feel sick."

She turned from the door and ran towards the steps. She hadn't cared if she left the door open or not. She had to get away from the woman before she said anything else. She couldn't bear to hear any more.

Chapter 10

Phillip Tomlinson

Mercy

Phillip drove down the beltline listening to K97.5. He rocked his head as he listened to the R&B tunes. On his way home, he stopped by the auto parts store and bought wax for his truck. The shine had started to dull.

He turned up the volume on the radio and sang along with R. Kelly. "When a woman's fed up . . ." He tapped his hand on the steering wheel and continued to rock his head to the beat.

His cell phone rang. Without looking, he reached over, retrieved and answered it.

"Hello?"

"Hello again, Phillip."

Phillip didn't recognize the voice. "Who is this?"

"It's Jeana."

"Jeana, how in the hell did you get my number? Didn't I tell you a couple of days ago, to leave me and my family alone?" Phillip clinched his teeth and tightened his hands on the steering wheel. "I'm sick of this harassment. You'll be hearing from my lawyer soon!"

"Don't be so mean, Phillip. I was just calling you as a favor," Jeana said.

"A favor. Don't call me. I don't know how you got this number, but you need to lose it. Don't call me anymore."

"Okay, Phillip. I am going to ignore your last remarks and be nice. I think you need to check on your wife."

"My wife? Jeana, I swear I am going to . . ."

"Save it, Phillip. You need to check on your little wifey. When I left your house about thirty minutes ago, she wasn't doing very well."

Phillip couldn't have heard her right. "My house? What were you doing at my house?"

"Well, you wouldn't talk to me. I gave you more than enough time. I had to talk to your wife. It's your fault. If you had just treated me with some decency, then Taren and I wouldn't have had to go over there."

"You took him to my house?" Phillip asked. He couldn't believe what he was hearing.

"I just told you that, Phillip. Aren't you listening? You and your wife are just the same. I tell her things and she asks me the same questions over and over."

"What did you tell my wife?"

"Oh nothing she didn't already know. She tried to play dumb, but I saw right through it. I have to give your wife a standing ovation; she acted like she didn't know anything about Taren and the child support. I told her I didn't appreciate the way you treated me in court and the other day when I visited your office."

"You told my wife about our going to court and about the child support?" Phillip asked in disbelief.

"And, you should have seen her face when she saw Taren. I'll just bet she's been wondering what he looks like. Now she knows," Jeana said.

"Jeana, tell me you are lying. Tell me you didn't go to my house and talk to my wife," Phillip said, hoping it wasn't true.

"Yeah. I went. You thought I was bluffing? I wasn't! I told you Taren was going to get all of his birthday presents and I meant it!" Jeana screamed.

"What did my wife say?"

"I told you she played along with you acting like she didn't know a thing. I have to admit, she looked pretty convincing. She should try out for Star Search or something. I mean, she showed all the emotions. First, innocence like she was a perfect little angel. Then, she was sarcastic with me and then got angry and told me to leave. She had the nerve to tell me she was going to call the police. And, she performed the best act of all. She was shocked. Her face turned pale. Ha, ha, ha," Jeana laughed.

"I promise you this, Phillip, by the time I left there, she knew I wasn't playing. She knew I meant serious business."

"What do you mean, Jeana, what did you do?" Phillip screamed.

"Just check on your little wifey, she wasn't doing to well when I left her," Jeana chuckled.

"You crazy B . . . ," Phillip started.

"Hold it now, Phillip, is that the way you want to treat the mother of your first born son?" Jeana asked.

"Jeana, leave me and my family alone! I mean it. Don't ever go near my wife or daughter again. Leave them out of this. Do you understand me?"

"Tell your wife she deserves an Oscar for her performance," Jeana said.

"My wife didn't know anything about Taren, or you for that matter. Now leave her alone!" Phillip said and hung up the phone.

"What is going on?" Phillip asked himself out loud. He dialed his home number and got a busy signal. He hit redial and got another busy signal. He couldn't understand why he was getting a busy signal when they had call waiting. Then he tried Shelby's cell phone number and didn't get an answer.

Something was terribly wrong. He could feel it. He pressed his foot harder on the accelerator. Before he knew it, he was flying at 100 miles per hour. He had to get home. He cursed when he had to slow down to 80 miles per hour behind a group of cars. As quickly as he could, he drove around to pass them.

He had to slam on his breaks once he got to the traffic light. Even though the law would allow him to turn right on red, the traffic was too heavy and he had to wait for the light to turn green.

He continued to curse under his breath in the interim. It seemed like an eternity before the light changed. He slammed his fist on the steering wheel.

What was going on at his house? Jeana had been there. She had told Shelby things he never wanted her to know. He tried calling his house again, but the line was still busy.

Once the light finally changed, he gunned the engine. He pressed the accelerator so hard that he'd left tire tracks where he had previously been waiting. He had only gotten 300 feet before he had to stop again. The traffic was relentless.

He thought quickly and turned onto a back street. He knew a back way to his sub-division. Normally it would take longer to use the alternant route, but today he knew it would be his savior.

He traveled the side streets and back roads until he came to the back gate of Barrington Estates. Barely slowing down, he flashed his pass to the unfamiliar back-gate attendant. Lucky for him another resident had just gone through the gate and it had not closed yet.

Even though the speed limit was only 25 miles per hour, Phillip sped towards his house at 50 miles per hour. He turned from street to street yielding at stop signs. His heart almost stopped when he turned onto his street.

He saw a fire truck, two police cars and an ambulance in front of his house. Within 20 seconds, he was in his driveway. Without turning the truck off, he jumped out and left the door wide open.

He ran past the firemen and the two police officers who were standing outside of his front door.

"Sir," the policeman said. "Stop, sir." The policeman ran up behind Phillip, trying to restrain him.

"Get off of me. This is my house. What's going on? Where are my wife and daughter?" Phillip asked.

The policeman moved aside, allowing Phillip passage. "Sorry, sir. Your wife is inside. The paramedics are preparing her for transport."

"For transport? Why? What's going on?" Phillip asked again.

"Daddy, Daddy!" Nyah said as she pulled away from a neighbor who was holding her hand to keep her back. She ran up and grabbed Phillip's leg.

"Nyah, sweetie. What's going on? What's wrong with Mommy?" Phillip wanted answers. He looked through the open door into his foyer. All he could see was Shelby's legs and shoes as she lay on the hospital gurney.

"Mommy fell down the steps, Daddy. She wouldn't get up. I called 9-1-1 like Miss Crystal told us to do in a mergency. Daddy, the fire trucks and the nice police man came," Nyah smiled. "They said they're going to make Mommy all better."

Phillip picked his daughter up and headed into the house. Laying on the gurney was Shelby. She was barely conscious.

"Shelby, honey, Shelby. Are you okay?" Phillip asked full of confusion and fear.

It took a second for Shelby's eyes to adjust on him. When they did he saw the same look on her face as it had been years earlier when he first divulged partial information about Jeana. There was distrust in her eyes. She looked at him as if he was a stranger. He wanted to cover his face in shame.

Shelby's voice was raspy. "Why didn't you tell me, Phillip? Why?" Shelby asked him the questions just before she passed back out.

"Sir, we need to get your wife to the hospital. You can meet us there if you'd like," the paramedic said.

Phillip moved to the side so the paramedics could get through the door with his wife.

"Are they going to make Mommy better?" Nyah asked.

"Yes baby, they are going to make Mommy feel better," Phillip said. He knew the doctors would help any physical injuries his wife had. But he wondered how he'd be able to repair the internal trust injuries he had inflicted.

Even in Shelby's semi conscious state, he knew the wounds were deep, maybe too deep to repair this time. He lied to his wife. Because of him, his wife was on her way to the hospital.

Phillip thanked the neighbor for watching Nyah and quickly locked up his house. He followed the ambulance to the hospital. It was going the speed limit with its lights on. Phillip figured whatever was wrong with his wife must not have been too bad, or else they would have been running their lights and speeding.

"Nyah, tell Daddy everything that happened."

"Mommy said I could watch Dora on your big TV," Nyah said.

"She did? What was Mommy doing while you were watching TV?"

"Mommy was talking to the nice lady."

"What nice lady?" Phillip asked.

"The lady gave me a gumball. I said thank you, Daddy."

Phillip knew his daughter would tell him what happened if he asked the right questions. "When did the nice lady give you a gum ball?"

"At the store," Nyah said.

"You saw a nice lady at the store who gave you a gumball?"

"Uh huh," Nyah said, shaking her head positively.

"Nyah, what does that have to do with your Mommy? I asked you what Mommy was doing while you were watching TV." Phillip pressed the importance of the question.

"Mommy was talking to the nice lady from the store."

"The nice lady from the store was at our house?" Phillip asked.

"Yes, Daddy." Nyah splayed her hands, gesturing with a that's-what-I've-been-trying-to-tell-you look.

"What did the lady say to Mommy?"

"I don't know, Daddy. Mommy told me to watch the big TV. She said you wouldn't get mad at me."

"No, baby. Daddy isn't mad at you." For further clarification Phillip said, "When you were watching Dora, did you hear Mommy talking to the lady?"

"No, Daddy," Nyah said.

"When did you find Mommy?" Phillip asked.

Nyah looked as if she was trying to process the question in her mind.

Phillip tried to simplify it. "How did you know to call 911?"

"I was watching Dora and I heard a big noise. I looked downstairs and saw Mommy on the floor. I shook her and she didn't say anything. Miss. Crystal showed us how to dial 9-1-1. Mrs. Crystal said don't call 9-1-1 unless it was a mergency," Nyah said, trying to say emergency.

"You did good, sweet heart. It was an emergency. I am proud of you and I know Mommy is proud of you also."

Phillip pressed the accelerator harder so he wouldn't be caught by the light.

By the time they arrived at the hospital, Phillip was told by the receptionist that Shelby had already been taken to the emergency area. While he waited to see her, he stepped outside to call Shelby's parents to let them know what was going on. He also called Crystal to see if she could meet him at the hospital and watch Nyah for a while.

Thirty minutes after he arrived, a nurse came out to tell him he could go back and sit with Shelby. He waited a couple more minutes and then Crystal and her husband Warren showed up with J.J.

"Phillip, how is she?" Crystal said as she rushed through the emergency room doors.

"I don't know yet. The nurse just came out to

let me know I could go back. She didn't give me an update," Phillip said.

"What happened?" Crystal asked.

Phillip thought for a second. He really hadn't known exactly what happened. Although his daughter was a very smart little girl, she might have gotten some of the facts wrong.

He didn't want to go into anything about the whole mess with Jeana. "I don't really know for sure. As far as I am aware, she might have fallen down the stairs."

"Oh, my God. I hope she's okay. And the baby . . ."

Crystal's husband placed his arms around his wife. "Everything will be fine. Calm down, Crystal." Warren turned his attention to Phillip. "Phillip, I know you're anxious and ready to go back and see Shelby, but I'd like to say a prayer, before you go. Is that alright?"

It was more than alright with Phillip. "Yes, please do. We need all the prayers we can get."

They all joined hands.

"Dear heavenly Father, we come to you as humble as we know how. We love you, Lord. We adore you, Lord. You are our Father and we thank you for your daily grace and mercy towards us. We know we fall short of your expectations daily, and we ask for your forgiveness. Even though we know we don't deserve it, you are so good to us. We thank you so much for loving us and caring for us as your sheep, you are our shepherd.

"Lord, you know why we are coming to you. Just as you know all things, but we know through prayer and faith you will take care of your child,

Shelby. You know the end just as you knew the beginning. We are just praying that our sister in Christ, Phillip's wife, and the baby on the way will be fine. It is in your hands, Lord, just as it has always been. We know you know best as to what will happen in this situation. We just thank you again for hearing our prayers.

"Lord, please bless each person standing here. Bless the other families waiting on word about their family members. Bless each person admitted to this hospital. And, Lord, if it is their time to go, I pray they know you as their personal Savior.

"Thank you again, Lord, for your awesome wonders. We pray this in your son Jesus' name. Amen."

"Amen," Crystal said.

Phillip felt awkward praying with them. Warren and Crystal were so strong in their faith with God. Phillip hadn't remembered saying a prayer in years. His prayer life consisted of a memorized prayer he said before he ate his food. And often times he only said grace for show when others were around. He let Shelby say the prayers or grace otherwise—especially since she'd rededicated her life to Christ.

"Thanks, Warren. You sounded just like a preacher. That prayer was powerful," Phillip said.

"It's all God. I just let Him use me as a vessel."

Phillip had no idea what Warren was talking about. He just wanted to thank the man.

"Don't worry about Shelby, she'll be fine. God has got it all in his hands," Warren said.

"I know He does," Phillip said. Trying to head

off a long conversation about the Lord, Phillip said, "I'm going to head on back."

"Don't worry about Nyah. Warren is going to watch the kids. I'm going to stay here with you and Shelby," Crystal said.

"Crystal, thanks. You don't have to do that," Phillip said.

"I know I don't have to, I want to. Shelby is like a sister to me. I wouldn't be able to rest at home anyway not knowing what's going on. I'm here if you need anything."

"And like Crystal said, don't worry about the kids. I've got it under control," Warren assured him.

Phillip felt bad about trying to ditch them so quickly when all they were trying to do was help. "Thanks," Phillip said. "I don't know if Nyah has eaten anything yet." He reached in his pocket and pulled out his wallet.

Warren patted Phillip on the back. "Don't worry. We've got it. You go ahead and see about Shelby."

"Thank you both so much. It really means a great deal to me." Phillip was truly touched by all Crystal and Warren were doing.

"Head on back. I'll be out here reading my book," Crystal said.

"Nyah," Phillip said. "I want you to be a good girl for Mr. Warren."

Nyah shook her head. "I will."

"Daddy is going to check on Mommy."

"Is the doctor making Mommy feel better, Daddy?" Nyah asked.

"I'm sure he is. I'll call Mr. Warren later and let

you know how Mommy is doing. And if Mommy is feeling better, you can talk to her too."

"Yipee," Nyah said. "Mommy is gonna feel better."

Phillip corrected his daughter just as Shelby would have. "Mommy is going to feel better, Nyah, not gonna."

"Mommy is going to feel better," Nyah repeated.

"Give me a hug and I'll see you later." Phillip hugged his daughter tightly. She was his link to Shelby. He hoped his wife was doing fine.

Phillip sat by Shelby's hospital bed. They had moved her from the emergency room to a private room. She was still unconscious. The doctor told Phillip her injuries were minimal. The bruises she had sustained to her head and arm would be sore for a while, but he didn't think there would be any permanent damage.

The doctor also said there was nothing wrong with the baby. Shelby's stomach, amazingly, had no detectable trauma. Shelby's prognosis was good.

Phillip had been relieved to hear the good news about her prognosis, but that was two hours later and Shelby still lay unconscious in her hospital bed. Phillip took the time to think about what really might have happened. He thought about the unfolding events of the recent weeks.

He couldn't believe what was going on. Jeana was making his life hell. Now, she had pulled Shelby into the whole fiasco.

It hurt him to know that because of him, his

wife was lying in a hospital bed unconscious. It was all, his fault. If he had been up front with Shelby in the first place, it would have never happened. If he had just talked to Jeana a little longer, maybe she wouldn't have gone to his house and hurt his wife.

Even though he was in the wrong, Phillip raged inside knowing Jeana had hurt his wife. He didn't know how, but he figured Jeana must have entered the house and pushed Shelby down the stairs.

He knew Jeana was a little off but even crazy people had do be dealt with as far as Phillip was concerned. He'd find out what Jeana had done and he'd make sure she paid one way or another.

Phillip heard a light tap at the door. "Come in," Phillip said.

The door opened and his mother-in-law emerged, followed by his father-in-law. Phillip had been expecting them.

Shelby's mother fought back tears as she looked at her daughter lying in the bed with bandages around her head and arm.

"Oh, Phillip, is there anymore news?" her mother asked.

"No, Mom, just what I told you on the phone an hour ago. She still hasn't woken up," Phillip was sad to say.

The tears Shelby's mother was holding back, poured forth. "My baby girl," she sobbed.

Shelby's father placed his arms around his wife. He was speechless to see his daughter in her injured state.

Phillip stood. "Mom, it's okay. The doctor said

it's not as bad as it looks. Her injuries will be a nuisance for a little while, but they'll go away. Nothing's broken and the baby is fine."

After crying a little longer, Shelby's mother wiped her tears. "I know she's going to be fine. I prayed to God and I know He is going to take care of my baby. It's just . . . seeing her in this state. I hadn't expected it. I'm fine now. I'll be strong for my daughter. I can't have her wake up and see me crying." She dried her tears. "Excuse me for a moment." She exited to the bathroom.

Once Shelby's mother closed the door to the bathroom, Shelby's Dad finally spoke. "Phillip, son, how are you doing?"

"Fine, Dad," Phillip lied. He felt awful. He just wanted his wife to wake up so he could hold her again and tell her how much he loved her. He wanted to explain why he hadn't come clean with her in the past about the son he had with Jeana.

"Shelby has always been a strong girl even when she was a toddler I knew she'd turn into a strong woman. And she has." Shelby's dad said.

"I know you're right. I know she'll pull through this with flying colors."

Shelby's mother returned from the bathroom. "Good I didn't mess up my make up too much," she joked.

She stood on the side of the bed opposite Phillip and held her daughter's hand as she spoke. "Shelby, honey. Daddy and I are here. Everything is going to be fine. You just rest and we'll be here right by your side."

She waited in silence for a response. None came.

The doctor returned to check on Shelby again. He checked her vitals, and stated that she was still doing well. He informed them that the pain medicine Shelby had been put on would start to wear off slightly and she should wake up soon.

Fifteen minutes after the doctor left, Shelby showed signs of consciousness. She squeezed her mother's hand.

"Shelby, baby!" Shelby's mother said with excitement.

Shelby opened her eyes to a slit trying to focus on her mother. She smiled when she realized who was holding her hand.

"Shelby, I'm here; sweetheart," her mother said.

"Mom," Shelby said. Her voice was raspy.

"It's okay, sweetheart. Don't try to talk. Dad and I are right here. We're not going anywhere."

"Daddy?" Shelby said a little stronger this time.

Her father moved around to the side of the bed next to her so that she could see him. "I'm right here, sweetheart." He put his hands around his wife and daughter's hand.

Shelby smiled at both of them.

Phillip was elated that his wife had finally awaken. He looked up and silently thanked God for coming through. He knew everything was going to be fine. All he needed to do was hug Shelby; tell her how much he loved her. Later, when they were alone, he'd explain the whole Jeana situation to her.

Phillip grasped Shelby's other hand. "Shelby, honey, I love you. I am so glad you're awake."

With a forced effort she turned her head towards him. Her eyes widened at seeing him. She recoiled from him.

"Why, Phillip? Why didn't you tell me?" she asked the same question she had asked hours before as she was being loaded into the ambulance.

"Shelby I . . . Let me explain . . ." Phillip started.

"Get out, Phillip," Shelby said. Her voice was still gruff but understandable.

"Shelby, please, I know I . . ." Phillip pleaded for her to listen.

"Get out, now! I don't want to see you. Leave now!" Her voice was stronger and clearer. There was no mistaking the meaning of her words.

Her parents watched the exchange. They didn't know what to make of it.

"Shelby . . ." Phillip tried to speak again.

"Get out!" Shelby screamed. She started shaking uncontrollably. Shelby's heart monitor pulsed at double speed. Beads of sweat popped out on the exposed portion of her forehead and on her nose.

"Phillip, I don't know what's going on, but you need to leave," Shelby's father said.

"Yes, Phillip, leave right now. My daughter is upset for some reason. Just leave so she can calm down," Shelby's mother said.

"I'll leave. I'll be right outside." Phillip didn't want to hurt Shelby.

"No, leave, get out of here. I don't want to see you again!" Shelby screamed even louder.

A nurse rushed into the room. "What is going on?"

"It's alright, I'm leaving," Phillip said. He

picked up his jacket and left the hospital room as swiftly as possible.

While walking down the hospital corridor, he could still hear Shelby screaming. Instead of waiting for the elevator, he ran towards the stairs. He couldn't stand to hear her pain and anguish.

He pushed the door to the steps open so hard that it slammed against the doorstop. He barreled down the stairs two at a time until reaching the bottom, then pushed through the ground floor door with the same force as he had previously used.

Once in the parking garage, he stopped. He gasped in deep breaths. The reaction from Shelby and the speed at which he had been moving together caused him to have difficulty breathing.

He stumbled towards his truck. When he reached it, he pounded both his fists on the hood and roared like a lion. He continued to pound his fists until he couldn't any longer.

He fumbled for his keys in his jacket pocket and pressed his remote to unlock the door. After slamming the door shut and causing the truck to vibrate, he turned the ignition. Once started, he quickly put the truck into reverse and then shifted into drive, barely letting the truck finish rolling backwards.

Phillip's anger continued to elevate the more he thought about how Shelby was feeling. It fueled his fury to know that Jeana had caused his wife to be in so much physical and mental pain. It was Jeana's fault Shelby was angry with him.

He'd find Jeana and she would pay dearly.

Chapter 11

Jeana Sands

Vengeance

Jeana pulled her Navigator around the curve of Phillip's parking garage. She had driven through all of the levels and couldn't find Phillip's pickup truck or his Yukon. It was the third day she had been at his job looking for the vehicles.

She'd called him several times at work but his secretary always told her he was out of the office. Jeana knew the woman had to be lying. Phillip told her to screen his calls. She couldn't believe his nerve.

She had also been canvassing the parking garage where Shelby worked, looking for Shelby's Navigator, but hadn't seen it either. When she sat outside Phillip's daughter's day care around the time the child was normally dropped off and picked up, she saw no sign of them either.

Numerous times, she would drive through his neighborhood, looking for signs of life from their house. At night she saw the same lights left on in the front window. It looked as if they had left town on vacation or something and left strategic lights on in the home to make it look as if they were home.

Jeana pulled back out of the parking garage and cursed, "They really are a pair going through such lengths to avoid me.

She looked at the clock on her dashboard. It was almost 2:00 p.m. and she had an appointment scheduled.

"I'll deal with you later, Phillip," Jeana said to herself.

"The crown molding in here is absolutely beautiful. I love the way they took the time to make the intricate carvings of the angels in each corner. It seems almost a waste of time since unless you are looking directly in the corners they are barely noticeable," Jeana's client said.

"Well, Mrs. Robano, as I assured you, this builder is like none other. This home is filled with little whatnots to make it special. We can't possibly adequately cover the whole 6,500 square feet in just a couple of hours," Jeana told her client.

"So, tell me again, this home has only had one other owner, correct?" Mr. Robano asked.

"Yes," Jeana replied.

"But, the development is so new. It couldn't be any older than a year," Mr. Robano said.

"You are correct. The previous owner only lived here for three months. I'm told she was a wealthy young eccentric from the west coast, who wanted to show Mommy and Daddy she didn't need them and could make it on the east coast without them.

"After about a month of being here she couldn't take being away from them, so she put the house back on the market. She moved out two months later saying she couldn't wait for it to sell. From what I hear, she was hardly ever here. She was always flying back to the west coast," Jeana said.

"It still looks brand new. Lucky for us," Mr. Robano said.

"The girl lived here all alone? In this massive house?" Mrs. Robano asked.

"Yes," Jeana answered.

"She must have been pretty well off."

"Very well off. She is the heiress to the Damonae family."

"Damonae, as in the clothing Mogul?"

"One in the same," Jeana replied.

"I'd love to see her closet. I can't imagine a closet full of Damonae clothing," Mrs. Robano said.

"Me either," Jeana said. "It is a gem of a home," Jeana continued, she needed to get the couple back on track. It was almost three-thirty and she wanted to be outside of the daycare and waiting by four-thirty.

"Right this way." Jeana led them into the living room. "As you can see, the living room has several focal points.

She walked over to the fireplace. "The fireplace is equipped with gas logs so you'll never have to cut one log or clean soot out of the chimney, Mr. Robano." Jeana had noticed the well-manicured hands of Mr. Robano. His nails had a shine that could only have come from clear nail polish. He also wore a pair of penny loafers, which didn't have a scratch on them and barely any creases from the bending the shoes would undergo while being walked in.

Mrs. Robano wore a wedding ring that had to have been at least three carats. She wore other jewelry, which suggested the couple had their own wealth. They had driven up in a late model two-seater Mercedes Benz which Mrs. Robano called her toy car.

Jeana could only dream of becoming that wealthy. She knew if she worked hard and continued to sell houses to the rich, then one day she too would have a toy car and insignificant trinkets. Then she would go back home and show her family that she wasn't a piece of dirt. Show them that she'd made something out of herself.

She couldn't wait for the day and could only imagine the look on her mother and father's face. Her sisters and brothers would be jealous with envy and would probably ask her for money, but she'd turn a deaf ear to them just as they had done to her.

She'd probably show them a little mercy. Maybe she'd let them work in one of her offices, cleaning and taking out the garbage.

"Ms. Sands?" Mrs. Robano said.

Jeana had lost herself in thought, forgetting about the couple for a second.

"Oh, I apologize. I was thinking about some business I need to take care of later," Jeana said.

"I was asking if anyone else had put an offer down on the house yet." Mr. Robano asked.

"Actually, we have three offers," Jeana said, lying.

"Honey, I want this house," Mrs. Robano said to her husband. "I don't care what it takes, I want it."

"We still have a couple more rooms to see and we haven't even seen the back lawn yet," Mr. Robano said.

"I've seen enough. If the rest of the house is like what we've seen, I want it. The front lawn is immaculate, so why wouldn't the back be?" Mrs. Robano pressed her husband. "If we wait too long, we could lose out on it. And, honey, one of the Daemonae heirs owned this house. That in itself is a major buying point."

"What is the asking price?" Mr. Robano asked.

"One-million five with a ten percent down payment," Jeana said.

"When can we do the paperwork? My wife wants this house. Who do I write the check to for the down payment?"

Jeana smiled with glee. "I'll have to submit the proposal first, of course, but I'm sure they'll be no problems, especially since you are willing to pay the asking price and the down payment upon request."

Jeana continued to show them the rest of the house and the back lawn.

"I'll call you as soon as I hear something," Jeana said.

She walked them to their car and saw them off. After they were gone, she looked back at her watch. It was four-fifteen. She still had just enough time to get to the daycare and perch in her usual incognito spot.

Jeana waited at the daycare for an hour, but saw no signs of Phillip or his wife. She wondered what was going on. She thought about calling Phillip's office again but knew the office was closed. Then she had an idea.

Jeana dialed the number for Phillip's office in hopes to get the office directory. She'd leave him a message. The automated voice prompted her to dial the last four letters of Phillip's last name. Her ears perked up as soon as she heard Phillip's recorded voice. Then she started to frown.

The recorded message stated that Phillip was out of the office and would not be returning for an indefinite amount of time. If there was anything of importance, all calls should be directed to his supervisor.

Jeana pressed the end button on her cell phone so hard that it remained mashed in when she released it.

"What is going on?" She said to herself as she cranked her Navigator and headed towards Phillip's house again. If she had to sit there all night this time, she would. They'd have to come home sooner or later.

She picked up her cell phone and dialed her son. "Taren, I've got to work late tonight. I want you to make sure the door is locked and don't answer it if anyone comes. If anyone calls, say I'm busy and I'll call them later. Don't let on that you are home alone. There are some hot pockets in the freezer. Microwave them for two minutes and they'll be done. I love you, son. I'm working hard for our future."

"Did you thank Steve's mom for bringing you home from camp?"

"Yeah, Mom. She said to give her a call when you get a chance," Taren answered.

"Okay. I will. Now if you need anything just call my cell phone instead of the office phone."

Jeana hung up the phone, drove to pick up a burger and fries and then headed towards Phillip's house.

It was dusk by the time she finally parked a couple of houses down from Phillip's house. There were dark rain clouds rolling in. It was just dark enough for her to notice that the lights, which had been burning for three days, had been turned off.

"Hum, signs of life," Jeana said to herself. "It must be my lucky day."

She settled comfortably in her seat, and chewed on her remaining fries.

As she watched the house, Jeana daydreamed about what her life would have been like with Phillip. The house she was watching could have been hers. She should have been pregnant with a second child. Jeana should have been the one with the white picket fence around her house.

Jeana drifted off to sleep while thinking of Phillip. She was jarred awake by her cell phone ringing.

"Hello?" she said curtly.

"Mom, Granny called," Taren said.

"Your granny called?" *That's a surprise. I wonder what she wants*, Jeana thought. "I'll call her tomorrow. Is everything okay there? Did you finish cleaning your room and folding your clothes?"

"Yeah," Taren yawned.

"Good, go ahead and get ready for bed, I'll be home in a couple of hours."

"Don't you want me to wait until you get home?" Taren asked.

"No, you don't need to wait for me. Go ahead and go to sleep."

"Okay, Mom. I love you."

"Love you too baby, bye," Jeana said.

She attempted to press the end button, but it was still collapsed from her earlier phone call.

She tossed the phone back into the passenger seat, and yawned from the nap she had mistakenly taken.

When she looked up at Phillip's house she saw his truck pulling out of the garage.

"Bingo!" she said to herself and cranked the Navigator. She waited until he was at the end of the street before turning on her headlights. Placing her foot on the accelerator, lightly she crept behind him. When he turned the corner, she sped up trying to catch him.

She followed his Yukon out of the sub-division, through downtown Silvermont and onto the Interstate 40. She continued to follow him as he entered the 340 beltline of the interstate heading north. "Where are you going at this late hour on a Friday night, Phillip? Not to the club I hope."

After a few miles, Jeana figured she might know where he was going, but wondered why. She also wondered why he was alone. *Where are his wife and daughter*, she thought.

Just as she suspected, he exited the beltline heading towards the hospital where Shelby worked.

Maybe he is going to pick Shelby up from work or something. Her hours must have changed, Jeana thought. *That must be why I've had such a hard time keeping up with them.*

"But why hasn't Phillip been at work all this time? Maybe they were on vacation and they're back," Jeana said out loud.

Jeana watched Phillip as he parked and got out of his truck. She couldn't believe what she saw.

Phillip was wearing a wrinkled pair of green jogging pants and a wrinkled t-shirt. His hair had obviously not been combed or cut in a couple of days and she could see the beginnings of a beard forming.

He walked with his head down, barely paying attention to the traffic as he crossed the street from the parking lot to the emergency entrance of the hospital. A car almost hit him and it barely seemed to faze him.

The driver of the car laid on his horn and mouthed obscenities Jeana couldn't make out.

With her mouth still dropped, Jean grabbed her purse and keys to follow Phillip into the building.

As she rounded the corner, heading to the elevators, she saw Phillip pushing a button as the doors closed. She looked up at the numbers as the elevator ascended. It looked as if he had gotten off on the third floor. But Jeana knew Shelby worked on the second floor.

"What the heck is going on?" She pushed the

elevator button to investigate further. She stepped off the elevator on the third floor and was face to face with the nurse's station.

A nurse flipping through her paperwork looked up. "Can I help you, Miss?"

"Uh, no. I'm fine. I know it's late, but I've been driving a long time to get here to see my Uncle who is ill," Jeana lied. She looked around as she spoke and saw the numbers for the rooms to the left and right of her.

"Ah, I see which way I need to go. Thanks for all your help." Jeana turned to the right and walked away from the nurse before she could ask the fake uncle's name. "You have a nice night."

"You too," the nurse said politely. "I hope your uncle is doing well."

"Un huh, thanks," Jeana said, picking up speed. She hadn't really known where she was going and didn't know what the third floor specialized in. She had just taken a guess that it wasn't the children's floor since there weren't any pictures of cartoon characters lining the hall.

She also knew it couldn't be the maternity ward, since that was where Shelby worked on the second floor.

The further she walked away from the nurse's station, the slower her pace became. She had no idea which way Phillip had gone and wondered who he would be visiting at the hospital so late at night. As nonchalantly as possible, she peeked into various hospital rooms.

She heard someone who sounded as like they were coughing up a lung. Most of the hall lights were off and it felt creepy. The low hums and beeps of the patient's machines didn't help calm her.

Mid-way down the hall, she came upon a waiting area. Sitting there in a chair with his back to her was Phillip talking to an older man.

Jeana retreated where she couldn't be seen, but she would still be able to hear the conversation Phillip was having with the man. She located a magazine holder mounted on the wall and pretended to look for a magazine.

"Phillip, have you gotten any rest?" The older man asked.

"I can't sleep. I just don't feel like doing anything," Phillip replied.

She heard what sounded like the older man patting Phillip on his back as he said, "I can tell. Look at you. You need to get some rest, take a shower and change clothes. You had the same outfit on yesterday."

"I know . . ."

There was a pause.

"Nyah is doing fine though. She is having the time of her life at her godmother's house. She's been asking about you," the older man said. "You need to give her a call."

"A call," Jeana whispered to herself. *Why is Nyah at her godmother's house having the time of her life? Why hasn't Phillip called his precious daughter?*

"I can't call her just yet. She's going to ask me questions I can't answer right now," Phillip said.

There was another pause. Jeana heard the older man speak again.

"Do you want to talk about it? I mean, I don't

want to pry into your business. I'm just concerned that's all."

Jeana's ears perked up.

"I can't, not now, Dad. I need to talk to Shelby first," Phillip replied.

Phillip's voice was barely audible. Jeana had a hard time hearing him. The man down the hall coughing didn't help matters either.

Why was Phillip calling this man, Dad? Jeana had seen pictures of Phillip's dad and this man looked nothing like him. And why did Phillip need to talk to him. Where was his wife, Shelby? Was she at the godmother's house also?

Jeana had so many questions.

The man down the hall coughed again. It was long and unrelenting.

Jeana had missed something they'd said. She heard the words "fall" and "paramedics" between the coughing breaths.

By the time the man finally stopped coughing, she realized someone was crying. It was Phillip.

She got closer to the corner to eavesdrop. Phillip was slumped over, sobbing on the older man's shoulder.

Jeana moved to the magazine rack, when she heard footsteps behind her. She saw an older woman, dressed in gray slacks and a black blouse. The woman looked to be the same age as the man consoling Phillip.

The woman made eye contact with Jeana for a brief moment and said, "Hello." Her smile was weary. Her hair was short and wavy with speckles of gray throughout.

Jeana returned the greeting and averted her eyes.

She listened as the woman continued to walk past her towards the waiting room.

The woman spoke no words at first. Phillip's sobbing and the man's coughing continued.

When the sobbing stopped Jeana finally heard the woman speak.

"Hello, Phillip."

Jeana listened as Phillip tried to stop his sobbing. The attempts were poor at best.

It hurt Jeana to see Phillip in the condition he was in. She always envisioned him as a man made of steel who couldn't be penetrated. After he dumped her years ago, she knew his heart was made of steel.

Now, she felt sorry for him. He had feelings. Phillip was human too.

Tears formed in her eyes. She discreetly wiped them with her forefingers.

"Phillip," the older woman said, "I asked her again and she doesn't want to see you. I'm sorry."

"What am I going to do?" Phillip asked.

"Just pray, Phillip. I have no idea what's going on. But, Shelby is extremely upset. I won't pry into your private business. That is between you and her. But, you two really need to talk about it. If not to each other, then someone you really trust.

"Keeping it all in, whatever it is, is tearing you both apart. I know my daughter, and she is trying to put on this armor of steel. But, I know it is starting to crack at the seams. Be patient and persistent. One day she'll agree to see you."

"I will. I'll keep coming up here and waiting until she decides she's ready to talk to me. When that happens, I want to be right here. I love Shelby and I would never hurt her intentionally," Phillip said with heartfelt sincerity.

"We know you love her, son. We have no doubt about that. You need to talk and pray about it. You'll come through this," the older man said.

Jeana realized who they were talking about. Shelby must have been in the hospital for some reason. *Maybe she had the baby*, she thought. But, Jeana didn't hear any mention of a baby and wondered why was Phillip crying so much.

"I will stay with her tonight," the woman said. "Phillip, you should go home. If I know my daughter, she probably won't change her mind tonight. You need to rest and change your clothes."

"I want to stay a little while longer. The house feels empty with Shelby and Nyah gone," Phillip said.

"OK. But, you don't want her to change her mind about talking to you while you are in the state you are in now. You don't want her to see you like this do you?" the woman asked.

"No, I guess you're right," Phillip admitted.

"Good then. Take my advice and go home take a nice long shower and get a good night's sleep. You'll feel one-hundred percent better, I guarantee it."

"I just want to stay a few more minutes. Then, I promise I will take your advice, Mom."

"Shelby will be fine. When you see her again, you won't believe the progress. Her eye is no longer purple and the doctor took her off of all the IV's they had her on. She is moving her arm more now also."

"She is?" Phillip said with audible hope.

"Yes. They've even taken the bandage from around her head," Shelby's mother said.

Jeana listened with intensity. Phillip's wife sustained injuries bad enough for her to be hospitalized. Phillip looked horrible.

Jeana wondered what happened to Shelby. She didn't want to admit it, but she admired Shelby. Even though she often felt twinges of jealousy, somehow she knew that Shelby might be a good person deep down.

Jeana remembered the last conversation she had with Phillip. He said that his wife didn't know anything about Taren. *Could it be true?* She thought. Maybe Shelby wasn't playing dumb when she confronted her. She wasn't acting.

"No wonder she kept asking me who I was after I told her my name," Jeana said under her breath.

Shelby must have been just as innocent as she herself had been years ago. Phillip took advantage of her also. Even though Shelby had everything Jeana wanted in life, Phillip wasn't any better to his wife either. He was still a liar.

Jeana didn't know why, but she felt guilty. She wondered what might have happened to Shelby.

Shelby was visibly upset when Jeana left her front door step. Jeana thought it was an act and dismissed the woman's distraught display.

Shelby had ran from the door and left Jeana standing there. She wanted to follow her, but thought her attempts would have been futile. She figured Shelby would just continue on her acting spree.

Not having time for silliness, she left the door wide open and figured Shelby would feel stupid when she realized Jeana wasn't going to run after her.

Jeana heard the shuffle of feet and one of the waiting-room chairs moving. She placed the magazine she was holding back into the magazine rack just before turning to return to the elevator.

She passed the same nurse sitting at the nurse's station.

"How is your uncle doing?" the nurse asked.

"Oh, he's fine. I talked to him for a few minutes before he dosed off to sleep. I didn't want to leave too quickly, you know, in case he woke up. But he didn't. I'll be back to see him tomorrow," Jeana said.

"Good. Have a good night," the nurse smiled with warmth.

"You too," Jeana said.

The elevator arrived and Jeana stepped into it. She heard a woman's voice call out to hold the elevator before it closed. Jeana didn't hold it. She didn't want to ride down with Shelby's mother. She was ashamed.

Jeana's gut told her that she had something to do with Shelby being in the hospital. It gnawed at her the more she thought about the confrontation at Phillip's house.

She felt awful. Her stomach did cartwheels and the back of her mouth tasted sour. As she made her way out to her Navigator, Jeana experienced bouts of dry heaves. The humidity of the night and the rank smell of an outside dumpster made her feel even sicker.

She needed fresh air. She cranked the Navigator and exited the parking garage as quickly as she could. She drove with all the windows rolled down and the air conditioning running. The fresh air helped a little, but the guilt continued to gnaw.

She drove to a nearby park, shut the engine off and made sure the doors were locked.

Jeana hadn't meant to harm Shelby. She just wanted what was hers, or what she thought was hers. The realization hit her that Phillip wasn't hers; he never was. It wasn't Shelby's fault and now, for some reason, the woman was in the hospital.

Jeana was sorry for causing any pain. She felt another one of her migraine headaches starting. Her head started to throb. The headaches were the worse when she thought about Phillip and the way he treated her. Phillip had caused her to become the person she'd evolved into and she hated him for it.

She had always been a determined person before going to college. She was hard working and diligent whenever it came to any task. But since Phillip jilted her, her hate for him had brought out an evil side of her.

It never made her feel good. Whenever she had evil thoughts, told lies or was manipulative, it always caused her pain. She knew her alter ego had caused the onset of the high blood pressure. And her headaches were also a residual effect.

She looked down at her hands, which had the remnants of scrapes and bruises from her many daydreams.

"What is wrong with me? What have I turned into?" Jeana asked herself.

As she sat in the dark deserted park alone, she'd felt a sudden surge of vulnerability.

She wanted the madness to end. She was tired of hating Phillip and his family. The rage and fury she'd allowed herself to feel was consuming her and taking a huge toll on her life.

The sound of an owl hooting startled her.

She no longer wanted to be the person she had evolved into over the years. Jeana wanted help and knew just where to get it.

Jeana's parents had unknowingly given her the resolve to exceed their expectations, which she knew in the long run had been a good thing. Her parents had also made sure Jeana went to church every Sunday and Wednesday night for mid-week service. While the other children played and sometimes mocked the way the preacher preached during the church services, Jeana sat and listened intently.

By sending her to church, her parents had also ended up instilling the invaluable love of Christ in her. She had strayed from Christ for much too long. Christ's love never left her with bruises and headaches. His love had always filled her with peace. It was time to ask for forgiveness and repent. She needed to return to the love, which no one else could compare. She bowed her head and clasped her hands together to pray.

"Dear Father, Son and Holy Spirit, Lord I thank you so much for your grace and mercy." Jeana wiped tears, which started streaming down her face. "Lord, you are awesome and magnificent. I praise your holy name I adore you. Lord, there is none like you anywhere and I thank you." The tears continued to flow.

"Lord, please forgive me for my sins. There are so many sins I can't even name them all. But Lord you know them, just as you know the exact number of all the hairs on my head. You, are all knowing, Lord.

"Lord, I have done horrible things and had terrible thoughts. I am ashamed of not respecting my parents, lying, cheating and stealing things in the past in order for me to get ahead. I know all those things are wrong and I feel the heaviness of conviction. I just ask you to forgive me. I want to repent for my sins, Lord." Jeana abandoned the attempts to wipe her newly forming tears.

"Lord Jesus, please forgive me for the way I've treated Phillip and his family. Forgive me for the evil thoughts and deeds I've done towards them.

"Lord, I pray Phillip will forgive me as well as his wife. Lord, I pray Shelby will make it through whatever she is going through right now. Heal her body, Lord, and make her better than new.

"Lord, please forgive me for not respecting my parents for who they are. I pray Lord that you will continue to keep them and the rest of my family safe and in your arms. And Lord Jesus, I pray I have not done some unknown, irreversible harm to my son, Taren. Lord, I thought my intentions were good but now I realize they were really warped. I ask you to forgive me. I can only pray that my wrong efforts have not cost my son a relationship with his father.

"Lord, I pray you comfort Shelby's family as she is going through recovery. Lord, bless Phillip's little girl, Nyah also. I hope I didn't do anything to harm her either. Lord, I pray for the new baby on the way. Protect him or her also.

"I know you are powerful. You can do all these things and more. I am asking in Jesus' name Lord. I know you don't have to do a thing. I just thank you for your grace and mercy.

"And I thank you in advance, Lord, for all the awesome works you will perform. I know you can and I know you will. Thank you, Lord! Thank you, Lord! Thank you, Lord! I will forever give your name the praise and glory. It is in your son Jesus' name I pray. Amen."

Jeana finally felt at peace. She opened her eyes. The sounds of the night creatures continued to hoop and howl, but she wasn't fazed. The Lord was on her side. She knew the Lord still loved her even with all of her shortcomings, and no matter what happened, everything was going to be all right.

Chapter 12

Phillip Tomlinson

Mercy

Phillip hugged his in-laws as they left him. He sat listening to the sound of their footsteps fading down the hall.

He looked grungy, or figured he did. He knew if he could smell the stench of his two-day old clothing, everyone else could also. Even though Phillip knew he needed to pull himself together for Shelby's sake, he just didn't have the strength to do it.

He thought about how recent events had turned his life up side down. The love of his life didn't want to talk to him. Because of his past indiscretions, she was lying in the hospital in pain. And it was all Jeana's fault.

In the days since Jeana had hurt Shelby, Phillip hadn't heard anything from the woman. He hadn't received any calls from her and hadn't seen the Toyota Tercel following him in his rearview mirror.

He knew Jeana must have been hiding. Phillip figured if she knew better, she'd continue hiding from him. It wouldn't be pretty if he got within arms distance of her. He balled his hands up into fists and released them methodically.

He couldn't believe Jeana had been crazy enough to hurt his wife and possibly kill her. He wondered if Jeana was in the process of making plans to kill him also. Jeana Sands had made herself a force to be dealt with and he was going to do just that as soon as he got the chance.

Thoughts about what he was going to do to Jeana overtook him. Before he knew it, an hour had passed and he was still sitting in the same place. He looked at his watch. It was almost midnight.

Figuring Shelby wouldn't have a change of heart at that late hour, he forced himself up from the waiting room chair. The days and nights of restlessness were starting to ware on him. His legs felt as if they loaded down with lead weights.

Making it to the elevator had been a large undertaking. He was even more tired than he realized. His eyes were heavy also. He wondered how he was going to make it all the way home.

Phillip's thoughts were dismal as he drove around the beltline trying to make it home. Exhaustion threatened to overtake him. He wondered if he'd even make it home without driving off the road. There were several times in which he had almost run off the road and run into other drivers. Somehow, forty-five minutes later, he was pulling into his garage. Most of the trip home he didn't even remember.

Not bothering to get under the covers, fully clothed, he fell across their king-sized bed. Even though he was in desperate need of a shower, he was just too tired to take one. Phillip's exhaustion ended up winning and overtook him completely. He had fallen asleep within minutes.

Phillip was awakened the next day by the ringing of the telephone. Groggily, he reached for the cordless phone located on its base on his nightstand.

"Hello?" Phillip said. His voice was gruff.

"Phil, man? What's up? Where are you?" Rick said.

"Rick?" Phillip asked, trying to verify who was screaming at him on the other end of the line.

"Yeah, man. What is up? You were suppose to meet me at the airport, remember?" Rick said.

Phillip could tell his friend was perturbed.

"I've been waiting for thirty-minutes."

"Oh, what time is it?" Phillip asked. "His stiff body turned towards Shelby's nightstand to look at the clock."

"It's one o'clock, man. I told you my flight would be in at 12:15. I don't want to spend my whole Saturday hanging out at the airport. You sound like you were sleep. Did you forget?" Rick asked.

"I did forget. Rick man, things have been crazy around here the last few days.

"Well, get your lazy butt out of the bed and come get me," Rick demanded.

"Rick, is there anyone else who can pick you up?" Phillip asked.

"No, everyone else is at work or too far away. Come on and get me."

"You just don't know, Rick. You just don't know . . ." Phillip's voice trailed off as he thought about the mess his life had turned into.

"Well, tell me about it when you get here. Get up. I'll be by the baggage claim."

"Okay, okay. I'll be there as soon as I can. Hold tight," Phillip said, realizing his friend was not going to take no for an answer.

"Hurry up; I'm not trying to hang out at RDU Airport all day. I've got a hot date tonight."

"Let me get up. Hold tight," Phillip said.

"Bye." Rick abruptly clicked his phone off.

Phillip sat up on the edge of the bed. His body was stiff from the much needed rest. He'd had a dreamless sleep.

He yawned and stood up, stretching his long body. The smell from his breath was rank. He shuffled to the bathroom heading straight for the toothbrush and toothpaste.

He picked them both up then turned on the hot and cold water. He looked up at the mirror and proceeded to brush his teeth.

The man staring back at him in the mirror startled him. It was an extremely bad variation of himself. His hair was uncombed and uneven from desperate need of a haircut. He had dried saliva residue, which had crept down his cheek and chin. In the corner and outer rim of his eyes there was sleep crust.

Phillip moaned to himself. He finished brushing his teeth and splashed luke warm water on his face. The water made the saliva residue disappear but the eye crust remained.

He abandoned trying to splash more water on his face. Time was ticking and he needed to get himself in gear. He turned the shower on and removed his clothing. He was tempted to throw them in the trash. Then he stepped in the shower stall.

He stood and turned around under the hot stream of water. It was slightly soothing as the water streamed over his entire body. He pulled the shampoo out of the caddy and squirted a generous amount on the top of his head. He vigorously lathered his hair. He rinsed it out and then repeated the process until he had a foamy afro. He let the shampoo set.

He then grabbed the bar of soap. With the same vigor he used to wash his hair, he lathered his skin. He rinsed once, re-lathered and rinsed again. Phillip felt good knowing the dirt was rolling off.

Just before turning off the water, he rinsed the foamy afro. He then stepped out of the shower, bypassed his old towel, and pulled a fresh one out of the bathroom's linen closet.

He quickly dried off and headed to the walk-in closet. He pulled out a Central State University t-shirt and a pair of jogging pants. He smiled as he pulled the shirt over his head- smelling its freshness. Shelby had neatly folded it as well as his jogging pants and placed them in their respective areas.

The outfit could have used a little ironing but since Shelby always folded the cloths before they had a chance to wrinkle, he didn't look too bad. It was one of the many things, he loved about his wife. She was such a good woman.

He pulled a pair of socks out of the drawer and put them on. Then he selected a pair of Nike sneakers from his shoe rack.

In the full-length mirror, he admired what sort of resembled the old Phillip except for the facial hair, which still needed to be shaved and the short Afro, which he'd combed and patted into a workable, round, shape. It wasn't perfect, but it would have to work.

He attempted to straighten the bed before grabbing his keys and heading downstairs to his truck.

Forty minutes after he'd hung up with Rick on the phone, Phillip was approaching the curb in front of the baggage claim for American Airlines at the Raleigh-Durham Airport. He hoped Rick was standing out front so he wouldn't have to park and find him.

His wish came true. He spotted Rick's lanky body stepping briskly towards the truck. Phillip couldn't have missed him if he was walking at a snail's pace. Rick wore a bright red jogging suit that had their fraternity's emblem sown into the jacket. He wore a baseball cap with the same emblem. The sun's rays intensified the color of the outfit.

Phillip could tell Rick was upset about the delay in being picked up, even though most people wouldn't have been able to tell by his smooth demeanor. Rick always emulated an air of calmness. He always looked like he was in control of a situation even if he wasn't.

The closer Rick got Phillip could tell his trip out of town had been good. He even looked like he had been able to get a hair cut before he came back. The diamond earring in Rick's left ear glistened with each step he took.

Phillip pushed the button to unlock the doors. Rick proceeded to put his bags in the back seat of Phillip's SUV, then he jumped into the front passenger seat.

"It's about time," Rick said.

Phillip turned on his signal light, looked in his rearview mirror, and headed towards the exit. "I'm here ain't I?"

"Only yeah, almost two hours later," Rick replied.

"I forgot, man. I've had a lot going on the past couple of days," Phillip said with a sigh.

"You told me. What is up with your hair and face? If you are trying out a new style, you need to drop it. It doesn't work on you. It looks like a bad wig," Rick commented.

"I know. I'm going to get a haircut and shave this afternoon."

"You're in luck. I am going to forgive you," Rick said.

"Oh really?" Phillip said without expression.

"Yes, and her name is Tai. Whew, man, she's got it going on." Rick paused.

Phillip gave no response.

Rick continued. "After I talked to you, I turned around and ran smack into Ms. Tai. I knocked her briefcase out of her hand and her purse off of her shoulder.

"Being the gentleman that I am, I bent down and helped pick up her things. I apologized profusely and introduced myself. To make a long story short, I got the digits. She is starting a new job in Durham and she is looking for a place to live. It's perfect, man. I'll be a good Samaritan and help her look for a place.

"You know I'll steer her away from Silvermont. Just in case things work out, I won't have to duck and dodge if I'm out with another woman. So thanks to you, my friend, I met Tai," Rick said pausing again. "Phil?" Rick realized Phillip wasn't paying him any attention.

"Huh?" Phillip had only heard bits and pieces of what Rick had said.

"Were you even listening to me?"

"You met some girl from Silvermont."

"No, you weren't listening to me," Rick said.

"Sorry. I have a million things on my mind. I've got to get my hair cut, pay some bills, and get back to the hospital."

"Definitely get the haircut and shave first," Rick joked. "What is wrong with Shelby's SUV? You gotta pick her up or something?" Rick asked.

"No." Phillip wasn't sure if he was ready to tell anyone about what had happened to Shelby.

"No, what?" Rick asked. He turned towards Phillip and looked at him squarely. "Enough about me. Something's wrong, isn't it? What's on your mind? What's been going on since I've been gone?"

Phillip was slow to answer at first. Rick was one of his best friends and fraternity brothers. They had known each other for years and Phillip knew he could trust him.

"Don't clam up on me," Rick said firmly.

Phillip opened up to his friend. "Shelby is in the hospital."

"Shelby went in already? I thought she wasn't due for another month or so," Rick said.

"She's not," Phillip said flatly.

"Is she okay? Is the baby okay?" Rick asked with concern.

"She is doing better and the baby is fine," Phillip replied.

"Better? What happened?"

"Shelby was hurt. The best I can tell, she was beaten and or pushed down the stairs. I'm not really sure exactly what happened."

"What?" Rick asked in awe. He dropped his mouth open. "Is she unconscious or something? Why don't you know what happened?" Rick asked.

"I don't know, because she won't talk to me. I only know what Nyah told me," Phillip admitted.

"Hold up, wait a minute. Tell me what happened from the beginning as far as you know."

Phillip told Rick part of the story; starting with some of the events of the past months. He told him about his ex-girlfriend who had been calling his home and following him around. Phillip left out the information about the son he had out of wedlock.

After he finished his story, neither said a word for a few minutes. Then Rick finally spoke. "Phillip, I don't know what to say. This is like some kind of mysterious mess that would happen on one of those movies of the week. You find Shelby being put on a stretcher, and she is asking you crazy questions, then she passes out. Then, the next thing you know, your wife won't even talk to you and she's treating you like the scum of the earth. What on earth are you going to do?"

"I don't know. I have to get Shelby to talk to me. It's killing me. Until this morning, I hadn't taken a shower in three days."

"I'm glad you decided to take one before you came to pick me up."

"That's why my hair looks the way it does. I've been at the hospital day and night since the accident, hoping Shelby would have a change of heart and talk to me. She does not even want me to come into the hospital room. I have to get updates from her parents or her friends after they visit her," Phillip said.

"What about Nyah? How is she taking all of this?"

"I haven't even seen my baby girl in three days. She is with Shelby's best friend. I guess she is doing fine." Phillip hunched his shoulders.

"This ain't you. Snap out of this. I know how much you love Shelby and Nyah. They love you too. Shelby needs time alone. She'll come around, you'll see. She loves you too much.

"And Nyah is just a little girl. She may not understand, everything but she will wonder why she hasn't seen or talked to you in days. I know how my little niece is when her father has to go on trips and he doesn't call for a couple of days. She always thinks he's mad at her or something.

"He spends five minutes at a minimum convincing her that he's not mad. So you need to call

Nyah. Even though she's young, you never know what's going through her little mind."

"You're right. I don't know what has gotten into me the past couple of days. I guess I'm just mad and hurt that my ex would go to the extremes she did and hurt my wife."

"Like I said, it's like something out of a movie. I thought Joy was crazy, but your ex takes the cake. She needs mental help from what you're telling me." Rick shook his head.

"She needs help alright, and if I see her, I'll make sure she gets it from "lefty" and "righty," Phillip lifted both his hands to emphasize the point.

"Don't do anything you'll regret later," Rick said.

"She hurt my wife, man. I can't just look past that. She'll have to answer for her actions."

"I know you're upset, but you really need to calm down," Rick reiterated. "Listen to me being the voice of reason. It's usually me needing this type of advice. I'm glad I can finally pay you back."

"I hear you, but I can't promise anything," Phillip said.

"Well, for this girl's sake, I hope she doesn't see you anytime soon. Hopefully, she moved on since you haven't heard anything from her in a few days."

"She's probably scared. Although, she sounded anything but scared the last time we spoke. She sounded cocky if you ask me."

"Just be careful. Watch your back. Crazy people don't care who they hurt."

"Well, all I gotta say is she better have some common sense and stay away from me."

Rick shook his head in agreement. "I hope, for her sake, she does also."

Phillip pulled into Rick's condominium complex.

"Thanks for the ride. I'm sorry. If I'd known what was going on, I wouldn't have pressed the issue so much."

"It's alright; I needed to get some of this off of my chest. Actually, I feel a lot better now. The fresh air has done me some good."

"And the shower too, huh?"

Phillip laughed. "That too."

Rick placed his hand on Phillip's newly formed afro. "Now you need to get this bush cut."

Phillip swatted his hand away. "Get off me," Phillip laughed. "I'm calling my barber right now."

Rick retrieved his bags from the truck.

After Rick had pulled the last bag from the back, Phillip asked, "Need any help?"

"Naw, I've got it now. Great timing."

"I know," Phillip laughed.

Rick walked to the driver's side of the truck. Phillip rolled down the window.

"Seriously, thanks again. Remember what I said. Give Shelby time to herself. She'll come around. Call your little girl."

Phillip held up his cell phone. "I will. Soon as I pull out of here."

The phone rang as he held it up. The caller ID displayed Shelby's mother's number.

"Hold up. Its Shelby's Mom," Phillip said. Hello? Yes. She is? She does? Are you serious? I'll be right there. Yes, I'm on my way. Tell her I'll be there in thirty-minutes. Okay, bye Mom, and thanks!" Phillip clicked the phone off and put the truck in reverse. "That was Shelby's mom. She said they're discharging Shelby!"

"That's good!" Rick said.

"No, the good part is she wants me to come and pick her up!"

"Good. See, I told you she just needed some extra time. Everything's going to be fine."

"Whew!" Phillip smiled. "I've got to get over there."

"Go, man. Get on over there and get your wife," Rick encouraged.

Phillip pressed the accelerator and moved backwards. "See you later."

"Call me later and let me know how things are."

"I will," Phillip yelled out of the window as he shifted the truck into drive.

Phillip smiled from ear to ear as he headed towards the hospital. He picked up his cell phone and dialed Kara's number to speak with Nyah.

The phone rang five times before anyone answered.

"Hello," Kara said.

"Hey, Kara, it's Phillip."

"Hey, Phillip. Any updates on Shelby?"

"She's doing better. They're discharging her in an hour or so."

"Oh, that is good! I know she's more than ready to go home. She told me she's tired of the hospital food."

"I'm ready for her to come home too. It's been so lonely without her and Nyah," Phillip said sadly.

"Speaking of Nyah, she's been asking about you."

"I know. I'm sorry it's taken me so long to call her. How's she doing?"

"She's doing fine. We've been reassuring her that you and Shelby are fine. We told her you've been at the hospital taking care of Shelby. She seems to understand," Kara explained.

"Do you think she's okay?" Phillip asked.

"What do you mean?"

"I mean do you think my not calling and not seeing her in a few days is going to stunt her emotionally or something?"

"No, Phillip. She's fine I assure you. You know this is like a second home to her. She's been busy playing with the kids. As a matter of fact, she's in the pool right now. That's what took me so long to answer the phone. I had to get my husband to watch them while I found the cordless."

Phillip was relieved. "Good. I was worried she might think I abandoned her or something."

"She's fine. You want to speak to her?"

"Yeah."

"Hold on."

Phillip heard Kara cover the phone and call Nyah's name out loud. A few seconds later he heard Kara telling Nyah her daddy was on the phone.

"Hi, Daddy!" Nyah's voice was filled with excitement.

"Hi, baby girl. What are you doing?"

"I'm swimming, Daddy! I can really swim. Godfather is helping me," Nyah said, giving her father a mini report.

"Good. Are you having fun?"

"Yes, Daddy, we are gonna see a movie after dinner."

"You are?"

"Un huh," Nyah answered. "Daddy, can I spend the night again?"

"You want to spend another night? You are having fun aren't you?"

"Yeah. The ice cream man comes tomorrow. Can I spend the night?"

"What about me and Mommy? We miss you very much. Daddy is going to pick Mommy up from the hospital in a little while."

"Mommy's all better now?" Nyah asked.

"She sure is. I know she misses you like I do."

"Yipee, Mommy's all better," Nyah squealed.

"I'm on my way to pick up Mommy now. We'll call you when we are coming to pick you up."

Nyah was silent for a moment.

"Nyah, honey, what's wrong?" Phillip asked.

Nyah whined, "I wanna see the ice cream man."

"Nyah, sweetheart, stop whining," Phillip told her. "Let me speak to your godmother."

Saying nothing else, Nyah handed the phone to her godmother.

"Hello?" Kara answered.

"Hey, Kara. Nyah is a little upset. I told her we were going to pick her up and she is whining about seeing the ice cream man or something."

"Yeah, the ice cream man comes every other day. The kids missed him yesterday and I promised I'd get them some ice cream tomorrow."

"Oh," Phillip said.

"You know Nyah is just fine here. She fits right in. And, it's nice to have my goddaughter all to myself. She can stay another night or two. I mean, Shelby needs some time to recuperate. Plus, you two can have some time alone. Once the baby gets here, it'll be a while before that happens again."

"Are you sure?"

"If I wasn't sure, I wouldn't have offered. Nyah's fine, I assure you. Tell Shelby Nyah can stay here for a couple more days so she can get some rest," Kara said.

"Thanks, Kara."

"You don't have to thank me. This is my godchild we're talking about."

"Do you need any money or anything?"

"Phillip, I should hang up on you. No, I don't need any money. Don't worry about her. Just get to the hospital and pick up my best friend. And take good care of her."

"Sorry," Phillip apologized for pressing the issue about giving Kara money. He knew Kara would never accept it and didn't need it. "I'll take good care of my wife."

"Okay. Let me get back out here with these kids."

"Tell Nyah I love her," Phillip said.

"I will. She's already run back outside."

"Talk to you later," Phillip said.

"Bye."

Phillip was elated; Shelby was going to talk to him again. As he drove the last couple of miles to the hospital he got an idea. He wanted Shelby's home coming to be a happy one. So he dialed information and obtained the numbers for a local florist. He ordered three-dozen pink roses. Then he ordered take out from Mama Lula's restaurant.

He finished the food order just as he reached the parking deck of the hospital. He quickly exited the truck and headed for the third floor.

The hospital room door was closed when he arrived. He tapped lightly on it. "Knock, knock. Anyone home?" he said in a cheerful voice."

"Come in."

He heard the sweet sound of Shelby's voice. He opened the door.

Shelby was sitting on the edge of the bed packed and ready to go.

"Hey, sweetheart." Phillip walked directly over to Shelby and gave her a light hug. He felt Shelby's body tense so he pulled back. "I didn't hurt you did I?" he asked with concern.

"No, *that* didn't hurt," Shelby said with coolness.

Phillip thought he detected coldness in her voice, but he dismissed it. Shelby was probably tired and ready to get into her comfortable king-sized bed.

He turned to greet his in-laws who were waiting with Shelby. "Hey, Mom and Dad." Phillip hugged them both.

"You smell good," Shelby's father joked.

Phillip chuckled, "Yeah, thanks for the advice last night. It came in handy." Phillip gave him a thumbs-up sign.

"Phillip, we are going to walk you all down, but won't be able to come to the house right now. We've got to get back home. We'll be back in a few days to check on Shelby," Shelby's mother said.

"Oh, okay," Phillip replied.

He directed his attention back to Shelby. "You ready honey?"

"Ready as ever," Shelby replied. Her tone was lifeless.

Phillip grabbed her bags and helped her to the awaiting wheelchair.

"I'm fine, I can make it." Shelby firmly pulled away from Phillip to sit in the wheel chair.

"Phillip, let me have those bags. You can push Shelby," Shelby's father said.

Phillip handed the bags over and the four of them headed for the downstairs lobby.

"I'll be right back," Phillip said as he parked Shelby's wheel chair just outside the entrance of the hospital. "Let me get the truck."

"We'll wait with her," Shelby's mother said.

Phillip left to retrieve the SUV and was back within ten minutes.

He exited the truck and opened the passenger side for Shelby. She stood as quickly as possible to try and get in the truck by herself without Phillip's help. Everyone watching noticed the deliberate display.

"That's my daughter, she's always been head-strong," Shelby's mother teased.

Shelby put her seatbelt on and turned towards her parents. "Mom, Dad, thanks for everything.

I'll see you in a few days." She hugged them both and closed the door.

Phillip hugged his in-laws again and thanked them also. He walked back around to the driver's side and got back in for the drive home.

He wasn't really sure where to start or what to say to Shelby. She sat silent as he pulled away from the hospital. He contemplated on what he should say and how he should say it. Should he tell her some kind of funny joke to break the solemn mood? Or should he broach the subject of what happened straight on?

He opted for making small talk. "How're you feeling?"

"Fine," Shelby said. Her answer was short and indifferent.

"Do you have to take any medication?" Phillip asked.

"No."

"You look good. Everything looks like it's healing well." He waited for a reply but didn't get one. "I ordered dinner for us. All your favorites from Mama Lula's."

Shelby shifted her body away from Phillip and sighed heavily.

Phillip tried to overlook the short answers and negative body language. He was happy Shelby had even agreed to talk to him.

"I spoke with Nyah and Kara. Kara said it would be okay if Nyah spent another couple of nights to give you some more time to recover." Phillip chuckled. "She said you know once the baby gets here, it'll be a while before we'll have time to ourselves again."

Phillip waited again for a reply but got none. Shelby continued facing the window. He gave up on trying to get her to talk and fell silent also. He wondered how long it would be before things would be back to normal between them. Or, if they ever would be.

Chapter 13

Shelby Tomlinson

Trust

Shelby slumped in the passenger seat, and her body was turned as far as she could get it from Phillip's direction. She wished Phillip would stop talking to her and just get them home. Even though she was uncomfortable in her awkward sitting position, she refused to move. The baby kicked her, letting her know he didn't like the position either.

The only reason she asked him to take her home in the first place, was so that her parents wouldn't suspect how bad things were. She knew they were suspicious. They'd witnessed enough. The last thing they needed was to see what was going to happen between her and Phillip.

Her skin crawled as she remembered Phillip touching her earlier. She was repulsed by his touch. She wanted to scream at him. He kept secrets from her over the years. He betrayed her trust royally, and now he was acting like nothing had happened.

If he wasn't man enough to bring up the subject, she would. She refused to pretend nothing happened. She never forgot the woman who knocked on her front door, confronting Shelby about her son—Phillip's son. She never forget what the boy looked like. He was the spitting image of his father. *There was no way it could be denied.*

She re-lived the moments of the woman named Jeana. Having nightmares about the woman lurking behind her in the grocery store, and following her home and accusing her about knowing Phillip had a son.

When she wasn't having bad dreams and was awake, words from the woman floated through her head. Jeana said her and Nyah's name like they were good friends or something. Shelby didn't believe the sarcastic reply she got about Jeana knowing Nyah's name. She felt there was something more to it.

The woman said Phillip's name like they were old buddies. Even though Shelby had no idea what was really going on, her intuition had thrown out red flags left and right. She realized that now.

Jeana said she knew where Shelby worked and personal things about Phillip. Shelby couldn't remember clearly but thought the woman said something about the mole on Phillip's inner thigh. A lot of the confrontation was still a bit of a blur.

Shelby remembered Jeana wanting to talk to her for years and the payments Phillip made to her son weren't enough any more. She thought she heard something about going to court with Phillip.

She remembered the visible pain and anger in the woman's eyes. Jeana called her callous. She called Shelby a good actress. But, Shelby wasn't acting. She had no idea why Jeana was standing at her door and why she was continuing to badger her.

Then things, which were first cloudy, became clearer. From out of nowhere came a boy who looked like the spitting image of Phillip. Shelby had to blink her eyes in order to make sure she was seeing correctly. The boy looked just like her husband. He came up asking his mother a question. He looked and acted as if he was oblivious to the exchange that was going on.

To clarify things Shelby asked the woman who the boy was. She told her unequivocally that his name was Taren and he was Phillip's son.

After three days of sitting in the hospital with the memories playing over and over in her head, Shelby intended to get answers to all the questions, which had been mounting. She'd wondered how Phillip was going to try and weasel his way out of this one. And she hoped he would answer her questions honestly so she could get to the bottom of the lies he'd told and the truths he had kept from her for years.

Phillip pulled into the driveway to minimize the rocking of the car as it ascended the initial hump. He pulled into the garage just as carefully. With ease, he opened and closed his car door. Shelby sighed in disgust, thinking if he had been more caring and honest years ago she wouldn't be in the predicament she was in now.

He opened the passenger side door and extended his hand to help her step out. She didn't want his help. She wasn't going to be treated as an invalid, especially by him. Instead, she held onto the door frame and carefully lifted her legs out, one at a time.

Phillip placed his hand on the small of her back trying to assist her. As soon as she felt his touch, she flinched, feeling the same wave of nausea she'd felt earlier.

"I don't need your help. I can do it myself."

Phillip backed, moving out of her way. "Honey, I was trying to be helpful. You know you need to take it easy. The doctor said . . ."

"I know what the doctor said, Phillip. The doctor told me to take it easy. That means avoiding things that are strenuous or stressful. I also need to avoid anything that will agitate or upset me," Shelby snapped. "And right now you are the one upsetting me."

"Baby, I just—"

"Don't baby me. Leave me alone, Phillip." Shelby struggled out of the seat and guided herself to the garage door by holding on to the truck then leaning on her car for support. She continued to hold on to things as she made her way up the steps and into the kitchen.

By the time she made it to the stairs, she was exhausted. All she wanted to do was crawl under her covers and get some rest. The whole time she made her way towards their bedroom, she avoided looking back, fearing she might break down crying at the sight of her husband. Her emotions had been running rampant the past few days. She'd thought she was strong enough to confront him, but she had been wrong. She couldn't do it.

Shelby bypassed her dresser, which held her pajamas, and crawled into her bed. Her eyes were heavy and she wanted to sleep. She hoped the recurrent visions wouldn't come to her again as they had been when she normally fell asleep. She hadn't had a decent nap or night's sleep in days.

When she'd told the doctor about the nightmares, he told her they were probably induced by the pain medications she was taking. He'd decreased the doses slightly, but the nightmares continued to haunt her.

She laid the pillow on top of her head then pulled the covers over it, to block out the bright light streaming through her sheer bedroom curtains. Her heavy eyes closed as a tear trickled down her face. She curled up in a ball and was sleep within minutes.

Shelby shot up into the sitting position in her bed. Beads of sweat sat on her forehead. Her heart was racing as she gasped for air.

Phillip rounded the corner of the bedroom door. "Honey, what's wrong? Are you okay?" He was by her side in a flash trying awkwardly not to touch her.

Shelby pulled the covers up under her chin. "I can't do this right now, Phillip." Shelby continued to gasp. "I thought I could, but I can't. I need some time."

"Sweetheart, I understand. I'll give you as much time as you need. I won't even sleep in here tonight. I'll sleep in the guest room. Just let me know when you're ready and we'll talk."

Phillip stood turning toward his dresser to pull out his pajamas.

"No, Phillip, that won't work," Shelby said.

"What, baby? What won't work? I know you don't want me to touch you and if I don't sleep in the other room, you won't be able to get any sleep." He smiled. "You know how I love to cuddle with you."

Shelby knew Phillip was only trying to be nice; trying to lighten her mood, but his attempts were futile. She stared at him and didn't crack a smile.

He'd lied to her for years. She thought, *Is his smile sincere or fake? Who is he? Do I really know?*

"Say something honey. What do you want? Just tell me and I'll do it." Phillip sat down on the bed by her feet.

"I want you to leave."

"What?"

"You heard me. I want you to leave this house. I need time alone to sort through all of this, and your being here; will only complicate things for me. I can't think straight right now."

"Shelby . . . Honey . . . Surely there has to be some other way we can work this out. How are we supposed to do so with you living here and me somewhere else?"

"I don't know, Phillip," she yelled at him.

"That's what I have to figure out. What I do know though is that the more you sit here and argue with me, the worse I feel. If you fight me on this, then I'll leave."

"No, baby. What about Nyah? Where is she going to be? What's she going to think? Don't do this to our family, honey."

"You have a lot of nerve. I didn't do anything to this family. You did. And now you want to think about Nyah? Her little life has already been turned upside down the past few days."

Shelby squeezed the covers in her hands, balling up her fists with anger. "I can't believe you're sitting here blaming me for our family being turned upside down."

"Baby, I didn't mean to say you were the reason for all of this. I just don't want us to be apart any longer," Phillip pleaded.

Shelby's head started to pound. The more Phillip spoke, the angrier she became. With the elevated anger came harder throbbing. She closed her eyes and put her head down placing the palms of her hands on her forehead. She rubbed her head, willing the throbbing to stop.

"Shelby, are you okay?"

"Just leave, Phillip. Just leave me alone."

She hadn't known how many minutes had passed before she looked up again. Phillip had left the room. She began to cry again. After a few more minutes, she heard the garage door open and Phillip's SUV crank up and pull out and down the street.

Shelby's unrelenting sobbing returned as she worried over her family's destiny.

Chapter 14

Phillip Tomlinson

Mercy

Phillip stirred on the futon he was sleeping on. Noises from above and outside were nudging him awake. Heavy footsteps thumped on the ceiling above his head, a door slammed and then heavy footsteps descended down metal stairs. For a couple of moments, he thought he was back in his dorm room in college, but then realized those days were long over.

He wasn't in college, nor was he on his own futon in his spacious recreation room. He was at his friend Will's, cramped one bedroom apartment, scrunched up an un-opened futon.

"Good morning," Will said.

Phillip turned his head toward his friend who was already up and dressed for work. "Morning," he grumbled.

"How did you sleep?"

"How do you think? I'd rather be at home with my wife, not scrunched up on this futon, looking at one of my best friends, first thing in the morning."

"You should have pulled the futon out. You might have slept a little better."

"I guess," Phillip said, trying not to sound so testy. "Thanks for letting me crash here last night. I really didn't want to go to a hotel."

"No problem," Will replied. "You know I am here for you."

"I know, and I apologize for being so short with you. It's just that I can't believe all this is happening to me. Things were going so great and now all this stuff has started crashing down on me all at once."

"I really can't say I understand what you are going through, because really I don't. But, I feel your pain if that makes any sense. I can see you're hurting, and as a friend, I hurt for you also."

"You're right; you can't even imagine how I am feeling right now. I wouldn't wish this on anyone. First, I am confronted by an ex-girlfriend I haven't seen in years. Then, my wife is hurt by her, now Shelby doesn't want to see me and kicked me out of my own house. And to put a cherry on top, I got a voice mail from my boss saying that he needs to have a conference with me to discuss the status of one of my biggest accounts, which I know can only mean trouble because normally he wouldn't call himself."

Will shook his head while listening to Phillip as he acknowledged his concerns.

"What am I going to do?" Phillip sat up and placed his head down in his hands.

"I know you're not going to like what I'm about to say, but I'll say it anyway."

Phillip's ears perked up. "Sometimes God has a way of getting our attention. And this may just be His way of getting your attention."

"Well He picked a fine way to do it. Losing my wife isn't funny." Phillip rolled his eyes upward. "The big man has a huge sense of humor. So why ain't I laughing?"

"Our ways are not His ways."

"What?"

"God doesn't do things the way we want Him to. He has a plan. We're the ones who often deviate from that plan."

"Well, maybe if He shared the plan with me I wouldn't deviate."

Will shook his head. "Phillip, it isn't a plan like one given by a football coach or like the plans you get from the builder of your house. His plans are laid out, for the most part, in His Word. By reading His Word in the Bible, you can use the Holy Spirit to guide you as to what God's plan is for your life."

Phillip shook his head this time. He had heard Will talk about God and the Bible numerous times, but had shunned away from him. He just wasn't ready to hear all the heavy stuff about the Bible and God. But now he wondered if he should have been listening all along. His friend always had a serene look on his face. Even when he faced problems and adversities, Will smiled and was always saying how good God was.

After a few moments, Will spoke, "Phil, man, I

know this is going to sound crazy but everything is going to turn out fine. I can just feel it. It may not be over night, but you'll see. It will."

"I hope so, but right now it doesn't seem that way," Phillip sighed before he felt his cell phone vibrate in the pocket of his sweat pants. He pulled it out quickly looking to see if it was his home number on the caller ID.

The display flashed the number as private.

He flipped his phone open. "Hello. Shelby?"

There was a pause before the person spoke. "No . . . this isn't Shelby."

Phillip didn't feel like being nice to someone who had obviously dialed the wrong number. "Look, you've got the wrong number." He pulled the phone away from his ear and was about to release the call when he heard the caller say his name.

Placing the phone back on his ear he asked, "Who is this?"

"Phillip, it's Jeana."

He couldn't believe his ears. "Jeana?" He took a deep breath. All the rage he'd felt wanting to ring Jeana's neck for hurting his wife, resurfaced with a vengeance. "What do you want, Jeana? Haven't you done enough already? What could you possibly want now?"

Will mouthed a question asking Phillip if it was the same Jeana that Phillip had told him about. Phillip shook his head in confirmation and disbelief.

"Phillip, I just want to talk," Jeana said.

"Haven't you said enough? Haven't you hurt

enough people? You better be glad my wife doesn't have any physical injuries because of what you did."

Jeana paused before speaking. "Physical injuries? What are you talking about?"

"Don't play dumb, Jeana. I know you country and all, but don't play that little country girl act on me. It won't work."

"Phillip, I don't know what you are talking about. What happened to your wife?"

"To tell you the truth, I don't really know what happened. You need to fill me in on what you did to my wife because she won't tell me."

"Honestly, Phillip, I don't know what you mean."

"Don't play with me. First, you start stalking me and my wife. Then, you hurt my wife. You better be glad you didn't lay a hand on my daughter or so help me God . . ."

"Phillip, all I did was try to talk to your wife. But, she kept playing dumb like she didn't know who I was. I told her Taren's birthday was coming up and he wanted to spend some time with you. But, she kept acting like she didn't know what I was talking about. It made me so angry that she kept treating my son like he didn't exist to her. If Taren hadn't been with me, I might have talked with her even longer, but I figured after a while it was a mute point."

"So you were so mad that you felt you had the right to beat my wife up?"

"What?" Jeana asked.

"You are a sick woman. When are you going to

get it through your thick scull that I don't want you and haven't wanted you in years? I can't believe you hurt my wife the way you did."

"Now hold on, Phillip. I didn't lay a hand on your wife. I may not like you. As a matter of fact, I've come to realize I don't want you anymore, so you can get that out of your head as well. I just want my son to have a chance to get to know his father. But, I would never hurt anyone intentionally."

"Stop lying! Stop lying! I don't want to hear your sick fantasies. You hurt my wife, and you'll be hearing from our lawyer. She's been hospitalized since the day you put her in there."

"I know I've done some really weird things. I've done things I wasn't proud of. I'm not a mean vindictive person. I don't want to hurt anyone. I did not hurt your wife," Jeana explained.

"You know you hurt her. You even called me after you finished beating her up to gloat that day."

"I didn't call you to gloat. I called because I was hurt. Hurt because your wife treated my son like he was nothing. Hurt because that was when I really realized I didn't want you anymore.

"I finally left your house after your wife became visibly upset. That's why I called you. I promise you I never laid a hand on her."

"You say my wife became upset? When and why?"

"Taren got out of the truck and asked me for my keys or something. When Shelby looked at him, it was as if the blood drained from her face.

Maybe her seeing him brought it all to reality for her. I don't know."

"She saw him?" Phillip asked.

"Yeah, I told you he was there with me." Jeana sighed. "Look, I didn't call you to argue. I just wanted to talk in a civil manner, that's all."

"Jeana. What else did you tell my wife?"

"Stuff she already knew."

"Stuff like what?" Phillip asked.

"The child support payments weren't cutting it and we probably need to go back to court to have adjustments made. I had to give it to her. I thought she was putting on a good act, pretending she didn't have a clue as to what I was talking about."

"She didn't," Phillip said almost in a whisper. "My wife didn't know anything about Taren." Phillip spoke talking more to himself than to Jeana.

"You never told your wife you have a son?"

"No, I didn't." Phillip's tone was softer now. He knew none of this was Jeana's fault. It was his fault. He was the true reason his wife was hurt.

He kept secrets from his wife and couldn't blame anyone else for that. His lies and past had caught up with him, like a speeding freight train.

"Look, I need to go. I can't talk right now." He paused. Guilt washed over him like a bucket of water being dashed on him.

"Phillip, I'm telling you, I didn't do anything to your wife. Please listen to me."

Phillip realized Jeana was probably telling the truth. He'd been channeling all his anger at her and the reason his wife was hurting so badly was his fault. Shelby was hurting not only physically, but emotionally. He had even started realizing how badly he must have hurt Jeana over the years, so badly that the woman had obviously almost gone crazy trying to get back at him.

Shame blanketed him. "Jeana, I've got to go."

"Phillip, we need to talk. You can't just keep avoiding me and your son."

"Jeana, I know. I realize that now. I just need a little while to think all of this through. I just can't talk to you right now. Give me a few days. I've got to sort some things out."

"Phillip . . ." Jeana drew a deep breath and paused. "Okay, Phillip. I'll give you a few days, but you've got to grow up. You've got responsibilities that go beyond just giving monetarily."

"All I am asking for is a couple of days."

"Okay, Phillip, a couple of days."

"Thanks, Jeana."

"Bye."

Phillip heard the click and dropped the phone on the futon. He buried his head in his hands trying to make sense of it all. "What have I done? What on earth have I done?"

"Phil, man? What's up? Is there anything I can do?" Will asked.

"Will, I think I've messed up pretty badly. So much so that I may have lost everything I hold dear."

"What did Jeana say?"

"She said she didn't hurt Shelby."

"Did Shelby say Jeana hurt her?" Will asked for clarification.

"No. Shelby didn't say anything. She never told me what happened because she won't talk to me."

"So you just assumed Jeana beat Shelby up or something?"

"Well, yeah. She must have . . . or least that's what I thought." Phillip shook his head. "I just don't know. Maybe I got it all wrong. Jeana said when she left my house Shelby was a little upset, but she was fine physically. She told me over and over that she wouldn't and didn't hurt Shelby."

"That's pretty heavy, man."

Phillip nodded his head. "I know. I know. I can't believe all this is happening to me. Why me?"

"Phillip, I don't want to sound like I am preaching to you or anything, but the reality is—we reap what we sow."

"I know that's true, but I did all that dirt years ago. I haven't been that kind of man since college. Why is this all coming back to me now?"

"Phillip, you're a good guy, a nice guy by man's standards, but with God, being just good and nice doesn't cut it. He is not pleased. You have some unresolved issues that need to be dealt with and instead of facing them head on, you put a band-aid on the sores and now they've festered and seeped through. It looks like its reaping time."

"I've hurt Shelby. She may never forgive me. And Jeana, it seems as though I've really messed up that poor girl's life also. Not to mention the boy . . . my son." Phillip shook his head in desperation. "What am I going to do?"

"What do you want to do?" Will asked.

"I just want to stop all the pain. I don't want to hurt my wife anymore than I've already hurt her."

"You need to make amends and ask for forgiveness."

"What if she won't forgive me?"

"I meant you need to ask forgiveness from God first. Phillip, you've got to ask God for forgiveness. That's where you start. I guarantee if you get it right with Him first and trust in Him, He will lead your path."

"This is all too much. First, all this stuff coming down on me, and now you're telling me to ask God for a pretty big order. I haven't talked to God in years. He probably doesn't want to hear anything I have to say."

"God loves you, no matter what you've done in the past. He's never stopped loving you."

"You're trying to be funny, right?"

"I am serious. Dead serious. Our Father in heaven is a forgiving God. All you have to do is come to Him and ask for forgiveness and He will give you a second chance."

Phillip eyed Will in disbelief.

"Try Him, I guarantee He won't fail you. You mark my words."

"Maybe for someone like you, Will. But for the dirt I've done in my past years, I'm pretty sure God won't forgive all of it."

"Try Him for yourself. You'll see."

Phillip put his head back down in his hands, rubbing his face and forehead up and down as if to rub the skin off.

"Let me give you some space. I've got to run out. There's an extra key on the kitchen counter. You can stay as long as you need to."

Phillip nodded but didn't look up. He kept his head down long after he heard Will leave.

Chapter 15

Jeana Sands

Vengeance

Jeana fidgeted her sweaty hands as she reached for the glass of tea from the waitress. The tiny booth she'd secured, sat next to the window of Mama Lula's restaurant. She'd chosen the area so she could see the cars pulling up in the parking lot as well as any one who entered the front door.

Every time she saw an SUV that looked like Phillip's, her heart began to race and beads of sweat formed on her forehead.

Three days passed, since she'd had the strange conversation with Phillip about his wife being hurt. She was still confused about the previous week's events. And Phillip's explanation only partly cleared things up for her. Shelby had been in the hospital because she was hurt and Phillip thought she'd injured his wife.

It hurt Jeana's feelings to know that Phillip thought so ill of her. He obviously didn't and hadn't known her at all. She almost hadn't recognized her own behavior over the past months though. Her obsession with Phillip had driven her to do things she never imagined she'd ever do, but deep down she was a good person.

Every since she'd prayed to God and gave it all up to Him, she'd felt an inner peace she hadn't felt in years. It was as if God wiped the pain away like a clean slate. Her hours and days hadn't been consumed with trying to figure out what Phillip was doing and where he was or how she could get back at him for all the pain he caused her over the years. She had also stopped worrying herself about trying to make Phillip meet Taren. She trusted in God to handle it all.

A huge burden had been lifted off her shoulders. She was sleeping better at night. And, she had been able to focus on the other important aspects of her life, like finding the real Jeana again. She had even resolved herself to the fact that if Phillip didn't call her, this time she wouldn't pursue it. If he didn't want to be in her son's life, then it would be his loss.

And, she didn't want any negative influences to be introduced to her son by his biological father. Taren had never known the man and she felt maybe her son didn't really need to get to know the man Jeana had pined over for years. The man she had made into an idol when he was just a mere flawed human being.

She let it go before it consumed her life completely. Jeana's focus was clearer than it had been ever before in her life. She felt if she kept her eyes on God, then somehow, He would make everything alright.

Now, as she sat in the tiny booth sipping on her iced tea, Jeana wondered why she was so nervous. Maybe it was because Phillip had just called to set up their meeting a little over two hours prior. The call she'd been waiting years for, had finally come. Phillip's voice held an urgency and something else she hadn't expected; Phillip seemed to have compassion.

He said he wanted to meet with her as soon as possible. There were things he wanted to discuss with her face to face. He asked if they could meet for lunch. And even though she was supposed to be showing a house around that time, she rescheduled.

During the end of their conversation, Phillip had asked how Taren was doing. The question had thrown her for a loop. Phillip had never said Taren's name before with out having to be reminded. He's always referred to him as "the boy". He actually sounded as if he was genuinely concerned.

Her heart almost stopped when she saw Phillip's SUV about to turn into the parking lot. She still couldn't believe that after all these years and recent months of wanting to talk to him, she was about to get her chance.

She pulled a paper napkin out of the metal napkin holder on the table and wiped the sweat from her forehead and neck. She took in a couple of deep breaths, willing her heartbeat to return to normal. Jeana closed her eyes, saying a quick prayer, hoping she'd be able to talk to him freely without feeling intimidated. Now was not the time.

As Phillip opened the door to enter Mama

Lula's, Jeana was surprised that the slowing pace of her heart remained steady without fluttering wildly like it usually did in Phillip's presence. The awe he once had within her, had seemed to dissipate—he wasn't a superman or an idol.

She waved her hand, letting him know where she was sitting. He looked over in her direction and smiled as he walked towards the table.

After sitting across from her he awkwardly said, "Hi."

Jeana did the same in return.

"Jeana, I don't know quite where to start, so I'll do the best I can and go from there."

"Okay," Jeana said, wondering where he was going to go from there.

"Jeana, I owe you an apology. I need to apologize for the way I treated you years ago and the way I've continued to treat you and," He paused, "My son."

"I'm still not sure what happened a few days ago at my house, but I know it could have all been avoided had I just told the truth to my wife years ago. And, if I had just been a man instead of an insensitive boy when you told me you were pregnant. I should have done the right thing by you. If I had, I wouldn't be sitting here right now asking for your forgiveness.

Just saying I am sorry really doesn't seem sufficient for all you've been through, but that's really all I can do at this point. For starters I mean. You don't have to forgive me, but I'm asking."

Jeana was speechless. She couldn't believe her ears. Had she just heard Phillip ask for her forgiveness or was she having some crazy dream?

Was this really happening? She knew God could work wonders, but this was almost too much for her.

After she didn't say anything, Phillip said, "I understand. You don't want to talk to me. And you probably don't want anything to do with me. But, I do want you to know how very sorry I am. If you can one day find it in your heart to forgive me, I will really be grateful. I know I have no right to ask this, but hopefully one day you'll find it in your heart to let me finally meet my son. I would really like that."

Now she knew she had to be dreaming. There was no way this was happening. Jeana took her finger and pinched her arm to make sure she was awake. The pinch hurt alright, and she was fully awake. She didn't know how to respond to all Phillip had come to her with. There were so many times in the past when she had a truckload of choice words for him. Now, she was speechless.

After a few more moments of her not saying anything, Phillip moved to leave saying, "Jeana, you've got my cell phone number. Give me a call when you've had some time to think about what I've said."

Jeana placed her hand on his arm. "No, don't go. I want to talk. I mean, I need to talk. I'm just speechless, that's all."

He slid back into the booth.

"Wow, I can't believe my ears. For years, I've wanted to talk to you, confront you really. I've wanted you to pay for treating me the way you did and these past couple of months for me have been the worst."

Phillip spoke before Jeana could say another word. "I know, and I hate that you went through all you did because of me . . ."

Jeana broke in, "Let me talk Phillip. I've waited for so long, just let me try to finish."

Phillip closed his mouth and let her speak.

"There were so many nights I cried myself to sleep over you. I felt bad for my son because he didn't have a real father around like so many of his friends. Not to mention the times I cried when Taren had to go without some of the basic things in life because I just couldn't afford them. For a long time I let my pride get the best of me.

"Then I realized enough was enough. That's around the time I took you to court. I had to do something for my son. He deserved new clothes for school each year just like his friends. My son should not have had to go without his school supplies and wait for some helping hands mission to give them to him. I knew you and your family had more than enough to help take care of him."

Phillip shook his head. Jeana saw the shame in his eyes, as well as a couple of tears welling up.

"Look, I'm not telling you all this to try and make you feel worse than you obviously already do. I am telling you all this because you need to hear it. You need to know. But I also want you to know I forgive you."

Phillip's mouth dropped and he looked at her in disbelief.

"I actually forgave you before you even called me. That is why I am so speechless."

"The days after I confronted your wife, I almost drove myself crazy trying to look for you. But when I couldn't find you, and didn't see your wife or daughter, I knew in my gut, something must have been wrong. I replayed the meeting in my head a thousand times.

"I also stopped and took a self inventory of myself. And when I did, I didn't like what the results were. I had to back up and think about a time when I wasn't so bitter and obsessed with thoughts of revenge. I had to pray and ask God to forgive me for the awful things I had done. I didn't want to be that evil woman anymore. I knew when I prayed to God that night, He forgave me. And I've felt such peace since then.

I knew God would work things out, I just didn't believe He would work things out so quickly. I can see He has obviously touched you in some way."

"He has. He has gotten my full attention." Phillip chuckled with slight irony.

"God has a way of getting our attention. Many times He is only patient with us for but so long until He's tired of our foolishness and then whatever it takes, He lets us know how serious He is," Jeana said.

Phillip nodded his head in agreement. "Believe me, I understand. And I wish I'd gotten the hint long ago. Now I've probably lost my wife because of all my foolishness."

"Is she that sick? How much longer do they think she'll be in the hospital?"

"No, she's home, but she won't speak to me. She kicked me out of the house." Phillip dropped his head in shame.

"Oh my goodness, I'm sorry to hear that. Why did she kick you out? Was it because of me?"

"I really don't know. That's the really bad part. She won't talk to me, so I can't ask her. I don't really know what happened the afternoon you came to my house."

Jeana broke in. "You see, that's where I'm confused, because like I told you on the phone, when I left your house she was fine, physically."

Phillip continued. "When I got home, the paramedics were at my house putting Shelby on a stretcher."

"What?" Jeana asked in disbelief. "What happened?"

"That's what I'm still trying to find out. I thought you hurt her and that's why you were calling me."

"Oh, my God, no. I was upset, I'll admit that, but I wouldn't have laid a hand on anyone."

"So what happened while you were there?" Phillip asked.

Jeana recapped what she remembered about the meeting.

"Okay, you're saying when you left she was visibly upset, but physically fine?" Phillip asked for clarification.

"Yeah. I thought she was putting on a good act."

"It wasn't an act. I never told my wife the truth about us. I told her you had a miscarriage and left school soon after that. I mean you left and I figured you had the abortion with the money I gave you. It was complicated, and I didn't want my wife to know I was the one who was going to make you get an abortion.

"When I found out I had a son, I couldn't tell her about him or the child support. I just wanted a quick fix. I hadn't seen you in years and I didn't know the child. I figured just sending the child support would be enough. So on top of what the court ordered, I had the payments set up for a little more in hopes that you'd just go away and leave me alone." Phillip shook his head. "Hindsight is 20/20. I should have told her everything as it happened as soon as I found out."

Jeana wasn't surprised to hear his words. She'd known Phillip had been a spoiled selfish kid in college and it sounded like he'd never grown up.

"Shelby really didn't know, and what makes it so bad is that I told her half truths. I've had more than enough time and chances to tell her the truth, but I didn't.

"It's amazing. Shelby has bruises all over her body. But it turns out, the baby is going to be fine," Phillip sighed with relief.

"I'm sorry. All this time I figured your wife was just like you and didn't want to acknowledge Taren existed. I understand why she looked like she'd seen a ghost when she saw Taren."

Phillip shook his head. "If only I'd come clean from the beginning."

"Phillip, there is no way to turn back the hands of time. But you can try to make amends. You've got to talk to your wife and tell her the truth, the whole truth. And I do mean everything."

"If she'll give me a chance I will."

"The whole truth, Phillip. I heard the stories about you after I left school. I heard about all the women you ran. I just wish I'd have known before hand. But, we can't go back and change the past. We can only partly control what happens in our futures."

"Believe me. If Shelby will give me the chance, I'll come completely clean with her. I am tired of hiding secrets. Secrets don't do anything but hurt people and I don't want to hurt anyone else."

"Pray, Phillip."

"You know, you're the second person in a couple of days to tell me to pray."

"Then what I am telling you is confirmation."

"I really don't think God wants to hear from me. Especially after all the dirt I've done."

"Newsflash, Phillip. The mound of dirt you've done can easily be covered up by someone else's pile. You're not the first to commit sins and you won't be the last. Heck, look at me. I've done some pretty mean things over the past few months and I asked God to forgive me and I know He has. Why? Because God loves me just like He loves you."

"If you pray to Him sincerely, God will hear your prayer."

Phillip nodded his head, "More confirmation I see. Much of what you are saying is what my friend said."

"See, Phillip, God is trying to tell you something."

"Thank you for forgiving me."

"Thank God, not me. He changed my heart," Jeana said.

Phillip quietly pondered the thought.

"Did you say you want to meet Taren?"

"Yeah, I do. And I have a lot of making up to do," Phillip admitted.

"I think that would be great. Taren has always wondered about his father. I told him you were dead. I didn't want to tell him the truth. I didn't want to hurt him."

"How do you think he'll react to finding out I'm not dead and that you've been telling him lies all these years?"

"To tell you the truth, I really don't know. My lies have to stop somewhere. Because I know that lies which fester too long, grow into ugly monsters, which take on lives of their own."

Phillip nodded his head in total agreement. And upon seeing the grief in Jeana's eyes, he placed his hands on hers. "With the help of God, we'll all get through this."

Jeana smiled at the words of reassurance.

Chapter 16

Shelby Tomlinson

Trust

"Mommy, I want some apple juice," Nyah asked Shelby.

"Hold on a second, Kara." Shelby pulled the phone down away from her mouth and looked at her daughter who was riding in the back seat of her car. "When we get home, I'll get you some juice. Mommy needs to stop by the restaurant and pick up some lunch first." She put the phone back to her ear. "I'm back."

"So you still haven't talked to Phillip?"

"No."

"Shelby, you need to talk to him. This isn't healthy. I can hear it in your voice. You're an emotional wreck, aren't you?"

"I am, but I just can't talk with him. Not yet. He lied to me. The boy that woman bought to my house looked like Phillip gave birth to him. He looked just like his pictures when he was a teenager. It was eerie."

"You won't know for sure until you talk with him. Give him a chance to explain."

"He's had a chance to explain, years actually. I never told you, but before Nyah was born, Phillip told me about an old girl friend of his who had gotten pregnant while they were in college. If I'm not mistaken he said her name was Jeana. The same name as the woman who came to my house."

"What happened?"

"He said he told her to have an abortion, but the girl had a miscarriage instead and that was it."

"What happened after that?" Kara asked.

"He said they broke up and she left college soon after."

"Why do you think he told you that much?"

"I figured it was because his ego was being tested. We weren't getting pregnant. I guess deep down he wanted me to know he was man enough to get me pregnant because he had gotten someone pregnant before."

"That doesn't sound right. It still seems like it was out of the blue to me. I wonder what really happened, especially since, it looks like the ex-girlfriend and the boy were just at your house a few weeks ago."

"I wish I could answer that, but I can't," Shelby said

"You'll never be able to if you don't talk with your husband."

"Deep down, I *know* this. I'll eventually need to talk to him, but I don't know when I'll be ready."

"Honey, the longer you wait and put it off, the

more you'll be racking your brain. All this isn't healthy for you, Nyah or the baby. You need some sort of resolution."

"What if he continues to lie? Or what if there are more lies he has yet to uncover? He might have a whole slew of children. Maybe I really don't know my husband at all. I may never be able to trust him again."

"Stop racking your brain. You're just going to make yourself sick. Call Phillip and set up a time to meet. I'll watch Nyah for you."

Shelby turned her SUV in to the parking lot of Mama Lula's to pick up lunch. "Should I talk to him?"

"There is no other way to get to the bottom of this," Kara said.

"Tonight after Nyah goes to sleep, I'll call him."

"You promise?"

"Yes, I promise."

"Okay, let me know so I can watch Nyah."

"I will," Shelby said. "With all this mess going on with me, I haven't asked you how things are going with Nate Jr. and his mom."

"Better, much better." Kara said. "Nate and I talked to her, on the phone of course, and told her she is not welcome in our house or anywhere in the vicinity of our home. From now on, we'll meet in a neutral place to pick up and drop Nate Jr. off. And, I let her know too that if she ever pulls anything even close to invading my personal space again, or coming near my kids, it won't be pretty."

"Has that deterred her any?" Shelby asked.

"Somewhat. I have to handle her with a long

handled spoon, as my auntie used to say. I'm not going to give her any wiggle room. As far as I am concerned we'll handle things in black and white, so there is no gray area for misunderstanding on her part."

"Good for you," Shelby said.

"In a way I'm sort of glad that whole thing happened with her coming into my house. I'd been giving her way too much power and it was really time for it to stop. If she's still craving for attention, then she's going to have to look elsewhere because I'm all out of quality time for her."

Shelby laughed. "Girl, stop."

"I'm serious. She's got to find a new hobby, because our scrap booking class is closed!" Kara laughed with amusement.

Shelby laughed along with her. "Okay, let me go so I can run in and pick up our lunch."

"I'll talk to you tomorrow then," Kara said.

As Shelby clicked the phone off, she noticed Phillip's SUV parked two cars down. With alarm, she looked through the front window of the restaurant and saw her husband sitting in a booth with the woman who had accosted her.

Shelby jumped, startled out of a nap, when she heard the telephone ring. The caller ID showed Kara's home number. With her heart racing, she picked up the phone. "Hello?"

"Hey, Shel. So what time do I need to pick up Nyah?"

Dazed Shelby asked, "Pick up Nyah? For what?"

"For your meeting with Phillip."

"What meeting with Phillip?"

"Don't tell me you've got amnesia. Remember last night you said you'd call him to talk?"

Shelby was reluctant to answer.

"Shelby? Did you hear me? What's going on with you?"

"I'm tired. I didn't sleep at all last night."

"Okay?"

Shelby could hear the confusion in her friend's voice.

"You're tired, huh? These last couple of months are really going to be uncomfortable especially trying to find a good position to sleep in," Kara said.

"Yeah," Shelby said absent-mindedly.

"That is all the more reason why you and Phillip need to talk. You really need him to be there with you for the rest of this pregnancy. You shouldn't have to go through all this alone.

Did you get cold feet? I know it's got to be hard. Sometimes life throws us curve balls and we have to duck, dodge or get the catcher's mitt and throw what life has back.

You two need to talk and get everything out. You need to give him the opportunity to tell you what is going on and you need to vent your feelings and frustrations," Kara said in almost one breath.

"I can't call him."

"Yes you can, Shelby. You can do anything you set your mind to do. You just have to do it and get the first part over with."

"No, I really can't call."

"Why not? What's stopping you?"

"It's that woman."

"Forget about that woman, Shelby. Focus on your husband. Focus on your family. Don't let some woman from off the street or maybe even from the far past come between you two."

Shelby closed her eyes and took a deep breath. "I saw them."

"You saw who?"

"Phillip. He was . . . with her."

"Huh? What do you mean? What on earth are you talking about, Shelby?"

"Yesterday, after I got off the phone with you, at Mama Lula's."

"You saw Phillip? Are you sure it was him?" Kara asked in disbelief.

"First, I saw his truck and when I looked at the restaurant, I saw him sitting with that woman, right there in a booth in front of the window."

"Are you sure it was the same woman? It could have been someone else." Kara paused. "Listen to me asking you if it was someone else. He shouldn't be sitting with any woman at lunch in the middle of the day."

Without doubt Shelby said, "It was her. I'm sure of it."

Kara took a deep breath. "Whoa, I don't know what to say. He was sitting right up front where you could see him?"

"Just as clear as day."

"Okay, okay, I've seen enough movies on TV to know that you can't always jump to conclusions, no matter how bad they may look. So we can't jump to any conclusions right now either.

"I mean, if it was him sitting there with . . . her,

then it couldn't have been anything too bad or important. Don't you think if he were trying to be inconspicuous then he would have sat in the back, in a corner? We know so many people who go to Mama' Lula's. Don't you think he would have gone somewhere else if he was up to no good?

"Obviously, he doesn't care who sees him." Shelby began to cry. "I guess he must figure the cat's out of the bag and now he doesn't have to hide it."

"Shelby, girl, please don't cry. You're going to make me cry."

"I'm so tired, Kara. I haven't slept in days. I cried most of last night and I know it's not healthy for the baby. He's been squirming and kicking more than ever, especially after I sped off from that restaurant yesterday.

Kara, I was so upset I almost hit a car. I couldn't get out of that parking lot fast enough. I tried to keep it together until I got home so Nyah wouldn't have to witness me getting even more upset than she'd been seeing me. I know she can sense when I'm upset. Her little emotions have been on a roller coaster mode also.

I got her some fast food for lunch instead, and when she took her nap, I cried like a baby. I pulled it together the best I could when she woke up, but when she went down for the night, it was all I could do to make it to my bed last night. I just wanted to curl up on my sofa and die. If it weren't for Nyah being in the car with me, I don't know what I would have done."

"Oh, my God, Shelby, this is a nightmare. And it needs to end."

The realization that everything happening to her wasn't a dream, but a living nightmare, hit Shelby. A flood of tears streamed through. She hadn't believed she could cry so many tears.

Kara sat on the line waiting patiently for Shelby to talk again. After what felt like hours, Shelby found the courage to speak.

"I don't know what I'm going to do. I don't know."

Instead of giving advice this time, her friend said, "I'm here for you. Whatever you need, a shoulder, a listening ear, anything; you just say the word."

Shelby appreciated Kara; she knew just what to say and not to say. She sniffled, "I know. Thank you."

"You don't have to thank me."

"Kara, do you mind coming over to pick up Nyah for a little while? I've—"

Kara cut her off. "Shut up, girl. Do I mind? You really are sleep deprived aren't you?"

Shelby chuckled. "Just a little."

She heard keys jingling in the background. "I'm on my way."

Chapter 17

Phillip Tomlinson

Mercy

Phillip's wondering thoughts returned when he heard a whomp, whomp just about the time he felt the back passenger side of his SUV start to vibrate. "What now?" He checked the rearview mirror and pulled to the side of the street.

When he got out, and inspected, he found one of his tires had gone flat. It had a gash in it as long as his forearm. "Aw, man! I really don't need this right now." He shook his head. "Everything seems to be going wrong."

As he opened the back of his truck, he rolled his eyes up remembering his jack wasn't in the car. He'd forgotten to put it back after using it on his pick-up truck.

He looked around to see where he was and realized he'd broken down a few feet from Shelby's church. The parking lot was full, but there wasn't anyone outside. *Wednesday night Bible study*, he thought. He wondered if Shelby had come. Hope filled his heart.

He looked up and down the street to see if there was anyone he could ask for help. There wasn't a soul around.

Returning to the driver's seat, he turned the ignition off, grabbed his keys, and locked the doors setting the alarm.

It had been months since he'd set foot in the church. Phillip thought back and realized it had probably been over a year. Shelby was always trying to get him go to with her, but he'd always come up with a convenient reason as to why he couldn't go; even though he knew his excuses were lame. Would it really have been so bad for him to have gone with her, every once in a while? "God, you sure do have a funny way of getting people's attention and getting them to do what you want." Phillip looked skyward.

He pulled the heavy glass church door towards him to enter. He looked down at his clothing. He had on a jogging suit and sneakers. He felt awkward stepping into the church dressed in such a manner. He knew people would probably look at him strange because he wasn't wearing a suit. Shelby had always told him he could dress down and not have to wear a suit all the time, but Phillip grew up in a church where you had to dress up or else the people would stare at you.

As a boy, he'd done the same thing. If a visitor came in wearing something that wasn't regular church approved attire, he'd look at them as if they were aliens from another planet, especially if a woman came in with a pair of pants on, or if a man was wearing jeans or shorts on a Sunday morning. Some Sundays, the older women in the congregation couldn't even pay attention to what the preacher was saying because they were staring so hard at a newcomer. Usually ten times out of ten, the visitors didn't return.

Self-consciously, he smoothed his shirt and jacket before opening the back doors which led to the actual sanctuary. Upon stepping in, an usher led him to a seat. Not wanting to be rude and draw any extra attention to himself, Phillip sat, figuring he'd ask for help as soon as the service was over.

"Okay, next question," Phillip heard Pastor Jordan say. Surprisingly, the pastor was not standing up in the pulpit. He was standing on the floor with a smaller podium. It reminded him of the podium the lady who did the announcements at his old church used to use.

He then heard someone asking a question, but he couldn't make out what they were saying.

"Did everyone hear that?" The pastor asked. Many in the congregation said they hadn't heard the question. "Sister, can you please step to the microphone so everyone may hear you."

Phillip watched as he saw a woman rise and walk past the people in her row moving towards the aisle. Her face was turning red with embarrassment with each step she took.

Once at the microphone, she asked her question again. "Pastor, you said God forgives us for our sins and that Jesus died for our sins. What I asked was this: What about a person who continually sins on purpose? Especially someone who knows better? How can God love and forgive them?"

"God loves us all. You ask how can God love a sinner? We have all sinned. Before many of us came to Christ, He loved us even when we didn't know any better. Of course when we learned better, most of us stopped our intentional sins. That is not to say that we are perfect," Pastor Jordan chuckled. "At least I know I'm not perfect. I can't speak for the rest of you. You may be perfect."

Phillip heard laughter and many of the voices say they knew they weren't perfect.

"God knows we aren't perfect, those of us who try our very best not to sin and even for people who sin over and over again. But, for those who continually sin, God is not pleased. You ask how can God forgive them. Well, that's up to the person. They have to want forgiveness in their hearts. Then they must ask for forgiveness and repent for their sins.

It doesn't matter how big of a sinner the person was. God will forgive you if you truly repent in your heart."

The young lady shook her head as if understanding. Her face had lost much of its redness as she returned to her seat.

"That was a good question, sister. I'm sure you weren't the only one who had that very same question. We've got time for one more question."

Phillip watched as a young man in a white T-shirt and baggy jeans stood and headed toward the microphone. To Phillip's surprise, the people in the congregation didn't gawk and stare at his thuggish appearance like they would have at his church at home.

"Uh, Pastor. What if you, well I mean someone, were to sin and ask for repentance, but they keep doing the same sin over and over. But, they don't mean to, it's like that particular sin pulls them or something. What do you do then?"

"You pray, my brother. If I'm hearing you correctly, you are saying the person is truly repentant but they have a proclivity or shall I say a tendency to be tugged towards certain sins."

The young man nodded his head, "Yeah, yeah, that's what I mean."

"As I said earlier, we've all sinned and come short of the Lord. Avoiding one sin for one person might not be so hard for another person. For instance, one person may have a problem when it comes to cursing. They may have cursed a great deal when they were in the secular world. Now even as a Christian, when things are frustrating or they get mad, a few of those words may come out. They don't mean to curse, but they do. Then they repent and truly mean it.

Now take another person. They might not have a hard time with curse words, but they have a tendency to lie or steal. Each person is different. That's why we have to pray and focus on the Lord. Pray that we'll do what is pleasing to His eye. He still loves us in spite of shortcomings.

Whew look at the time. It's nine already. I'm going to let you all go in just a moment. But first I want to give you another scripture to study along with the others I gave earlier. I want you to read over Psalm 32, the entire chapter. This Psalm speaks of the joy of being forgiven. Read it and study it. For those of us who remember back in the day when we would sin left and right without a care, this passage of scripture will bring us joy.

And for those people who are still in this world of sin, it will give you hope and an assurance that God can bring you joy in his forgiveness of your sins."

The pastor closed his Bible. "Let us pray."

Phillip bowed his head but the prayer the pastor prayed didn't register. Instead, his thoughts were on the discussion about God forgiving people for their sins. God was really pulling out all the stops to get his attention. Everything the pastor said was right along the line with what Will and Jeana had been telling him. He decided when he got back to Will's apartment he'd check out the 32nd Psalm as the pastor suggested. He wanted to read about the joy of being forgiven.

Phillip turned the key to open Will's apartment door. It was well past ten by the time he got back. The young guy who had asked the last question of the pastor wasn't parked far from Phillip and he ended up helping Phillip with the tire.

The man's name was Darrian. He told Phillip he'd been saved for about three months, and was learning a lot in New Hope's ministry. After changing the tire, the two made small talk about how much Darrian felt his life had changed since his coming to Christ. He told Phillip he studied the 32nd Psalm a couple of nights before, and was pleased because he knew where to find that particular passage in the Bible without flipping aimlessly to find it.

Phillip saw the glow of joy and peace on the young man's face. It was the same serene expression Will normally had. He could tell by Darrian's clothing, street language and walk that the young man had probably had a pretty rough life. But judging by the aura that surrounded the young man, it seemed as though the man's past prior to being saved wasn't a hindering factor.

Upon their parting, Darrian told Phillip he looked forward to seeing him on Sunday at church. Phillip surprised himself by saying he would see him on Sunday. He meant it. Just listening to the little bit of the Bible study he had attended, made Phillip want to learn more about God's love and how much God could love a sinner like him.

"What's up, man?" Will asked. He was sitting at his dinette table reading the Bible.

"Nothing, what's up with you?" Phillip asked.

"I thought I was going to have to put an All Points Bulletin out on you. I was concerned. I called you, but I kept getting your voice mail."

Phillip pulled his cell phone out of his pants pocket and saw where he missed Will's calls. "Sorry, man, I must have still been at Bible study."

"Bible study?" Will asked incredulously.

Phillip grinned. "Yeah, man. I was at Bible study."

"Where?"

"New Hope."

"I didn't know you were planning on going."

Phillip took a seat across from Will. "I didn't know I was going myself. And, you were right. When God wants to get your attention, He doesn't hold any stops."

"What happened?"

"I got a flat tire right in front of New Hope. When I got ready to change it, I realized I didn't have my jack. New Hope's parking lot was full so I went in to find some help.

"I stepped in the door and an usher directed me to a seat," Phillip laughed. "I felt bad because I had on a jogging suit. But to my surprise, Pastor Jordan had one on too."

Will smiled. "New Hope is come as you are."

"Well, I *had to* go as I was. There was no other choice." Phillip made the joke and laughed. Will laughed along with him.

"So how was it?"

"It was pretty strange in a way. The topic was about being forgiven for our sins. It's like it was confirmation for what's going on with me right now."

Will smiled knowingly. "God is good. He really does know how to get our attention."

"He got my attention. He gave us, I mean the congregation, a scripture to study."

"You said it right the first time. That *us* does include you. God was speaking to you through Pastor Jordan." Will's face perked up. "What scripture did he give you?"

"The 32nd Psalm; it's about the kind of joy you can feel by being forgiven by God."

"I know the scripture." Within a couple of seconds Will turned to the Psalm. "My favorite part is *'Blessed is he whose transgression is forgiven, whose sin is covered.'*"

"I hate that I missed Bible Study," Will said.

"Why weren't you there? If you were, then you could have helped me."

"I went out on a date."

Phillip's eyebrows shot up. "You went out on a date, on a Wednesday night? And, skipped Bible Study? She must be pretty hot." Phillip said.

"Whoa, hold up. You're starting to sound a little like Rick. It's nothing like that. Not that the young lady isn't what you guys would call hot. I think she looks very nice."

Phillip stared at Will, waiting for the punch line.

"She is fine, single and saved. Her church has Bible study on Thursday nights. And me being the gentleman, skipped mine instead of her having to skip hers."

"Fine, single and saved, huh? Does she have a name?

"Her name is Morgan," Will readily said.

"What's the catch?" Phillip asked.

"No catch."

"There's always a catch. Let me know when you find out what it is." Phillip laughed.

Changing the subject, Will said, "Anyway. That's why I'm sitting here reading scriptures." He slid the Bible over and pointed to the first verse of the 32nd Psalm.

"What does that part mean?" Phillip asked.

"The first part means, the one who God forgives for the sinful acts is a blessed person. The last part means that those sins are then washed away by God."

"That makes sense. It's hard to understand the *thees* and *thous*. I'll probably need you to translate the whole scripture. I never really could understand the King James Version."

"Me neither," Will confided. "There are other translations of the Bible you can read as a reference. Then, you can compare them. This will help you better understand the word of God.

"I've got three other versions of the Bible in my room. You can borrow them if you'd like."

Phillip was glad for the offer. "Thanks. I'll probably do that."

"If you want, I can go over the rest of this scripture with you to break it down."

"Yeah. I'd like that. I'm curious about the kind of joy that forgiveness can bring."

Chapter 18

Shelby Tomlinson

Trust

Shelby stood on the porch of her childhood home, waiting for someone to answer the front door. Just after she saw her mother peek out of the side curtain, the door swung open. "Shelby, honey? What on earth are you doing here?" Vanessa extended her arms to pull her daughter in for a hug. Shelby clung to her as if her life depended on it.

She pulled away from her mother's warm arms, after it seemed like they'd been there for a few minutes. "What, I can't visit anymore?"

Vanessa rolled her eyes. "You know what I mean." She looked past Shelby towards the car. "Where are Phillip and Nyah?"

Shelby walked past her mom towards the den, and sat on the loveseat. The tears she dried a couple of miles before reaching her parent's house returned, streaming just as freely as they had during her two hour trip. "Nyah is at Kara's for a couple of days and I don't know where Phillip is," Shelby admitted through tear-drenched sobs.

Her mom sat next to her on the couch and took Shelby back in her arms. "Oh, honey. What's wrong? I'm not trying to pry, but do you feel like talking about it?"

Shelby nodded her head, "I do. I need to tell you something. I've been dealing with some pretty complicated emotions the past couple of weeks."

Vanessa sat back patiently, giving Shelby the freedom to talk at her own pace. Shelby loved the way her mother instinctively knew when she needed her space or when she needed to be nudged. She always knew the right words to say to encourage her. Her mother's supportive ways were one of the reasons she got in her car and stopped by. She didn't want to call first. Knowing if she tried, she probably would have broken down on the phone. Plus, Shelby didn't want her mother to worry about her.

"It's Phillip. He's been living a lie." Shelby took a deep breath. "I need to tell you what happened the day I ended up in the hospital."

Shelby told her mom about the woman coming to her house and confronting her with information claiming to be the mother of Phillip's child. She explained how she saw a boy who looked like Phillip's younger twin. Then she told her mother how upset she was, and that she tripped going up the stairs and the next thing she knew she was waking up in the hospital. Shelby finished recapping the story, she told her mother how she kicked Phillip out.

As she waited for her mother's reaction and any words of wisdom she might have, Shelby felt like a huge burden had been released.

Her mom wasn't surprised by the news. She didn't yell or bad mouth Phillip. Calmly she said, "Shelby, honey, I know you're hurting. I can see the pain in your eyes. I saw it each day I visited the hospital. I hear the pain in your heart." Vanessa paused for a moment. "Do you know what else I see?"

Shelby shook her head having no idea.

"I see the strong woman in you. The pain you hold in your eyes and the pain I see on your face isn't as intense as it once was. Believe it or not, time heals all wounds. We all have events to happen to us in life, which throw us off. And you're going to get through this."

Shelby stared at her mother, wondering what she was talking about. She also wondered if her mother had heard anything she said.

"Do you remember years ago, before Nyah was born, and we were sitting on your couch? As I remember it, we were sitting in these same positions pretty much." Vanessa smiled.

Shelby remembered, "Yeah."

"Communication is still the key, Shelby. You need to talk to your husband. You can't avoid him forever. Talk and give him a chance to tell you what's going on. Get his side of the story."

Shelby sighed. "But according to this woman, he's been sending child support payments to her for years. So it's not like he can say he doesn't know her or the boy. And . . ."

"And what?"

"I saw him with her the other afternoon."

"You saw him with the same woman who came to your house?"

"Yeah, at Mama Lula's. They were sitting in a booth near the front window like two teenagers, for the whole world to see."

"Whew, baby. Look, I don't know what is going on, so I'm not going to try and speculate or pass any judgment on Phillip. But the only way you're going to know what is going on is if you talk to your husband and get to the bottom of this. You can't keep letting all of this continue to eat you up."

"Kara told me the same thing."

"She's right, baby. You've just got to face all of this head on."

"Mom, that's easy for you to say. You're a much stronger woman than I am. Don't take this the wrong way, but I'm sure it's easy to say from people looking from the outside to the inside."

Her mother looked directly in Shelby's eyes with love. Shelby could see her mother's features soften with understanding. She patted Shelby's lap then stood and said, "Sit right there. I think its time we had a talk. It's the right time for me to tell you a little bit more about how I came to be such a strong woman." Vanessa Adams headed in the direction of her kitchen.

She returned a few minutes later with tissues and two cups of warm spiced tea. Shelby's curiosity was suddenly piqued. What was her mother about to say? The tone had been one of some type of long kept secret.

After her mother settled comfortably on the

couch next to her she said, "You know I was young like you once, don't you? I'm about to tell you something that I never wanted to tell you, but none the less, some things happened in the early years of my marriage to your father, which helped me to be the *so called* strong woman you see before you today."

Shelby looked at her mother with concern. Somehow she knew whatever her mother said next would change her life forever.

"Your father had an affair."

"Daddy did what?" Shelby asked in pure disbelief.

"You heard me correctly. It happened when you were three-years old."

Shelby's mouth dropped, "When I was three?"

"Yes."

"Why? I mean I can't believe it. What happened?"

Her mother took a deep breath. "Ultimately I forgave him."

"When I was three? I don't remember anything." Shelby thought back.

"And I hoped you wouldn't. In some ways I'm glad you can't remember."

Shelby shook her head. "I can't believe Daddy cheated on you."

"Well believe it. He is a man, human—just like you and I."

Shelby sat speechless. Her father had cheated on her mother. He was the last person in the world that she would have ever expected to cheat.

"I know it seems easy for me to let these words

roll off my tongue, but let me assure you it wasn't easy twenty-five years ago.

"I was hurt. I had been the best wife I knew how to be, but it seemed as though it wasn't good enough and hadn't mattered at the time. I heard from a couple of my friends that they saw your father at various places with a particular woman on a number of occasions.

"Of course, when I asked your father about it, he told me my friends were busy bodies who had nothing else to do and for me to stop listening to their nonsense. So I listened to him and did as he said for a while. But deep down, my intuition told me something wasn't right. A woman's intuition is normally right. Don't ever underestimate it."

Shelby listened intently. For a few moments she'd been able to forget about her own pressing problems.

"One night I trusted my intuition and followed your father. He claimed, for days at a time, to be working at the office late. It sounds crazy now, but I was desperate for real answers. I put you and your brother in the car and drove over to his office building. I saw him leave and I followed him to a hotel where he met a woman in the parking lot."

Shelby shook her head exclaiming, "No, Mom?"

"Yes. And I guess one of them must have gotten the key early because they went straight to the room. I sat in that car for at least two hours and it felt like an eternity as I waited for him to come back out. But he never did.

"I drove back home in a daze. God was looking

out for us that night, because I didn't even remember driving back."

In astonishment Shelby asked, "What did you do?"

"I put you two in bed and then I balled up as many of your Dad's clothes as I could and threw them out on the front lawn. When he came in three hours later he was furious, asking me why his clothes were on the lawn.

"I confronted him with what I'd seen and he looked like a cat with a canary's feather sticking out of his mouth. I kicked him out and told him to never come back."

"You kicked Daddy out? I don't remember that."

"You thought he'd gone on a business trip."

"You mean that business trip he took to New York?"

"I think that's what I told you."

"I do remember. You were crying a lot. I thought it was because Dad was in New York and you were sad."

Vanessa chuckled. "I was sad alright. And mad at the same time."

"Your father called and called so much, I finally pulled the cord out of the wall."

"So how did you get from there to where you are now? You and Dad seem like one of the happiest couples I know."

"And right now we are. It took a while and a great deal of counseling, but with God's grace and mercy, our marriage was saved. Amazingly enough, our marriage is actually closer than it was before the incident. That same test also brought me closer to God. I ended up rededicating my life to Him."

"Wow," Shelby said in amazement.

"It made me a stronger woman quick. And, what you're going through is going to make you a stronger woman too." Vanessa stroked Shelby's cheek.

"We all have our crosses to bear. My cross may have been too big for someone else to bear. Just as yours might be too big for another person. But your cross can be bore. God won't give you more than you can handle.

"Take your problems to God. Give them to Him and He will lead your steps. And I promise, you'll come out stronger than you could ever imagine."

"Do you really think so?" Shelby asked in disbelief.

Vanessa pulled Shelby in close for a hug. "I know so."

Chapter 19

Phillip Tomlinson

Mercy

Phillip awoke on the futon with a notebook and pen still clutched in his hand. He looked towards the clock wondering what time it was. The last time he'd checked, it was close to three in the morning.

Will had read the 32nd Psalm with him and broke it down into terms he could understand. Then his friend pulled out a couple of his other Bibles, which were written in different versions. Phillip found one in particular that had three different translations of the word side by side so he didn't have to keep flipping pages on the various books.

Will had had also given Phillip a few more of his favorite scriptures to read. And he'd been utterly surprised to find the scriptures fascinating. Many of them seemed to speak directly to him.

The clock on the fireplace mantel read 9:30 a.m. He couldn't believe he'd slept so late. He stood and stretched his long body- hands only inches from the ceiling.

On the refrigerator, being held by a banana fruit magnet was a note from Will.

Phil, Give me a call when you wake up.

Phillip looked around for his duffle bag, filled with the things he'd stuffed in there before last leaving his home. It had almost been a week and a half since Shelby had kicked him out. He hoped she'd soon have a change of heart and let him come back. Sleeping on Will's futon was getting old.

Once he located the bag, he pulled out his toothbrush and toothpaste. After he brushed his teeth, he took a shower and slipped on a jogging suit. He then took his cell phone off the charger, grabbed his keys and set out for his truck.

Even though his message display didn't say he'd missed any calls, he checked the message counter to see if maybe Shelby had called. The display read no messages. His heart sank a little.

As soon as he flipped the phone shut, it began to ring. Without looking at who was calling he answered with anticipation. "Hello?"

"What's up, man?"

"Oh, Rick." Phillip's heart sank even lower.

"You don't have to sound so happy to hear from me."

Shaking his head in disappointment, Phillip said, "Where have you been?"

"Hiding."

"Hiding? From who?"

"Joy."

"You still dealing with her?"

"Hiding." Rick clarified. "There is a difference."

"Just tell her to leave you alone," Phillip told his friend.

"If it was that easy, she'd be gone. I've told her on numerous occasions, but she won't leave me alone." Rick lowered his voice a little. "To tell you the truth, I think I might have to put a restraining order out on her."

"Is it that bad?" Phillip's voice went up an octave.

"Ah, you're finally understanding what I'm saying?"

Phillip shook his head, feeling sorry for his friend. "I told you to be careful and watch your back."

"I am, believe me. I haven't been out on a date in weeks. I never know when Joy might just show up and run one of my women away. I mean, I've still got a few who don't know I'm being stalked, but if Joy keeps this up, I'm going to have to rebuild my little black book."

Phillip sighed heavily. "All jokes aside, you need to do something about Joy. You seriously need to slow down. Take it from someone who should be giving seminars on the subject of running women."

Rick laughed at Phillip. "That was years ago. You couldn't hang now, especially doing some of that lame stuff you did in college. Women are smarter these days."

"Don't worry, I wouldn't want to try and hang now. The past can catch up with you. Most times, the results aren't pretty. Just take my word for it and slow down."

"You sound a lot like Will."

Phillip laughed to himself, realizing Rick's words were true.

"So, where have you and Shelby been? Your secretary said you were out for an indefinite amount of time and I called the house a few times, but you guys are never there."

"I go back to work Monday." Phillip paused, closing his eyes before he answered. "I'm not living at home right now."

"What do you mean, you're not living at home right now?"

"Shelby kicked me out."

Rick became silent on the other end of the line. Phillip figured his friend probably didn't know what to say. He knew if the shoe was on the other foot, he probably wouldn't know what to say either.

Awkwardly Phillip said, "It's a long story. One I don't feel like recapping right now. But just trust me, when I say, you need to slow down."

"Whoa, man. I don't know what to say." Rick fell silent again. "So do you need a place to stay or something?"

"No, I'm alright for now. I've been staying at Will's."

"Why didn't you call me? We're boys. You know if you need me I'm here for you."

"Except for when you're hiding from Joy, right?"

"That's real funny."

"Just kidding, man. I know you've got my back if I need it. I've just been trying to work through things on my own. And having my wife kick me out of the house, wasn't exactly something I wanted to talk about."

"Hold on a second," Rick said. "Ahh shoot!"

"What?"

Rick groaned. "That's Joy calling on the other line. I'm not answering it."

"Don't take what this woman is doing lightly. Get a restraining order if you need one, change your phone numbers and move if you have to. Don't be nice, smile at her or try to reason with her. Crazy people can't be reasoned with. Cut her off and pray she'll get the message and finally leave you alone."

"Good advice. I swear you're sounding more and more like Will."

Phillip smiled feeling good about himself for giving good advice. "Thanks for the compliment."

"Hold on . . . Joy is calling again. I need to call my cell phone company. I'll call you back later with my new number."

"Alright. Later."

Phillip clicked off and called Will. "Hey. You wanted me to call?"

"Yeah, you were sleeping so good all cuddled up with your notebook and pen, I didn't want to wake you up."

For two nights in a row, Phillip had fallen asleep while studying scriptures in the Bible. He found them comforting and intriguing—especially when using the versions of the Bible, which broke it down for him. Proverbs spoke wisdom and most of the people he was reading about had all types of drama going on in their lives. Phillip wasn't one to watch soap operas, but he figured if some of the writer's took some of the stories from the Bible for their scripts, they'd have some of the best Neilson ratings.

Phillip laughed lightly. "Cuddled up, that's real cute."

Will laughed. "Anyway, I wanted to invite you to Men's Fellowship tonight."

"Men's Fellowship? I thought only women had fellowships?"

"No, the men do too. The church has it the third Friday of each month. I don't get a chance to go that often but I have a good time whenever I do attend. And I think you'd like it. Plus, it might keep your mind off the heavier things going on in your life."

Phillip thought about it. He was tired of moping around. And the offer actually appealed to him. "What time does it start?"

There was no hesitation in Will's voice. "Seven."

"Sounds good. Do I need to dress up or anything?"

"No, man. Jeans, jogging suit, but no spandex biker shorts."

"Darn, I was hoping to wear my red ones." Phillip laughed.

Will laughed too. "It's not that kind of party. I'll meet you there. How about a quarter of seven?"

"That'll work. I need to show my face in the office for a few hours. Then, I'll go get this afro cut."

"Good, you're starting to look a little like one of the Jackson brothers."

"Which one? Marlon or Jermaine?"

"Michael."

"Man, I'm about to hang this phone up on you."

"Gotta go," Will said quickly.

"Yeah, I just bet you do. I'll see you around seven."

Phillip stood outside the church talking with Will and Darrian after the fellowship was over.

"The fellowship was pretty cool," Darrian said.

A couple of guys Phillip had played a round of spades with walked out past them towards their cars. One of them said, "It was good meeting you, Phillip and Darrian. See you all Sunday at church."

"Yeah, alright," Phillip said as the men continued on towards their cars.

Darrian shook his head. "I wasn't expecting to have so much fun at the fellowship. I thought we were gonna sit and listen to Pastor teach us like he does in Bible study." He smiled. "It was cool watching the fight and playing cards." He shook his head again. "The food was good too. I felt like I was at the Golden Corral Buffet." Darrian held up his doggie bag of food.

Will agreed. "The food is always good. Since this was your first time, you didn't have to bring anything, but next time, bring a little something. Everyone does. That's why we end up with so much. And you saw the spread; it doesn't have to be home cooked, you saw I brought chips and dip."

"I'm like Darrian. I was ready to take notes tonight," Phillip said.

Will said, "The fellowship is meant for us to get to know one another on other levels. Sometimes it's hard to do after church or Bible study. This way we can all relax."

Darrian nodded his head with pleasure. "I am definitely coming back next month.

The door opened again and the pastor along with one of the ministers, stepped out. "Still hanging out gentlemen?"

Will answered, "The fellowship was so good, I guess we still want to keep it going out here in the parking lot."

"Feel free. I'm headed home myself," the pastor said.

Darrien spoke. "I really enjoyed the fellowship, Pastor Jordan. Usually when I get together with friends to play cards and watch a fight, I have to watch my back in case someone breaks bad and wants to start a fight of their own. Tonight I didn't have to do that. It was really cool."

"I'm glad you enjoyed it, my brother. You'll have to come again next month."

Darrin nodded, "Oh, I will, you can believe it."

"What about you, Mr. Tomlinson? Did you enjoy the fellowship?" Pastor Jordan asked.

Phillip was taken aback that the Pastor knew him by name. "I had a good time too. It wasn't what I expected at all."

Conviction covered Phillip's heart. "Uh, Pastor, my wife told me you might want me to help with the Pee Wee football. I apologize for not talking to you before now, but if you still need my help, I'd like to do so."

"Wonderful, we do need help with the Pee Wee team. How is sister Shelby doing?"

Phillip dropped his head for a moment. "She's . . .

well . . . she's doing okay." He stammered, not knowing exactly what to say and how to say it.

The pastor extended his hand and patted his shoulder with a knowing look in his eye. "Young brother, if you pray and seek God about the things that are going on in your life, He'll lead you in the right path." The pastor stopped speaking for a moment. "Phillip, God has special plans for you. He's got work for you to do." He patted Phillip's shoulder once more and bid them all good night.

Once they were back in Will's apartment, Phillip asked, "What do you think the Pastor meant by his last comment?"

"Pastor Jordan was speaking a prophetic word to you. And from what I've seen in the past, when Pastor Victor Jordan speaks prophetically, what ever he says usually manifests."

"So what is it suppose to mean?" Still unclear Phillip asked.

"It means get ready. God has something in store for you."

Phillip nodded his head more to himself than to Will. He wondered what kind of work God had for a sinner like him.

Phillip tossed and turned on the futon, because he couldn't stop thinking about what God might have in store for him.

People were telling him he needed to pray and ask God for forgiveness. This weighed on his mind also. He wasn't good at praying. He wasn't like his grandfather. His grandfather could pray for hours on end to God. Especially at meal time when he would go on and on in prayer thanking God for the many blessings and safe travels on the highways and byways. His prayers seemed to flow from his lips like water traveling downhill in a brook.

His parents prayed, but their prayers were silent. He had no idea what they were praying about. Phillip didn't know if there was some kind of special formula for praying, but he figured he'd better go ahead and try something. He needed to ask for forgiveness and make sure God was on his side. He could use all the help he could get.

He'd seen people in various positions when they prayed. Some people knelt while others merely bowed their heads wherever they were. Phillip wasn't sure what position would allow him the best receptiveness from God.

Pushing himself up into a sitting position, Phillip slid off the futon and got on his knees, clasped his hands together and bowed his head.

Awkwardly he began to speak. "Hello, God. It's me, Phillip Tomlinson . . . but of course you know this already. I hope you can hear me. I know it's been a long time since I said a prayer." Phillip paused, re-thinking his last statement. "Okay, a long time is an understatement. I've never prayed to You, not as sincerely as I am praying to You now. It is with the utmost sincerity that I am praying to you from my soul. There are many things I need to confess and ask you to forgive me for.

"I really don't know where to start, so I guess

I'll just say things as they come to mind. Forgive me, God, for not respecting one of your most beautiful of creations. Forgive me for all the women I have disrespected over the years. I should have told Shelby about my ex and the child. But I guess I let my ego and pride get in the way.

Please forgive me, also, for disrespecting Jeana and not taking the responsibility I should have taken years ago. I hope you will forgive me and give me a chance to make some kind of amends to her and my . . . son. Please forgive me for cutting that person off the other day while I was driving. I was in a rush and they did actually have the right of way. And while I'm mentioning that, thank you for my not getting in an accident. I don't know what I was thinking. If something happens to me, I'll never be able to ask Shelby for forgiveness. And my daughter and son . . . sons . . . wouldn't have a father.

God, there are so many things I know I've left out. So, I ask you to forgive me for the things I've mentioned and the things I've done wrong that I can't remember.

I am learning that you are very caring and forgiving. I hope you can forgive me for taking so many years to pray like this to you. I promise right here and now, it won't take decades for me to pray again.

And God, thank you for Shelby's recovery and for keeping the baby safe. I think that's it for now. If I think of something else, I'll do like I'm doing now and kneel and pray.

Thank you for listening."

His prayer wasn't as smooth and didn't flow like his grandfather's prayers did. But, God had heard him. It was a start.

Phillip extended the futon to finally get some rest. Less than five minutes after his head hit the pillow, he was fast asleep.

Chapter 20

Shelby Tomlinson

Trust

Shelby tossed and turned, waking from a nightmare. She fell asleep on the couch the evening after returning from her two-day stay at her parents' house. She picked up the phone and checked the caller ID. The display showed 15 calls had come in during her absence and while she was taking her nap. Phillip called several times; three of his calls came in while she was sleep. Because she'd turned the ringers off before leaving to visit her parents, she hadn't heard them ring.

She waddled around the house rubbing her lower back as she turned all the ringers back on.

She shook her head. The dream was still fresh on her mind. Phillip was standing at the altar in a tuxedo and his ex-girlfriend was coming down the isle in a wedding dress to meet him. The vivid sight caused her to let out a low moan.

The conversation with her mother played over and over in her mind also. There was no way she'd be able to deal with everything in her own strength. It was time for all the confusion to end and she knew there was only one place to get the answers she needed.

She looked up towards heaven. "Lord God, what on earth am I going to do? I can't go on like this." Tears streamed from her eyes. "What is going on? Why is all of this happening? Why me?"

Things like this happened to other people, not her, she thought. She felt bad for thinking that way. She remembered the story about Job in the Bible. Even though Job was an extreme example, he endured much worse.

Job had been put to a test she thought. "Am I being put through a test? I know you won't put anything more on me than I can handle. Honestly, it feels like this test is too hard. At times it feels as if all of this is going to consume me and it's like I just can't go on. And I don't want to feel that way."

Shelby let the tears stream down her face. "Lord, I accepted you as my Lord and Savior long ago and I trust you. I trust that you will never leave me alone. I trust you will be my comforter. And most of all, I trust that you will help me to get through this; the hardest test of my life. I have faith in you, Lord, and most of all I love you. I thank you for covering me, walking with me and carrying me. I thank you for what you are about to do in my life, because above all, I know you love me too."

She wiped the tears from her cheeks with the palms of her hands. "Oh, dear God," she cried out. "I need you, I need you, I need you," she repeated over and over again. "Give me the strength. I know You can do this. I know only *You* can do this."

Shelby felt the remaining heavy burden she'd been carrying around lift. She knew God had taken it onto His shoulders, and if she would continue to trust in Him, He would help her through the seemingly impossible trial in her life.

She waddled to the end of the couch and picked the phone back up. She didn't plan on letting this situation continue to get the best of her. She clicked the phone on and listened to all the messages.

The messages Phillip left made her heart cry. He'd pleaded over and over for her to talk to him. He said he really needed to talk face to face. Message after message he said the same thing. With each message he sounded more and more desperate. She'd even thought she could hear him crying on the last message.

She rubbed her belly and took a deep breath before dialing Phillip's cell phone number. "There is no time like the present," she said to herself.

"Hello?" Phillip's voice was groggy on the other end. Shelby missed talking to him so much. Since they'd met and were an official couple in college they'd never gone more than a day without speaking to one another. So even though it had only been a couple of weeks since she'd kicked him out, it felt like an eternity.

"Hello, Phillip."

Without a second of hesitation, Phillip answered, "Shelby, honey? Please tell me I'm not dreaming. Is that you?"

"Yes. It's me."

Fearing he lost the connection on the phone, Phillip continued. "Shelby, baby, it's so good to hear your voice. I need to talk to you. There are some things I need to tell you; things I should have told you about years ago."

Shelby cut him off, "Come home."

She heard what sounded like his sitting up. "I'll be there in thirty minutes."

"Okay. I'll see you then," Shelby replied.

"And, Shelby, honey?"

"Yes?"

"I love you so much."

Shelby closed her eyes as the tears formed, this time due to a happiness that filled her heart. Even though deep down she knew he loved her, hearing the words some how gave her confirmation. "I love you too," she said and hung up the phone.

It had been twenty minutes since Shelby had spoken to Phillip. She'd felt like a nervous teenager waiting to be picked up for her first official date. She checked her hair in the mirror, splashed cold water on her face and changed in to her favorite silk pajamas.

She figured it might be a long night and she wanted to be as comfortable as humanly possible with a basketball for a stomach. Several times she had flipped back and forth in her mind as to where they should talk. She finally settled on the sitting area of their bedroom, which had two matching recamier sofas, in which they could talk comfortably face to face.

Her emotions ranged from excited to pissed off, and from unconditional love to distrust, then back again. She took a deep breath. "Lord, I know you can help us through this. I know You can do exceedingly and abundantly. I am depending on You."

She heard the garage door open. Within a couple of minutes of hearing the car pull in, Phillip was standing in the doorway of their bedroom. He'd looked better than he'd ever looked to her.

With three long strides he was within arms reach. "Shelby, you don't know how much I've missed you and Nyah." He pulled her into his arms as if his life depended on the embrace. "Baby, I love you." She could hear the urgency in his voice and felt his tears trickle down her face as he rubbed his cheek against hers. Then he pulled back to look into her eyes. "Let's sit down. I need to tell you some things."

Shelby turned towards one of the chairs in the sitting area and sat while Phillip pulled the other closer and positioned it directly in front of hers so they could hold hands while he spoke.

"I should have told you what I'm about to tell you a long time ago. And, I should have come clean about some other things a while back also."

She looked into his eyes. There were so many things she wanted to say, so many questions she wanted to ask. But she remained patient, wanting to hear him out. When the time was right, she'd speak.

"Whew," Phillip let out a deep breath. "Let me start at the beginning. I want tonight to be the start of something new for us. That being said, I am going to come clean with you about everything. I am about to tell you some things that don't even have anything directly to do with why we are having this conversation. By the time I finish, you'll know everything there is to know. There will be no secrets between us."

Shelby's heart quickened. *What did he mean by things that didn't directly have anything to do with the most recent events of their life? How much had he kept from her? How many lies had he told her over the years? How was she going to get through all this?*

"Back in college, well really starting in high school, I was a pretty popular guy. Not just on the football field but . . . with the women."

Phillip continued to tell her about his escapades in college with all sorts of women. He'd told her about his promiscuous lifestyle, and that there were times he played Russian roulette with his life by not always using protection. He told her he was lucky he never caught anything deadly.

He went on to explain that when Jeana had gotten pregnant, he gave her the money to get an abortion and he never changed his mind on that original decision. He told Shelby a lie about the miscarriage, so she wouldn't continue to be upset with him. He thought Jeana went ahead with the termination.

He also came clean about the summons he received for child support and the DNA test, which proved that Jeana's son, Taren, was his son.

Phillip told her about the secret bank account he set up to make the monthly child support payments, and he told his lawyer he didn't want to be contacted by Jeana for anything else.

By the time Phillip finished talking, it seemed to Shelby that he'd told her everything he could possibly think of to come clean about his deceptions over the years. He even caught her up on the days since the accident.

Without her having to ask, he told her about the meeting with Jeana at Mama Lula's. Throughout his confession, the look on his face was that of the utmost sincerity.

Once he was done, he looked lovingly into Shelby's eyes for her reaction. She was speechless.

"I know it's a lot to take in for one night. I need you to know that I love you and I'll do whatever it takes to make up for all of this. I don't want to lose you. I was stupid and thought if I just ignored certain things, my past really didn't matter. But I was wrong, dead wrong."

All the questions Shelby wanted to know before Phillip started his confession had been answered. She now knew what Jeana had been babbling about at her home. She knew Jeana had come there thinking Shelby knew about Taren. And, her instinct told her, her husband didn't have any feelings for his ex-girlfriend.

There was the fact that Phillip had been going to Bible study and hanging out with the men at the Men's Fellowship. He quoted one of the Bible scriptures to her.

"Whoa, this *is* a lot for me to digest in one sitting." It was all so overwhelming for her. She'd asked God to help her through this and for answers. He had exceeded her expectations.

"I'm asking for your forgiveness. If you can find it in your heart, please forgive me. I don't want to lose you over my past stupidity."

In her heart, Shelby loved her husband. He wasn't perfect and neither was she. Deep down she'd forgiven him. But she wondered, as she had a few years earlier, how long it would take for her to have complete trust in him again. And how long it would take to forget the turbulence their lives were in the process of undertaking.

Bending over to hug him she said, "I forgive you."

"What? Really?" Phillip asked in disbelief.

"Yes, I forgive you. I'm not saying I've forgotten everything. And I'm not going to promise that I'll be happy go lucky from now on. We've just had a major blow to our marriage. It is all going to take some time. But I do forgive you. I can't go on being unforgiving and hating you for being human."

Phillip looked directly into Shelby's eyes. "You're right and I don't expect you to forget all that's happened. And I guess everything does happen for a reason. My love for you has intensified tremendously. And I've been reading so much about God and Jesus over the past week or so, I feel like I've been studying for exams or something."

"They say be careful what you wish for, because you just might get it," Shelby said.

"What did you wish for?"

Shelby smiled. "I hoped and prayed that you'd come to church with me and get to know Christ. From what I'm hearing, you are learning about Christ, and if you keep it up at the rate you're going, you'll probably know more than me by the end of the summer."

"If I keep all this up, I'll probably know more than Will, and that's saying a lot."

Shelby yawned.

Phillip caressed her cheeks with his hand. "I know you've got to be tired. Are you ready to lie down?"

"Yeah, I'm exhausted." She rubbed her back. "And my lower back has been killing me."

"Let's go lay down," Phillip suggested.

"Are you sleepy too?"

"No, I just want to hold you and look at you."

She watched as Phillip pulled the covers back for her. After she laid down and got as comfortable as humanly possible, she allowed Phillip to lay next to her in a snug embrace.

The morning light beamed through a crack in the curtains of Shelby and Phillip's bedroom, causing Shelby to stir awake. Her husband's arms were still embracing her snuggly.

It had been the best night's sleep she'd had in weeks.

"Good morning," she heard Phillip say as he squeezed her intently.

"Morning, did I wake you?"

"No, I've been awake for a little while. I've just

been laying her thinking about how thankful I am to have a second chance. Your love and trust are priceless and I would have given just about anything to win them back."

Shelby confessed her own feelings. "I realized how much I loved you also. I was scared of losing you. I wondered if I was married to some stranger all these years."

Phillip gave her a squeeze. "This is me. All of me; everything you did and didn't want to know. I don't want you to have any doubts about us."

Shelby yawned. The last few weeks had been so emotionally draining. Even though she'd slept well, she could use a few more hours of uninterrupted sleep.

"You still sound like you're pretty tired."

"I am, but I promised Kara I'd pick Nyah up this morning. They've got to get her stepson . . ." Shelby trailed off.

As if reading her mind, Phillip didn't miss a beat in saying, "I know what you're thinking. You have a stepson too."

"Oh, you're a mind reader now?"

"Am I right?" Phillip asked.

"Yeah, you're right."

"That's something else I wanted to talk with you about." Phillip stopped for a response.

"I'm listening." Shelby waited for him to continue.

"You know I told Jeana that I want to meet Taren. I do, but I don't want to do anything you won't be pleased with. I should have discussed it with you first, before I spoke with her. I was so set on asking for her forgiveness. I didn't think everything through. So, I need to ask for your forgiveness again."

"I accept your apology. I would appreciate in the future if you'd talk with me first, especially on major and even some not so major decisions. I hope you are not apologizing for wanting to see . . . your son." Her pause, even though unintentional, was still noticeable.

"Honey, I know this isn't going to be easy for you, but thank you for understanding," Phillip said.

"I'm not going to act like I'm a superwoman or something. I know it won't be easy. But it's past time for you to meet your son. And that child has a right to meet his father."

Phillip hugged her again. Even though Shelby knew the road ahead wasn't going to be easy, she was glad God was watching over them.

"You rest. I'll pick up Nyah. We'll probably go somewhere for the day. I want to spend time with my little girl. Tomorrow I'll call Jeana and see about setting up the meeting with Taren."

Phillip paused for a moment. "I wonder how Nyah is going to be able to accept not just one new brother, but two?"

Shelby hunched her shoulders and sighed. "Who knows? I guess time will tell."

Chapter 21

Jeana Sands

Vengeance

Jeana fiddled with the buttons on her cordless phone. She held a post-it note with the number for a counselor who specialized in anger management. She copied the number down from the yellow pages a couple of days ago and debated if she should make the call or not.

She thought about her conversation with Phillip, and she replayed as much of it as she could in her head. During some points of her recollection, she felt bad about the way she'd confronted his wife, especially knowing his wife had been totally innocent when it came to knowing anything about Taren.

Even though she had forgiven Phillip for what he had done to her, there were times when she experienced uncontrollable bouts of anger. The waves of anger seemed to wash upon her like an unexpected tidal wave. Jeana knew something wasn't right. She shouldn't be having such strong emotions. She thought about her bouts of anger, and she realized she hadn't always had them. They seemed to have slowly increased as the months progressed. And it wasn't only where Phillip was concerned. She realized she had issues when it came to her family. She didn't know why she had so much hatred for them.

Her father could be a bull, but he was consistent in the way he treated all people. He didn't treat her any differently than he treated her other brothers and sisters had left Edgecomb and go to college.

In the past couple of weeks, she experienced bouts of depression, which were causing her to cry at the drop of a dime. Jeana wished she could take the hurtful moments back, like when she lashed out at her mom when things didn't seem to be going right for her. When she thought about her mother and the way her mother had truly tried to love her, crying spells went on for what seemed like hours. Jeana admitted that she had been the one to push her mother away. Her mom had no choice but to back off.

Her stomach churned thinking about all the times she put her mom and family down and called them 'Country Bumpkins.' She had no right to call them that. They were hard working people who tried to get by the best way they knew how. The hurtful comments they made to her were in retaliation for what she was saying to and about them.

Jeana had wasted some of the best years of her life focusing on others and what they did or didn't have. She was unhappy with the way her life was turning out. She didn't want to keep feeling sorry for herself and blaming others for the bed she made and was continuing to lay in.

After days of contemplating she dialed the number for the counselor without having to look at the piece of paper. She had it memorized from looking at it so many times.

When the receptionist picked up the phone Jeana said, "Hello. I'd like to make an appointment with Dr. Katz for a consultation."

The receptionist booked the appointment. Her emotions seemed to be on pause for the moment. She never knew what to expect lately as each hour rolled by. She sat back on her sofa, pulling her legs in as if getting ready to do a tumble in a preschool gymnastics class.

Exhaustion blanketed her body. Silently she prayed, willing her rampant emotions to stay on pause for a little while longer.

"Mom . . . Mom."

Jeana felt the pressure of hands on her shoulder and heard her name being called. She opened her eyes and found that she was lying in a prone position facing the back of the love seat.

"Taren, honey? What's wrong?" she asked with sleepy alarm.

"Telephone."

Jeana sat up so quickly. Her head started to spin a little. "Who is it?"

"Granny."

She took the cordless phone from her son. "Hello?"

"Jeana, baby. How are you?"

"Mom . . . I'm fine." Awkwardly Jeana said, "How are you doing?" It had been months since she had last spoken with her mother. She felt ashamed.

"Oh, I'm doing alright. My gout is flaring up a little, but other than that, the Lord is taking care of me just fine."

"That's good. How is Dad doing?"

"You know your daddy. I believe he isn't feeling too well, but you'll never hear it come out of his mouth. The doctor told him he needs to get some exercise and eat more vegetables, but he ain't going to do it. He's just set in his ways."

"How's everybody else?" Jeana asked with sincerity.

"Well let's see, your big sister, Pauline, is taking up some classes at the community college."

"Pauline?" Jeana was genuinely surprised. Pauline had been one of the smartest ones in the family and probably could have gone to any school in the nation, but she'd never valued education.

"She takin' up some cosmetology classes," Jeana's mother said.

Jeana laughed. "It's about time. She's done hair for people all these years, and never charged them anything. She better get paid for the good work she does."

"Your cousin, Sunny Boy, has finally come home."

"Sunny Boy?" Jeana had no idea who her mother was talking about.

"Oh, you too young to remember Sunny Boy.

He's your great Aunt Mary's son. He left when he was 18, and said he was never coming back. Mary's sick, she might not make it through the next couple of months. Sunny Boy finally came back to see his mama after 30 years in California."

"Aunt Mary is sick?" Mary was one of Jeana's favorite great aunts. Now she really felt bad about neglecting to call home over the past months.

"Yeah, it's her heart. Weak hearts run in our family."

"I hate to hear that. I need to make a trip down there. I feel really bad about . . ." the words stuck in her throat.

"About what, baby?" her mother asked.

"Mom . . . I feel bad about a lot of things. Especially where you and daddy are concerned."

"What you talking about, Jeana?" Her mother asked as if she really had no idea.

"A lot has been on my mind lately. I haven't been so nice over the years. Mama, I want you to know, I love you and I'm sorry for being so difficult. I'm sorry for treating you and daddy so bad all these years."

"Oh, baby, I love you too. Never stopped and always will. You been on *my* mind a lot lately too. That's why I called. I wanted to see how you and my grandson were doing."

"We're doing good. I'll be doing better after I work through some things." Jeana fell silent.

"Honey, you gonna be just fine."

"Mama, just pray for me, please."

"Baby I've been praying for you for years. I'll just send up a few extra ones. But with the Lord's help, everything is gonna be just fine. You just mark my word."

Jeana's eyes filled with tears. Sniffling she said, "Thank you, Mama. Like I said I need to work through some things here, but as soon as I get a chance, Taren and I are coming home to visit."

"That'll be good. I know Taren is growing like a weed."

"He sure is, Mama. You won't believe it when you see him."

Jeana heard her phone beep. Looking at the caller I.D. she saw Phillip's home number.

"Mama, I've got a call on the other line. I'll call you in a day or so to check back up on you all."

"Okay, honey. Love you."

"I love you too, Mama." Jeana hit the release button and the phone immediately rang. "Hello."

"Hello, Jeana?" Phillip asked, his voice sounding uncertain as to if he had gotten the right number.

"It's me, Phillip."

"Oh, sorry. I couldn't read my own handwriting. I wrote your number down so quickly that day in the restaurant, I couldn't tell if the seven was a seven or a one."

Jeana wondered what the call was about. "I see you're calling from home. Is everything okay?"

"With the grace of God, it is," Phillip said.

"I'm really glad to hear so."

"Well, I was calling about what we discussed the other day at the restaurant. I'd like to meet Taren."

Jeana took a deep breath. "I'd like you to meet him."

"Are you both busy this Saturday?"

Jeana chuckled.

"What's so funny?"

"We are going to be just a little busy. It's Taren's birthday."

"Is it?" Phillip asked.

"Yep, July 28th," Jeana said.

"Wow, I'm sorry, I should have already known that."

"We'll just look at all of this as being a fresh start. Now you know, and from now on you won't forget."

"Were you all planning something special? I mean, I don't want to intrude or anything."

"Phillip, you are the one birthday present Taren has been waiting a while for. I can't think of a better present than his finally being able to meet his dad."

"What time and where?" Phillip asked.

"Well, I was planning on taking him out to lunch. Why don't you meet us at Ginny's. The reservation is for 1:00."

"What does he want for his birthday?"

"Besides meeting you? He wanted a game player 3000 and a pair of Kelsey Jackson sneakers," Jeana said.

"Did you get the gifts yet?" Phillip asked.

"Yeah, I bought them months ago."

"What else does he like?"

"He likes sports, music and he loves to read," Jeana said.

"Okay, that helps. I've got a few things in mind. I'll see you on Saturday."

Phillip hung up the phone with gift ideas swirling in his head. His heart beat with nervous anticipation. After all this time, he was about to meet his first born child, his son.

Chapter 22

Phillip Tomlinson

Mercy

"Honey, do you think you went a little overboard with the gifts?" Shelby asked.

"No, not really. I've missed quite a few birthdays and other important days in Taren's life. I guess, in a way, I'm trying to make up for it," Phillip admitted.

"It's going to take some time. But you don't want him thinking you're trying to buy his love or anything. Plus, you don't want him to think you're made of money and every time he sees you he'll be getting a gift or money."

"I don't want him thinking that either, but it just felt right. It is his birthday."

"Don't get me wrong, I think the gifts are great. But you might want to save some of your gift ideas for Christmas."

They walked out of the bookstore. Phillip slipped the $50.00 gift certificate in the gift bag, which already held five game player 3000 games and another gift certificate of $50.00 for one of the local music stores."

"Okay, that's it. I'll stop." Phillip smiled, pleased with his gift choices.

"I think he'll love his gifts," Shelby said.

"Nyah is going to love her gift too," Phillip said, looking at the gift bag Shelby held with three jigsaw puzzles.

"Maybe this will keep her from talking so much about the jigsaw puzzles J.J. has. Now she can share hers with him."

Once in the SUV, Phillip asked, "Are you sure you don't want to go with me to meet Taren today?"

"No, not this time. Nyah and I will meet him the next time. Meeting you might be more than enough to swallow in one day. Let him get use to having a father in his life first. Then, he can meet his new step-mother, little sister and eventually his baby brother."

Shelby rubbed her belly. "Besides I've been so tired lately the whole thing might really wear me out."

Phillip agreed. "You're right. I just don't want you to feel left out.

"Don't worry, I don't. And if I do start feeling left out, believe me I'll let you know, Mr. Tomlinson."

"Yes ma'am, Mrs. Tomlinson."

* * *

"Right this way, sir." Phillip followed the hostess back to the table where Jeana and Taren were sitting."

As he approached the table, he had to blink his eyes a couple of times. Taren looked just like he did as a pre-teen; pimples and all.

"Phillip, hey." Jeana greeted Phillip with a warm hand wave.

The table was set for three and he took the seat unoccupied.

"Hey, Jeana, Taren." Phillip extended his hand for Taren to shake.

Awkwardly, Taren extended his hand, giving Phillip a solid hand shake.

Phillip sat the items he held down on the floor next to his chair, and turned his attention squarely on his son.

"Taren, it's good to meet you."

Taren nodded his head without saying anything.

Jeana looked at Taren. "Does the cat have your tongue, Taren? Just a minute ago you were Mr. Twenty Questions."

Taren gave his mother a give me a break look.

"Phillip, I told Taren last night that we were coming to lunch and that you'd be coming to meet us. Needless to say he was surprised, excited and confused—not necessarily in that order."

Phillip nodded his head in understanding. He couldn't believe how much Taren looked like him. He had so many of the Tomlinson traits.

Jeana continued, "Neither one of us could really sleep last night. But every since I told him, he's had a lot of questions. Not just about you, but about the lies, I told him about your not being alive." Jeana's face turned red with embarrassment.

Phillip felt her pain. "Taren, your mom did what she thought she had to do at the time. Please don't hold that against her. Just as I made some decisions in the past which were not the best, I hope you'll be able to forgive me for not being in your life for so many years."

Taren nodded his head to let his parents know he was listening.

"You can ask me what ever you want to ask," Phillip told his son. "And don't feel like you've got to ask all of your questions today, because you'll be seeing me more. Your mom and I will be talking some later about making arrangements for you to visit."

Taren's face softened with relief, as if he was hoping to see his father again.

The waitress came over to their table. "Okay, I see Dad has joined you. Wow, you and your son look just alike."

Phillip looked at the waitress and smiled. "He sure does."

"One of these days you two might be able to pass for twins."

Taren held his head up, full of pride in his eyes.

"We already ordered," Jeana said.

Phillip skimmed the menu. "Well in that case, I'll have the grilled chicken sandwich with steamed vegetables instead of fries. And let me have lemonade also." He handed the menu back to the waitress.

"I'll be right back with your drink, sir."

Phillip smiled at Jeana, pleased the meeting seemed to be going well. He turned to Taren. "I know all of this is pretty awkward, but soon it won't be that way."

Taren smiled with more reassurance.

"Your mom has told me a little about you. And I know you want to know about me and my side of the family, so I brought something to help a little with our getting to know each other."

Phillip bent over and picked up the photo album he'd placed on the floor only minutes before. He set it on the table, turning it toward Taren. "I don't know just how much your mom told you about me."

"She told me you used to play football," Taren said, finally speaking.

"I sure did. I started in Pee Wee football right up to college. I wanted to go pro, but sometimes things don't always go the way you plan."

Phillip pointed to a baby picture of himself and several grade school pictures. "This is me as a bald headed baby; and here you can see where I had needed a few visits from the tooth fairy."

The waitress returned with the lemonade and refilled Jeana and Taren's glasses.

Taren looked at the pictures with interest. "These pictures look just like me when I was little. Don't they, Mom?"

Jeana smiled and nodded her head in agreement. "Phillip, I didn't think to bring any pictures of Taren."

"Don't worry about that right now. Like I told, Taren, we'll have more than enough time and I'll see them soon." Phillip turned the page. "Here is a family picture. This is your grandfather, Gordon, and your grandmother, Glenda. And sitting next to me is your uncle, Gordon, Jr."

Taren eyed the photo closely.

Excited about sharing the photo album with his son, Phillip continued to describe picture after picture. "And this is a picture of my wife, Shelby."

"Did your mom tell you I'm married with a daughter?"

Taren nodded his head yes.

On the next page he showed Taren a family picture of himself with Shelby and Nyah.

"Your sister's name is Nyah. She's three years old."

Taren looked closely at the pictures of Shelby and Nyah as if they looked familiar.

"What is it, Taren?" Jeana asked.

He shook his head. "Nothing, Mom."

Jeana squirmed uncomfortably. "Do they look familiar to you?"

"A little," Taren admitted.

"You have actually seen them before. We went by their house a few weeks ago."

Taren shook his head as he remembered. "Why didn't you tell me that lady was my dad's wife?"

Phillip looked at Jeana, feeling sorry for her having to answer so many difficult questions, but he kept silent. Only Jeana could make her own amends. Taren had to hear the truth from her.

"It wasn't the right time. One day when you are older and better able to understand everything, I'll explain it to you in more detail. I made that trip to your father's house in hopes that you two would be able to meet." Jeana took a deep breath. "In ways I hadn't planned, my wish came true."

Taren shook his head again as if he understood.

Bringing the subject back to the photo album, Phillip said, "This photo album is for you. We scanned the pictures so you'd have copies." He handed the album to his son.

Taren accepted it and handled it as though it was gold plated.

The waitress returned with their food. Too excited to focus on eating, they talked, all eating their food intermittently.

Near the end of their meal, the wait staff surrounded the table and sang Happy Birthday to Taren. Afterwards, Phillip pulled out the gift bag and gave it to Taren.

"Here's your birthday gift from Me, Shelby and Nyah. I hope you like it."

Taren pulled out his birthday card first. It was signed by the three of them. "Thank you," he said after reading it.

"You're welcome."

Then he pulled out the gift cards. "Wow, $50.00 for music and for books!"

Jeana looked at the gifts with approval.

Then Taren pulled out his five new game player 3000 games. His face lit up like it was Christmas. "Wow, I can't believe it, five games. Thanks."

"You're more than welcome. We put the gift receipt for the games in the bag. Your mom told me you were getting the game player but I didn't find out what games she'd gotten you. So if you have any duplicates, you can just exchange them without a problem."

Jeana smiled with a look of pleasure and peace on her face. She mouthed the words thank you to Phillip.

"This is so cool. I can't wait to play them," Taren said.

"Maybe you and I can play a few games," Phillip suggested.

"Yeah, sure."

"Your mom and I will talk and set up something for our next meeting. My wife, Shelby, is looking forward to meeting you."

Jeana nodded her head. "I think that would be good. I think this meeting went pretty well."

"I agree." Phillip looked at his son as he admired the games for his player.

The waitress returned with the bill.

Seeing there was only one bill generated Jeana said, "Oh, waitress, I'm sorry can you put my son's and my meal on a separate ticket?"

The waitress looked confused.

"No, don't worry about that," Phillip interjected, "this one is fine."

Jeana looked at Phillip with questioning eyes.

"I've got it."

"Thanks," Jeana smiled.

"No problem."

Phillip's cell phone vibrated in his pocket. "Hold on one second," he told them. Looking at the display, he saw Shelby's cell phone number. "Hello?"

"Phillip?" Shelby said panting.

"Yeah, baby? What's up?"

"How's the lunch going?" she asked.

"Fine, sweetheart. Why are you breathing so hard?"

"I think I'm in labor."

"What?" Phillip exclaimed. "You're not due for another two weeks."

"My water broke."

"Where are you? Where's Nyah?"

"We're on the way to the hospital. Crystal was here helping me with the baby's room."

"I'm on my way. I'll meet you all there."

Phillip clicked the phone off. "That was Shelby. She's in labor."

"I heard, I heard. Go to the hospital. We'll talk in a few days."

Phillip looked up at the waitress and the bill.

"Go ahead, Phillip, I'll get the bill," Jeana said.

"Are you sure?"

"I've got it. But you owe me one," Jeana smiled.

"I owe you more than one, but believe me, I'm good for it. I'll pay you back later."

He turned his attention to Taren, "Okay, Taren, I'll see you in a few days."

"Okay," Taren replied.

With that Phillip sprinted towards the parking lot.

"Knock, knock." Phillip's parents knocked, opening the hospital room door. Phillip hugged both of them.

Shelby looked up from breastfeeding her son and smiled. "Hi, Mr. & Mrs. Tomlinson."

"Ohhh, look at my little grandson." Phillip's mom walked closer to the hospital bed. "He's beautiful, absolutely beautiful; my first grandson."

Phillip and Shelby looked at each other.

"Mom and Dad, Shelby and I, well mostly I, have something to tell you."

Phillip's parents gave his serious tone their undivided attention.

"Phillip Junior is actually your second grandson."

"Huh?" his mother said.

"It's a long story and I don't want to go into the details, but I have an older son. His name is Taren and he is fourteen-years-old."

Phillip's mother looked up and started counting on her fingers.

"It happened in college years ago. A lot of this information is still pretty fresh, especially for Shelby. I don't want to cast a negative light on the fact that I have an older son, but for a long time I wasn't truthful about a few things. And my deception almost caused me to lose the people I hold most dear in my life.

I learned the hard way and I don't intend on making the same mistake twice. So today we will celebrate two grandsons. One you're meeting today and the other you will meet in the near future."

Phillip's mom was speechless. Her husband rubbed her shoulders to help loosen her stiffness.

"Son," Gordon Tomlinson said, "You let us know when we can meet our other grandson. We'll be ready."

"I need a drink of water," Phillip's mom said.

She stepped out of the room and walked down the hall.

Phillip's dad hunched his shoulders. "Give her some time. Before you know it she'll be spoiling both her grandsons' silly." He turned towards the door, "Let me go check on her."

"Thanks, Dad." After they left Phillip smiled and said, "Mom took it better than I thought she would."

"Yep," Shelby said as she stroked her baby's curly jet black hair.

"That takes care of my parents and your parents. Now that they know we can start telling others," Phillip said. "And I've got the perfect way to tell them."

Raising her eyebrows, Shelby asked, "How?"

Phillip picked up a plastic Partyrama bag. "With these." He pulled out a box of cellophane covered blue bubble gum cigars.

"Instead of giving out one, I'll give out two. Then I'll tell everyone we have two additions to the family not just one."

Shelby smiled at her husband. "It's un-orthodox, but so is our situation. I like the idea."

They heard another knock at the door just as Will and Rick entered, both carrying flowers and balloons.

"Hey, we heard someone had a big head baby boy," Rick laughed.

Shelby eyed Rick.

"Sorry, Shelby; just kidding. Congratulations." He set the vase of roses he'd brought in on her tray.

Playfully, Shelby hit his arm with her free hand.

"Congratulations, both of you," Will said. He shook Phillip's hand and gave Shelby a hug.

"I've got something for you both also," Phillip said, pulling four cigars out of the box. "Two for you. And two for you."

"Obviously you haven't done this in a while," Rick said, trying to hand one of the cigars back to Phillip. Let me help you before you run out of cigars with your poor math skills."

"Naw man, keep it. Shelby and I are giving out two cigars. One is for little Phillip Junior here. The other one is for my older son, Taren."

Rick did a double take. "Who?"

Will said nothing as he put his cigars in his shirt pocket.

Phillip pulled Rick to the side towards the bathroom. He lowered his voice so no one else could hear them. "Long story. Let me impart some words of wisdom to you right now my friend. Be careful when it comes to all these women you are playing. If you aren't, the past can come back and bite you—hard. The past doesn't stay in the past."

Epilogue

One Year Later

Shelby and Kara sat wrapped in spa robes and slippers ready for their Queen for a Day spa treatment. Both women were set to spend the next few hours enjoying all the amenities that came with their spa packages.

"This is nice," Kara said as she relaxed on a velvety soft chaise lounge. She admired the marble floors and gold plated ceilings, as well as the artwork of peaceful scenes that adorned the walls. "Really nice." Kara flipped thorough the brochure Shelby had given her as soon as she pulled up in the parking lot of the spa.

Shelby took a sip of her sweetened iced tea. "I told you you'd like it." She sat next to her friend on a matching chaise lounge.

There was a fountain shaped like dolphins behind them. The trickling water, along with the classical music, which was playing, had already begun to relax both women.

"When you said to clear my schedule for this Saturday and that the men were going to watch the kids, I didn't know what to expect. But this . . ." Kara paused for a moment, looking around again at her surroundings. She rubbed her hands against the plush robe she was wearing and also on the chaise lounge. "I never would have expected this." Kara took a sip of her fresh squeezed lemonade.

"We deserve it," Shelby said.

"I already feel good, and all I've done so far is put on this robe and slippers." Kara pointed to the inside page of the brochure. "It says here that we'll be getting a facial cleansing, a one-hour massage, the spa pedicure with a foot mask and a spa manicure. This must have cost you a little bit of change."

"You can't put a price on quality time and friendship." Shelby took another sip of her tea. "We'll eat lunch here too. The menu should be on one of those pages."

Kara beamed. "Shelby, did I tell you that you're my best friend in the whole wide world?"

"Not lately," Shelby answered. "But it's always good to hear it."

Kara closed the brochure and let her body fall back into the soft pillows of the chair. "I feel like I've died and gone to heaven."

"No, wait until you meet the twins," Shelby said nodding her head.

"Twins? What twins?"

"Jock and Brock. They're identical twins from Sweden and they'll be giving us our massages. After our hour long session with them, you'll know you're in heaven."

Kara closed her eyes tightly. "I can't believe this is happening. Somebody pinch me please."

Shelby sat her tea down and laid back in her own chair to relax.

"I can't believe a year has flown by already. It seems like Phillip Junior was just born," Kara said.

"I can't believe it either. Time seems to have slipped by quickly," Shelby told her friend.

"I'm glad you set this up for us. I feel so bad about not spending more time with my godchildren over the last few months. We've just been so busy with work, and Nate Jr.'s mom is still trying her little tricks here and there." Kara rolled her eyes up towards heaven. "If the Lord wasn't on my side, I don't know what I'd do."

"You'll make it through. And what doesn't kill you will only make you stronger. Believe me, I know," Shelby confirmed.

"Oh, yeah, I'd say I'm stronger for the wear." Kara had to laugh in spite of herself.

"Do you need me to bring anything else for P.J.'s party next week?" Kara asked.

Shelby shook her head. "Not a thing. Just you and the family will be fine."

"Is Taren coming to the party?"

"Yeah, later on that night he's going to hang out with some of his friends to celebrate his birthday."

"How's everything going with his mom?"

"Pretty good actually; even though it all started out a little rocky."

Kara sat up, staring at Shelby in disbelief. "A little rocky?"

"Okay, real rocky, but after the truth came out,

things are going much smoother." Shelby shifted the pillow behind her back. "Jeana is a nice person. She went for counseling and found out her hormones were out of whack. During the time she was stalking us, they were at their worst. If she didn't have the hormonal problems, I might not have known Phillip had another child."

Kara shook her head. "God works in mysterious ways. Or shall I say mischievous ways"

"Huh?" Shelby asked.

"That's the way my grandmother used to say it."

Shelby laughed. "Our ways are not His ways, that's for sure."

"How is divinity school going for Phillip?" Kara shook her head. "I still can't believe he's actually in divinity school."

"Sometimes I can't believe it myself. But every since we returned from that couples retreat on Lake Turner, he's literally been a changed person," Shelby said. "You know, Phillip doesn't even call it Lake Turner anymore. He found his redemption there, so he calls it Redemption Lake."

Kara nodded her head. "Getting saved—accepting the Lord as his personal Savior. Yes, I'd say that's a change."

Shelby shook her head. "Mysterious ways that God of ours works in."

Kara nodded in agreement. "Yep. Mysterious ways."

Soul Confessions

Reading Guide

1. In the Prologue, Phillip says, "Let the past, stay in the past." Do you agree with the statement as a whole, or are there times when other people need to know about someone's past?
2. Rick has a promiscuous lifestyle, which is running rampant. Do you think he'll heed the advice Phillip gives him?
3. When the storms of life arise and we are faced with trials and tribulations, they often make us stronger and wiser. In what ways do you think each of the following character's lives became stronger and wiser? Shelby, Phillip and Jeana.
4. Will and Rick were both equally good friends with Phillip. Why do you think Phillip leaned more towards the advice Will gave him after the fallout with Shelby, especially since in the beginning of the novel Phillip felt he was the king of his own destiny?
5. Often people think the grass is greener on the other side-Jeana thought so. What do you think was Jeana's pivotal point in realizing her grass was just fine?
6. Do you think Kara was justified in how she handled the situations with her stepson's mother?

7. No one is perfect, as Shelby found out during her heart to heart talk with her mother. Each of us needs to recognize imperfections in our own lives. Is there anyone who revealed a secret to you, in which you've been holding a grudge and haven't forgiven them? If so, can you forgive them now understanding they, too, are mere humans?
8. Phillip's first meeting with Taren seems to have gone well. What do you think the future holds for Taren as he adjusts to find out his father abandoned him and his mother lied to him for years?
9. Even though Phillip lived in sin for so many years, God still had a plan for him. Do you agree with the statement, "Everything happens in its own season?"
10. Do you believe God works in mysterious ways? If so, how has he worked in mysterious ways in your life?
11. Will finds a woman who is fine, single, and saved. Phillip asks him what the catch is and states there is always a catch. Do you agree that there is always a catch?
12. What is the overall message of this novel?
13. Were you surprised to find out Phillip accepted the Lord as his personal Savior and ends up going to Divinity school?
14. Who was your favorite character?
15. What was your favorite part in the book?

Redemption Lake is the follow-up to ***Soul Confessions***! It is the third book in a three-part trilogy.

Redemption Lake

By
Monique Miller

Prologue

Xavier & Charlotte Knight

Charlotte sat poker faced in the dining room chair. She had no idea how much time had passed, since she sat down at the kitchen table. She stopped hearing the ticking of the kitchen clock. There were copies of the papers—evidence she'd been gathering for months, spread across the table. Evidence proving that without a shadow of a doubt, her husband, Xavier, was cheating on her. He was not only doing it in cyberspace, but as close as the neighbor three houses down.

The grandfather clock, in the living room, chimed three times. *Three o'clock*, she thought. *In just a little over an hour, he'll be home.* To her surprise, she was unbelievably calm. No, maybe calm wasn't the right word. She was numb. After three months of collecting information about her husband's infidelity, nothing could surprise her anymore, not even the letter she'd just received from her doctor's office confirming she tested positive for gonorrhea.

In an hour, she'd confront him with what she knew. Just enough to let him know, that this time there would be no forgiving him for the lies he continually told her. Charlotte wouldn't let him know all that she was privy to, until the time was right.

Travis & Beryl Highgate

"Don't worry, baby. I'll be there to pick you up. I promise I'll be there waiting in the parking deck before you get off."

"Whatever, Travis. Don't make promises you won't be able to keep. Bye." Beryl hung the phone up before her husband could respond.

Beryl was tired of hearing his sorry lies and pathetic excuses. Her patience meter hit its breaking point months ago. Why she kept giving him chance after chance to prove himself, she didn't know. It was for her two little boys. Maybe it was that she wanted to believe in her husband so badly. She knew he had potential, but he needed to apply himself more. She spent so much time coaxing him and stroking his ego, that it felt like she had three sons instead of two.

Beryl was at her wits end. She didn't want to give up on their marriage, but he was draining her. She could see it each time she looked in the mirror. And she saw it when she compared herself to many of the pictures she took before she got married five years earlier. Her glow was gone. The sparkle in her eyes, had fizzled. No matter how much she tried to bring the glow back with make up, it didn't help. The stress was weighing on her like a lead weight.

Continually, she chastised herself for giving him so many chances to lie to her or to selectively feed her little bits of information here and there. She was tired of feeling stupid and listening to his ever-growing lame excuses. He had an excuse or answer for everything, even if it wasn't necessarily the right answer. She wished her intuition would have knocked her up side the head when she first met him.

Her instinct let her know things were amiss. Too many things weren't adding up. The miscalculations were causing checks to bounce, bill collectors to call, and the lights to be turned off.

Beryl finally admitted enough was enough.

Nina and George Jones

"Pastor Jones, here is the report you asked me to pull. Do you need anything else?" Pastor Jones's secretary, Jennifer, asked.

"No, Jennifer, that will be all. I'll let you know if I need anything else."

"Okay, sir." Jennifer turned to leave.

"Jennifer, if anyone calls, please take a message. I don't want to be disturbed for the next couple of hours."

"Okay, Pastor. What About Mrs. Jones?"

A sharp pain surged through George Jones's head. Wearily, he took a deep breath before answering. "If Nina calls, just let her know I'm taking care of some important business and can't be disturbed. I'll call her when I'm done."

Once his secretary closed the door, George flipped through the pages of the bank statements Jennifer compiled for him. Seven months of statements had been neatly put together and categorized by date. They were the bank statements for the church.

He pulled his keys out of his pocket, and unlocked his desk file drawer, which he stored personal bank statements, and credit card statements and other billing information. He shook his head in dismay. The devil was attacking their lives in the three areas that meant the most. Satan was making blows against their marriage through their finances, spiritually, and in the bedroom.

Nina had a problem with spending. It was a problem that was ruining their credit and affecting the church he founded, and was pastoring. This had to end.

George opened his rolodex and pulled out a business card given to him by a friend. It was for a very exclusive and secluded Christian couples retreat in the mountains. Their marriage needed both spiritual and professional help. Being the pastor of over 5000 members in the heart of Greensboro, NC, he didn't want anyone to find out about his marital problems. He didn't want the various Bishops and Pastors he knew to find out.

Pastor George Jones picked up the telephone, and called the number on the card. They needed to be present on the first available date. He prayed their marriage would make it until then.